~ Acclaim for Keith Melton ~

For *Ghost Soldiers*

"Nonstop action, relentless pacing, brutal organized crime warfare, nightmarish monsters, black ops missions, and, above all else, an utterly readable narrative that is addictively entertaining. Melton's narrative is unrelenting.

...[I]ntermeshed amongst the action and adventure are some really profound lines and memorable imagery. ...[A] hugely underrated author and his Nightfall Syndicate saga is an addictive blend of noir fiction, dark fantasy, and mainstream thriller."
—Paul Goat Allen for Explorations: The BN SciFi and Fantasy Blog

"Keith Melton has written a masterful book (and series) that shatters all the stereotypes of good and evil, right and wrong. All of the characters are complex and intricately-drawn, and the reader is sucked into all the shades of black and gray that envelops their lives. Mr. Melton is a storyteller of the highest order and his writing is sharp, vivid and engrossing."
—Bitten By Books

For *Blood Vice*

"...a raw, gritty and masterful tale...This book absolutely blew me away..."

—Bitten By Books

"Enthralling! ...will hook you in the first paragraph and keep you ensnared throughout... The paranormal has never been so sexy and ruthless... The realistic inside look into the mafia is fascinating... Blood Vice is a paranormal work of art."

—Teagan, BookWenches

"...[T]urf war dramas, vampire politics, women with big guns, and other fun stuff to make sure that this one doesn't have a dull moment... Blood Vice is a charming fast-paced and action-packed tale that allows the bullets to fly free and the blood to flow..."

—Mrs. Giggles

"...Karl Vance is a baddie—mysterious, lethal, intense. ...[P]lenty of unexpected twists to keep the story very interesting. For those who enjoy dark urban fantasy with romantic tension, this is a must."

—Smexy Books

Look for these titles from Keith Melton

9MM BLUES

Thorn Knights Book One

Keith Melton

Etopia Press
1643 Warwick Ave., #124
Warwick, RI 02889
http://www.etopia-press.net

9mm Blues

Print ISBN: 978-1-949719-25-3
Digital ISBN: 978-1-936751-20-4

First Etopia Press electronic publication: October 9, 2015

First Etopia Press print publication: June 2019

~ DEDICATION ~

For K and C

CHAPTER ONE
Hunt-Kill-Run

Cranston, Rhode Island
20:39 hours

The crunch and clack of teeth gnawing on bone were sounds Christopher Hill could happily go the rest of his life without ever hearing again. Even worse than the crunching was the contented, happy humming that drifted from the pit dug out of the graveyard earth. That damn humming made his skin crawl and his hands clamp down on the submachine gun he carried.

The moon hadn't yet risen. Oakland Cemetery huddled in the dark, pressed between busy Broad Street and the black-glass-calm of Edgewood Lake around Roger Williams Park. A short chain link fence on the opposite side of the cemetery separated the gravestones from the steady stream of traffic. But the business lights and headlights, engine noise and the whisper of tires on asphalt, all these familiar city sights and sounds seemed strangely disconnected from him as he and Tashelle Parker hunted in the dark.

Except for Tashelle, he was alone here and knew it. Ordinary people went about their ordinary lives completely ignorant of what he and his fellow knights suffered to keep the wolves from the door and the monsters at bay.

He didn't blame those people. He envied them.

He covered his friend with his suppressed MP7 from behind a marble tombstone as they leapfrogged positions, advancing toward the gaping hole through the scattering of headstones. They steadily closed in on the sounds of crunching and gnawing and the delighted cooing. It was time to buckle down, quit bitching, and focus.

His night vision goggles transformed the world into a ghostly green. He wished the rest of the team were here watching his six instead of it just being him and Tashelle, asses in the wind while they stalked a humming, hungry ghoul in the middle of a cemetery. Then again, wishes were for civilians. Soldiers got shit done.

Tashelle took cover, resting her crossbow on a

granite tombstone. He advanced, scanning methodically, gun barrel always tracking back to the hole and the scattered dirt. Adrenaline popped and jumped in his veins. He fought to keep his breathing steady and his heart rate down but had no luck with it. The dark shape of a mausoleum rose beyond the feeding ghoul, a huge two-and-a-half story monument of crumbling mortar, missing granite blocks and busted out windows. The building loomed over the graves. He couldn't shake the feeling that it was aware of the hunt and watching.

A dog began to howl. It sounded very close.

He took cover next to an obelisk spire. The disturbed grave was now only ten feet off. He glanced at Tashelle. Her dark skin shone almost sickly in the green of his night vision device. The upper part of her face was hidden behind the NVD hanging off her helmet. She wore the standard Thorn knight assault gear the same as he did: Kevlar body armor reinforced with ceramic plates, black fatigues, combat boots, web harness with ammo and gear, pistol holster strapped to her upper thigh. She carried a PSE TAC 15 crossbow. A long, weird, but effective weapon that shot arrows instead of bolts and used an AR-15 upper receiver. Very quiet, and—except when reloading—beat out any suppressed firearm for silence that he'd ever run across.

A falcata hung in a sheath over her shoulder, and near her lower back dangled a sling with her Benelli semi-auto twelve gauge, just in case things went sideways on a rocket. Lots of gear. Moving silently in lots of gear was always a righteous pain in the ass.

Tashelle turned toward him, pointed two fingers at her night vision goggles and then pointed toward the dug-up grave. She made a flanking motion with her free hand.

He took one hand off his submachine gun and formed an OK, then followed with an exaggerated double nod so she could see his affirmative. This close, they had to run radio silent if they hoped to surprise their little ghoul buddy. Last thing he wanted was to spook the bone-chomper and end up chasing it through residential neighborhoods or into the damn zoo.

Before they advanced again, a brown and white dog trotted into view at the far end of the pit. Tashelle motioned for him to hold tight as the dog paced around in a nervous circle, whining, with its ears flattened and its tail down. It loosed a couple of mournful "barroooo" sounds. The humming from the pit stopped. The dog whined again and scurried backward, but didn't flee the graveyard.

Chris realized he was gritting his teeth and holding his breath, waiting for the monster to scramble out of the pit and go for the dog. From this position, he wouldn't have a good shot, because the dog would be in the fire zone. He breathed out quietly and glanced over at Tashelle, hoping she had an idea on how to handle this new problem.

"Shit," she whispered, her word nearly inaudible over the city sounds and the dog's strange, yowling *barooos*. But the ghoul returned to its humming song and bone-crunching, apparently indifferent to the noise outside the pit. The dog looked at Chris and his curled tail wagged briefly before stilling again. Beautiful dog, but he didn't recognize the breed. Brave little bastard, too. It refused to run away from the monster in the hole.

"What's the plan?" he whispered to her over his headset microphone.

"Damn mutt's gonna blow our cover." She scanned the street and buildings beyond the graveyard fence.

"Can't risk hitting the dog. Maybe I can lure him off."

"We're not blowing this hunt over some stray. We get close, stay radio silent, and get this done. I don't miss."

He bit down on his reply. Tashelle had primary shooter designation on this Hunt-Kill-Run because of the silence of her crossbow, so she was calling the shots.

Ideal outcome: they'd whack this filthy carrion eater with a two-foot arrow through its brainpan, destroy its body, and withdraw with no civilian ever hearing a sound. Anyway, that was the perfect world scenario. Since nothing ever played perfectly—as shown by this dog who'd wandered into their killzone—Chris carried a suppressed Heckler and Koch MP7. His weapon was straight up sierra hotel, but even shit hot and suppressed, the weapon's armor-piercing rounds weren't subsonic and would crack like an unmistakable rifle shot as soon as he popped off. They were also likely to rip right through that monster and hit the poor dog, and no dog was getting killed on his watch.

Tashelle moved out again. Chris followed, swinging around the obelisk with his MP7 up as he scanned left to right in short arcs. He shifted so the dog was no longer in his field of fire and moved toward the target. Slow and steady. The dog stared at him and whined, took a couple of steps toward the hole, then darted back and uttered that weird yowling noise again.

If only they'd had a mage to throw down some silence wards and seal off the area then this would've been cake. There'd be no need to worry about the noise from the dog or the humming ghoul or the blast of gunfire. But magicslinger Richards was with Captain Garcia on Specter One team, and Sergeant Drake and the rest of the Thorn knights had spread through Cranston and South Providence neighborhoods chasing down leads on the broodsire making all these damn ghouls. So no dice on the easy mode for this game.

Tashelle advanced on his left, twenty feet off as they executed the pincher maneuver, coming in from the flank so the dog stayed out of danger. The dog paced in circles, glancing from them to the pit again while growling low in its throat. The humming in the pit stopped again. Something made a disapproving "Shhhhhhh…" sound.

The hair on the back of Chris's neck stood up and his hands tightened on the weapon grips.

Recently, people had been disappearing in the neighborhoods north of the cemetery, most of them past the I-95 freeway on rundown South Providence streets. He had no idea why the ghouls had escalated, switching from feasting on corpses to eating live, fresh meat, but he was here to bring the hammer down. Hard.

This particular ghoul seemed happy enough on the usual corpse diet, but that didn't mean they'd be letting it go. He was very close now, each step revealing more of the unearthed grave, which was nothing like the neat, squared-off holes he always saw on TV. This hole resembled a bomb crater, nothing more than an uneven pit with dirt flung everywhere around it. The stench of rot and decay grew thicker, and the humming started again. The note of contented bliss in the humming caused the same deep revulsion as a spider crawling across his eye. The sound of tearing meat now added to the clash of teeth on bones, followed by gulping, then more atonal, happy humming.

He and Tashelle cleared the top of the hole in perfect synch. The ghoul squatted over the corpse in the casket. The top half of the coffin had been wrenched off its hinges. The ghoul clutched the dead man's arm and chewed along the bicep.

It had been male once, lean, with short, dirty yellow hair, but its cheeks were flayed back from its jaws, revealing pointed teeth and a blackened tongue. The ghoul's jagged, claw-like fingernails cut into the corpse's arm, leaving smears of dirt on the dead flesh. As Chris watched, the ghoul ripped a bite of muscle away. It didn't chew, but tossed its head back and gulped down the meat like a bird swallowing a fish. Lacerations scored along its ears and nose in angry red slashes. The ghoul was naked except for shredded, filthy blue jeans. Dirt covered it to the elbows and gore was smeared around its mouth. The grayish-white skin of its face, chest, and arms was scarified into strange, abstract patterns that reminded him of odd, fractal art.

The ghoul stopped humming. It lifted its head and sniffed the air, peering up from the shadows filling the hole. It flinched when it spotted them. The way its mouth had been flayed back gave it the look of an eternally grinning shark.

"Sorry," it whispered, the word distorted by ravaged lips. "From inside. Sorry from inside."

Tashelle stood at the edge of the hole, staring down at it, her finger on the crossbow trigger. Chris glanced at her, frowning. Hesitation was never a good sign.

The dog moved to the edge of the hole and began to pace back and forth, looking from them to the ghoul as if confident they'd do something to set this craziness to rights. The ghoul craned its neck and peered at the dog. Its black tongue seeped from its mouth in a dark, curling stain.

"Waste that scrote," Chris said. He kept his voice calm, despite his heart thundering away and the adrenaline crashing through his body.

The ghoul jerked at the sound of his voice and it whipped its head around to stare at him. Drool poured from between its sharp teeth because it didn't have any damn lips. He had it dead center in his gun sights, but he waited, because it wasn't his shot. The ghoul rose from its squat and scrambled up the dirt slope toward him.

The dog whined again. It stepped too close to the edge. Its hindquarters lost traction and it started to fall into the pit. The ghoul spotted the motion and lunged for the dog. Chris aimed for the ghoul's head, cursing the damn thing, cursing how fast this operation had gone sideways, increasing his pressure on the trigger—

Tashelle's crossbow arrow hissed through the air and took the ghoul in the side of the head, straight through the temple. The ghoul went limp at once and slid in a small avalanche of loose brown dirt into the coffin, lying atop its meal. The arrowhead had pierced out the other side of its skull, making the ghoul look hideously absurd, as if it wore one of those stupid joke arrow-through-the-head props for a Halloween costume.

Chris ran to the dog and grabbed it around the middle and hauled it back onto stable ground. The dog began to lick his cheeks, its tongue flapping against the lenses of his night vision goggles. He pushed the goggles out of the way and tried to keep the trembling dog from climbing into his lap. He scanned the graveyard again, making sure nothing was sneaking up on their flanks or six o'clock while they'd been dealing with this ghoul.

The place stood empty except for tombstones

and grass and decaying flowers. The crumbling mausoleum brooded behind its chain link fence, a silhouette in a sky brightened by the lights of Providence. The night was quiet except for the far-off rotor chop of a helicopter and the constant noise of traffic. He wanted to find those sounds comforting. Big cities always sounded of traffic, as unending as the rush, crash, hiss of waves at the beach. It meant people and technology and that things were right and normal…but he also knew that was an illusion.

"You all right?" he asked Tashelle. He did his best not to sound worried as he let his weapon dangle on the sling and petted the dog. It was dancing around him and trying to lick his hand off.

Tashelle pushed her night vision goggles up and flashed him a look that could've sparked tinder into flame. "I'm fucking fantastic, Hill. What do you think?"

Now there was the Tashelle he knew. "I think I want a beer, some pizza, and to watch the Yankees game I'm missing because of this shit." The dog stared up at him with a worshipful expression, as if it were eager to come along for the food and the game. "Me and my new pal here."

"I just spiked a monster eating a rotting corpse and you can think of food?" She shook her head and then frowned at the dog. "And forget about adopting a stray basenji. The captain'll never let you keep an untrained dog."

"This little fella's part of the team now. Ain't that right, boy?"

"That's a bitch," Tashelle said.

"Yeah, *life's* a bitch."

"No, you absolute dimwit. That dog is a bitch. A girl dog. Honest to God, Hill, do I need to draw you pictures?"

He bent down and rubbed the dog around the ears while she panted happily. "Hell, I knew that, pretty girl like this could never be mistaken for anything but a lady."

Tashelle gave a disgusted grunt and shouldered her crossbow on its sling. Then she unstrapped her shotgun from where it rode at the small of her back and looked as though she was searching for an excuse to blast something. She'd always taken this stuff hard. His attempts to lighten things up rarely worked. He wondered if they'd work this time and decided to hell with it, he'd try anyway. God hated quitters and people who thought twice.

He gave her a wide grin. "So who's gonna climb down there and drag that poor bastard out? Since you got to do all the shooting, I think it should be something like: you make the mess, you clean it up." He shrugged.

"Besides, I have my new dog to protect."

"Tell you what. I'll call it in. You do the manly heavy lifting. Boys like to play in the dirt, right?"

"You're a terrible friend, you realize that?"

She favored him with a full-on smile and turned on her radio. "Specter One Actual, this is Specter Two-Zero, target neutralized, retrieving now, over."

"Copy that, Specter Two-Zero," Captain Garcia's raspy voice came back over the encrypted frequency. "Cover your tracks and head to rally point, over."

"Roger that. Specter Two-Zero out."

Cover their tracks…easy to say. Chris scowled at the dead ghoul and the rotting corpse it had been eating, then he eyed the dirt scattered all around the hole. Mounds of it. In some places it had been flung in wide fanning patterns. Damn thing had made this mess digging with its claws like a frenzied animal. Bastard must've been hungry.

"I'm gonna need a bulldozer," he said.

"Maybe your new pet can help."

He glanced at the dog. "You gonna help, pretty lady?" The dog blinked at him, mouth open, tongue out. He could've sworn it was grinning. "I like your enthusiasm, fur-face."

"Hate to break things up with your new girlfriend," Tashelle said, "but we don't have time to screw around filling the grave back in. Just get the ghoul. I'll cover you so you don't bust your ass and then get jumped by another monster sneaking up." She flipped down her night vision goggles and gave him a mocking thumbs up before turning away and scanning their surroundings.

He muttered a curse and scrambled down into the hole. Twice he lost his balance and nearly fell onto the bodies. The stink of decaying flesh and damp earth filled his nose, so thick it was nearly suffocating. He fought back a wave of nausea that threatened to have him spewing every meal he'd ever eaten. So much for his appetite. The dog watched him from the edge of the pit. After a moment, she tried to follow him until he told her to stay. And she did. So at least one thing had gone his way tonight.

He confirmed the ghoul was dead by poking it in one staring eye with the suppressor on the barrel of his submachine gun. No reaction, so it wasn't playing possum. Not that he'd doubted it, with that arrow sticking through its dome, but this was protocol. Some monsters still twitched with a bit of life, even after taking a truckload of damage. He didn't want to end up a midnight snack.

He slung his weapon and flipped the ghoul over onto its face. Small avalanches of dirt slid down around him, scraping and pattering off his legs and into the coffin.

"Hurry up, Hill." Tension crackled in Tashelle's voice.

"Give me a sec."

His boots kept sinking into the loose dirt, and there wasn't much room. He grabbed the ghoul by the back of its filthy jeans. Climbing out again while hauling the ghoul was like trying to forge a trail up a mountain slope through drifts of new snow. For every couple of feet he climbed, he slid back half a foot. His shoulders burned with the strain of dragging the awkward dead weight. More than once he nearly lost his grip, and the ghoul almost tumbled to the bottom of the grave again.

The top edge of the hole was the worst, crumbling and falling away beneath him. Tashelle had to hurry over and help pull him up while the dog circled and growled at the dead monster. Chris grunted as he heaved the ghoul the rest of the way out of the hole, then he plopped down on his ass, breathing hard. The burn in his muscles slowly faded. Wet dirt covered him from the waist downward. He smelled like a swamp.

"Thanks for all the help," he said sourly. "What a team."

She flipped up her NVD again and gave him an evil grin. "What's protocol? Someone always on overwatch, guarding your back, so quit your bitchin." She pointed at the ghoul. "Bad enough we're leaving a dug-up grave with a chewed-on corpse. Can't leave a monster to end up all over the news."

"No shit, but I've got incendiaries. Just burn and go."

"Too public, too risky." She flipped down her night vision goggles again and raised her assault shotgun. "C'mon, let's bug the hell out."

"What about the dog?"

"I know you're lonely, Hill, but that ain't your dog." She turned and started through the rows of graves and tombstones, sweeping her shotgun barrel back and forth as she advanced. He followed, dragging the ghoul by the feet and struggling not to make much noise. The dead ghoul bumped and thudded against the ground and scraped through the grass. The dragging would leave a trail even the greenest forensic tech or rookie cop would spot, but he and Tashelle would be long gone by then.

The dog padded quietly alongside him. Her ears twitched at the sounds of traffic. She kept glancing up at him as if to ask: what now?

They made their way toward their SUV parked

on the empty, tree-lined FC Greene Memorial Boulevard. He dragged the body past the last of the tombstones and into the deeper darkness of the oak trees. Their black Chevy Suburban sat on a carpet of oak leaves and acorns. The water on the other side of the street reflected the few stars that outshone the light pollution.

A cop cruiser rolled slowly up the street with its searchlight on, sweeping along the trees on the cemetery-side.

Shit. He hauled the ghoul behind a cluster of thick bushes while Tashelle darted behind a tree trunk. The dog turned to look at him with its head cocked to the side.

"C'mere, girl," he whispered, gesturing her toward him. His heart was pounding so hard he could feel the pulse in his temples, seeming to hammer against the sides of his helmet. The dog watched him for a long moment more, then she glanced at the cop car before casually padding over to him.

Good girl. He stroked her head and pulled her closer. She squirmed a bit, but didn't try and break free of their cover.

The cruiser rolled along, its tires whispering on the road. It was a Crown Victoria with "City of Cranston" emblazoned beneath the bold blue word

POLICE on the side. Tashelle pressed up against the tree trunk as if trying to merge with the bark, her shotgun held close to her body. He stayed low to the ground and held his breath as the searchlight beam swept past. They weren't cleared to engage civilian authorities—it was always avoid and disengage ASAP protocols. He didn't want to imagine what would happen if the entire mission was burned because they'd stumbled into contact with the cops during their sortie.

The white beam of light jerked over to a thicker stand of trees, throwing shadows against the mausoleum. The cruiser slowed as it closed in on their SUV. Chris's heart thudded in shotgun kicks. His mouth tasted like metal shavings. The stink coming off the ghoul made it hard to breathe without coughing or gagging.

His headset burst to life, making him flinch. "Specter Two-Zero, this is Specter One Actual, what's your status, over?"

Tashelle gave a hushed reply. "Specter One Actual, this is Specter Two-Zero. Visual on a police unit stopped in our area, probably running the plates on the SUV. Confirm rules of engagement, over."

"Specter Two-Zero, you are cleared for limited engagement. Tires and engine block damage only. No casualties. I repeat, no civilian casualties, over."

"Copy that. Tires and engine block only. Specter Two-Zero out."

Chris risked another look. The cruiser had stopped behind the SUV, flooding it with the searchlight.

Dammit. He glanced at Tashelle. She still pressed against the tree truck, hiding from view. Her night vision goggles made her appear strange and insect-like.

The cruiser's door squealed as it opened. The cop climbed out and walked around their SUV with his flashlight raised, shining the beam inside. All their gear and weapons were concealed, but it still raised the hair on the back of his neck at having a cop this close. The officer finished circling the SUV and turned his flashlight toward the cemetery. Right in their direction.

Chris slowly raised his weapon, taking care to aim only at the cop cruiser. It might've just been dumb bad luck that had landed a cop here when they'd been on active hunt. Either that or some civvie on the road had seen something and called it in. He hated when things went tits up for no discernable reason.

The officer's radio squawked. He turned away and answered as he hurried back to his cruiser and scrambled inside. A moment later the car pulled onto the road and raced away, up to a roundabout and then it vanished into the distance. Chris sucked in a deep breath and let it out slowly. Too damn close. The dog licked his face, giving him a wet cheek, soggy chinstrap, and a healthy appreciation for the power of dog-breath.

Tashelle signaled him. They broke from cover and advanced toward the SUV again. He moved as fast as he could while dragging a ghoul and keeping to the deeper shadows of the trees. If the cop was playing games and circling around for another pass, then things would get really interesting, really fast. But Chris thought they'd finally caught a break. Their fake license plates must've checked out, and the cop had either received a call more important than this one or he really hadn't wanted to go stumbling through the cemetery at this hour.

Tashelle reached the SUV first. She checked it, then scanned the street, trees, and lake for threats before giving him the all-clear signal. He hauled the ghoul the rest of the way with the dog trotting along at his side. Tashelle popped open the back of the SUV, and together they heaved the body onto a blue tarp covering the floor. They used the extra flaps to conceal the corpse and secured the tarp with bungee cords before quietly shutting the hatch.

"Poor bastard." In his mind he could hear the ghoul pleading "Sorry from inside," followed by the *thunk* of the arrow piercing its skull.

"C'mon," Tashelle said. "Let's get gone before that cop decides to roll through again."

They tossed their weapons and gear into the SUV. The stink of graveyard mud filled the air. The dog whined, watching Chris with plaintive eyes.

He squatted down and petted her again. No collar. Out at this late hour. He didn't want to leave her behind. "My dog's coming with us."

"That's not your dog, you moron." She closed her eyes, took a deep breath, and continued more calmly. "Tell you what. If that dog is dumb enough to get in here with you and that stinking ghoul, then by all means, have yourself a new pet that's just as fool-headed as you are."

"I'm really feeling the love tonight, Tashelle," he said as he climbed into the SUV's passenger side. He patted his thigh and whistled. The dog clambered into the SUV. Her tongue flopped out and her curved tail wagged like mad. Chris looked at Tashelle with his eyebrows raised.

"The captain's gonna shit bricks." She started the engine, cracked the tinted windows, and swung a U-turn onto the road. She headed south, away from the cemetery and the cop.

He closed his eyes, petted his new doggie friend, and tried not to breathe through his nose. The sooner they ditched this ghoul, the better. The night wasn't even over yet and already he was tired of smelling horrible things.

After a moment, he lowered his window far enough so the dog could put her head out in the wind. He only wished he could do the same.

CHAPTER TWO

Rally Point

The white cargo van that served as the team's command vehicle had parked in the empty lot of a grungy brick warehouse off Poe Street. The van was half hidden down the slope from the I-95 freeway by huge mounds of gravel in a stretch of South Providence industrial wasteland near the harbor. Chris could smell the water, all pungent brine and dead seaweed. Tashelle pulled into the lot and killed the headlights. She cruised toward the van in the dim yellow wash of a single street lamp.

Rusted chain link encircled the lot, with tall weeds growing against the diamond-shaped wire and litter trapped against the fence bottom. He shifted in his seat to glance at the overpass that rose over the mountains of gravel held in place by concrete blocks and center lane barriers. Traffic raced along the freeway, cars and semis, in a never-ending red taillight blur. He'd never been able to get over how blissfully the world slouched along, happy to know nothing of the low-intensity war in its dark streets and forgotten holes. Not blissfully ignorant for much longer though, if things kept carrying on like they were nowadays. The Silence wouldn't hold.

He returned his attention to the non-descript van parked near a Dumpster. He tried to keep the dog's wildly wagging tail from smacking him in the face as he keyed his encrypted radio. "Specter One Actual, this is Specter Two-Zero. We are approaching from your six, over."

"Roger that, Specter Two-Zero, I have visual. Park it and sit tight, out."

"Copy that." He muted his mike and gave Tashelle a sour glance. "More waiting."

She snorted as she parked their SUV behind the van and killed the engine. "How many times I have to hear you whine about waiting? Just be easy and keep your booties on, Hill. If the captain wants us to chill with a dead ghoul in the back, he must have good reason."

"Yeah, yeah, hurry up and wait." The dog licked the window glass next to him and shifted around, nearly planting a foot in his crotch as she sniffed the night air. "Hey girl, you heard the lady. Be easy, like me." The dog whirled around and began to lick his face, and he laughed.

"What are you gonna call her?" Tashelle asked.

"Don't know. How about...Bullet?"

"Bad luck to name things bullet. And it's a stupid name for a dog."

"You're an eternal sunbeam, Tashelle. I mean that. You glow."

"Shit," was all she said, and turned to stare out the window as they waited on their orders.

Their assault team, call sign Specter, had been deployed to this part of South Providence for almost a week, hunting for ghouls here and in bordering Cranston. Search and destroy, following up on police reports of break-ins to funeral homes, corpse mutilations, and desecrated graves. What the police had intentionally suppressed from the news media was that some of the graves had been emptied and some of the dead bodies had been partially eaten—facts that funeral home owners were equally eager to keep quiet. Chris didn't blame them. What family would want to send Grandma to a mortician at the risk having her spleen chewed?

Soon, both his grim thoughts and the ominous stillness started to grate on his nerves. The old warehouses, asphalt lots, and rusting cargo containers seemed empty of life but filled with shadows. A clipped squawk of chatter burst over their police scanner and made them both flinch. From the codes, some robbery in progress in Elmwood.

"Ugly part of town." Tashelle leaned her head against the glass of the driver side window and stared toward the gravel mounds and the dump trucks arranged in rows like sleeping dinosaurs. "But it sure as hell doesn't compete with Cleveland for straight up ghetto."

Industrial slums all looked the same to him. Peeling paint and rust. Trash and weeds and junk. All gritty wastelands full of metal, decaying buildings, and high-tension wires. Newark, Detroit, or Gary, Indiana, it never mattered. Only the names changed, and maybe the weather, but he didn't feel like debating the point.

The van's back doors remained tightly shut. Still, he could feel someone watching him through the deeply tinted rear windows—the creepy prickle of somebody's gaze crawling across his skin. The dog had noticed something too. She was sitting at attention, her head tilted, watching the white van intently. He glanced at Tashelle, wondering if she'd noticed. Her face was haggard, her eyes tired and grim.

"You think Weeger's in there staring at me?" he

asked, trying to break the mood. "Jealous because you get the honor of running with me instead of him? Or maybe he envies my dog." He scratched the dog behind the ears. "And who can blame him?"

"Your ego should come with a warning label. Just remember who had the kill shot."

"I ever tell you we make a great team?"

"Yeah, I do all the thinking and you do all the whining." But she grinned, so mission accomplished.

Maybe he was overdoing the clowning around routine, but he'd seen her staring at the ghoul, hesitating to fire. He'd only wanted to shake her out of it—get her mind back on insulting him and not dwelling on the fact they'd just shot down a monster which had once been human. A monster that had still been sorry from the inside.

"So what do you think of the new guys—" he began, but both their encrypted radios crackled to life, cutting him off.

"Specter Two-Zero, this is Specter One Actual. Area around us is now clear of eyes. Toss your package but hold off on erasing it. Repeat, negative on erasing package at this time, over."

"Copy that, Specter One Actual," Tashelle radioed back. "Negative on erasing at this time. Specter Two-Zero out."

Without another word, she climbed from the SUV and headed to the back. He followed with the dog, annoyed the radio call had interrupted his question. He'd been meaning to ask her about the new guys for a while now, but the timing had never seemed right or his new squad mates had been in earshot. He wanted to know because he valued her opinion and hell, he had some worries. Nothing definite. Just...worries.

Together they heaved the tarp-wrapped ghoul out of the SUV. They carried it to the Dumpster with Chris walking backward and the tarp bowing in the middle, almost scraping the concrete. The dog trotted alongside, sniffing at everything. When they reached the Dumpster, Tashelle threw back the lid. She helped him swing and toss their special package into the bin. The corpse hit the metal side with a dull, reverberating *clong*. Chris glanced around, but there was no sign the sound had drawn any unwelcome attention.

Tashelle ran back to the SUV for the accelerant—the trusty old standard: gasoline—in two red plastic gas cans. They didn't speak as they drenched the ghoul's body and the trash inside the Dumpster and then shut the lid. She carefully splashed an ignition trail away from the bin while he held the dog back. The stink of gasoline always gave him a headache. No matter how careful he tried to be, he always managed to get some on his gloves.

"Specter One Actual, this is Specter Two-Zero," Tashelle said into her mike. "Ready to light on your command, over."

"Negative, Specter Two-Zero. Hold off. More blue eyes entering the area, out."

Blue eyes was code for police units. Bad luck with cops tonight. Instead of lighting the gasoline trail, they returned the gas cans to the SUV and double-timed it to the van.

The van's back doors swung open, and Captain Garcia waved them in. Chris picked up the dog and set her inside before he climbed inside. The van was empty except for the captain and mage Richards, who sat in the driver's seat with his boots up on the dash. Richards glanced at them without interest, snorted at the dog, and then returned to staring out the window as he sipped from a Dunkin Donuts coffee cup. Chris did his best to ignore him right back. Damn arrogant magicslingers.

The captain glared at the dog. "What the hell is that animal doing here?"

"Hill found a new girlfriend," Tashelle said. "Now he doesn't go anywhere without her."

Chris took a moment to pull the van doors shut and give him time to think up a good reply. "She helped us take down that ghoul, captain."

"You expect me to believe that, Hill?"

"Yes, sir." Better to keep his responses short and lacking detail. Captain Garcia was far from one of those rear echelon motherfuckers afraid to bleed in the gutters and slog through the shit. He sure as hell was no fool either. His brown eyes were soldier eyes: hard, wary. He wore black fatigues, body armor, and his helmet sat on the floor near his SIG 553 assault rifle and a sheathed long sword. He was clean-shaven, with short black hair and deep lines around his eyes and cutting across his forehead.

"Fine, the dog's a hero," Captain Garcia said, his expression betraying that he didn't believe a word of it. "Give me your report."

"We engaged and destroyed the ghoul in Oakland cemetery," Chris replied, careful to keep it formal since he was already on thin ice. "The target had dug up a fresh grave and was feeding on the corpse. We're good to go on burning it, just waiting for the green light."

Captain Garcia's frown deepened. "Status of the Silence?"

"Partially compromised, sir," Tashelle said. "No known civilian contact, but the police stopped and sniffed around our vehicle."

"We heard him on the scanner," the captain replied. "He called in the plates and got nothing. We spoofed a homicide call to pull him off you."

"They'll connect it as soon as someone discovers the grave and the desecrated corpse. That license number is burned."

"Bad luck. When we're done here, change out the plates with a set the DMSA has scrubbed."

They both nodded. Each vehicle kept at a half dozen or so registered, valid plates on hand to switch out if something like this happened, all courtesy of the Thorn's Data Manipulation and Security Arm hacking into DMV databases.

Captain Garcia looked at the dog again and let her sniff his hand. She licked his fingers. "What's her name?"

"I'm thinking Tracer."

"That's a crappy name for a dog," the captain said over his shoulder as he moved back to the command terminal behind the driver's side seat. The terminal consisted of a low spring chair hard-mounted to the floor, and a computer with two flat screen monitors. One screen showed a satellite image of Providence. The other streamed a constant flood of data and words, jacked into the Thorn's Data Manipulation and Security Arm intel streams. "But good work tracking the ghoul down. None of the other teams have reported contact yet."

"Be nice if we had watchers, sir," Tashelle ventured. "Sure would help with the hunt for the broodsire."

Captain Garcia gave her a tight smile. "Astral jumpers are a crutch. Use them too much, you start to wither and your hunter skills atrophy. We do this the old fashioned, ground-pounder way."

From the front seat, Richards slurped his coffee. Too loudly.

Chris eyed him and his damn coffee. Richards was the unit's resident magicslinger. Mages got to lounge around through all the shit work until they finally grabbed their magical walking sticks and did a few fireworks and took all the credit. Fucking casters. In any kind of hot situation they needed bodyguards to keep them safe while they tapped their eldritch powers or whatever showy bullshit they did. He wouldn't have minded so much, but Richards gave off a vibe as if he believed himself better than the rest of the line animals. As if he bought into that crap about mages being a higher breed, a distinguished and intellectual order superior to the trigger-pullers and blade-swingers.

Still, he should probably cut the guy some slack. He didn't really know Richards. The mage was one of the new additions from Sergeant Drake's team, when Command had merged two under-strength units. Maybe the guy suffered from chronic coffee-slurping syndrome and couldn't help making obnoxious, attention-grabbing noises.

Maybe.

Captain Garcia's voice cut through his annoyance. "I'm sending you both back out on another HKR. If we don't waste this broodsire, it'll just keep churning out new ghouls." He ran a hand through his black hair, staring at the map of Providence with narrowed eyes, his face appearing weary in the blue-tinged light. "Keep frosty. We find the big, bad nasty, don't engage. We'll need the full team to take it down."

So much for baseball and beer. Chris wouldn't have enjoyed them anyway. Not if monsters remained out there, hurting people. Sometimes he had problems sleeping, knowing that.

The encrypted radio squawked, startling them with Sergeant Drake's voice. "Specter One Actual this is Specter Three-Zero. We have sighted primary hostile at the following location." Drake rattled off a stream of GPS coordinates.

Captain Garcia grabbed his headset from where it dangled next to a computer screen. Eagerness yanked at his voice, dragged the words out fast. "Roger that,

Specter Three-Zero. Secure the area and do not engage. All other search teams stand by for pick up. Specter One Actual, out." He turned back to them. "Burn the ghoul, then follow me in the SUV. We'll finish this before the sun comes up."

Chris and Tashelle scrambled out of the van, but he had stop and call the dog, who seemed fascinated by Richards…or maybe with his coffee. She finally came, her tail wagging, now looking eager to head to the next round of excitement. Once they were clear, Richards started the van engine and drove to the end of the lot and stopped, waiting on them.

"Start the SUV," Chris told her. "I'll do this."

She nodded and hurried off. The engine turned over as he pulled a matchbook from a pocket of his fatigues.

"Stay back, pretty girl," he warned the dog. She watched him with her head cocked to the side and her ears up.

He lit a match, then torched the entire book and tossed it onto the stream of gasoline leading to the Dumpster. The flammable vapor had dissipated since they'd poured it, but enough remained to finish the job. Flames raced along the line of fuel. He grabbed the dog, turned and ran for the SUV. The dog started to lick his face, her tongue rasping against his helmet strap when she missed.

A very low bass *whump* sounded as the rest of the gasoline ignited, followed by a loud *clang* as the lid blew open and then slammed back down. Firelight flickered from inside the trash container. Smoke streamed from the edges. The ghoul body wouldn't be incinerated as completely as it would've been if they'd used thermate, but the flames would do enough damage to hide most of the deformities. The medical examiner would have a hell of a time determining how long it'd been dead, though.

Tashelle popped the door open for him as he reached the SUV. He set the dog inside, and when she was safe, he swung himself into the passenger seat. The van took off fast. They followed right behind, racing away from the fire, headed out to destroy the broodsire and put an end to this nightmare so they all could go home.

CHAPTER THREE
Late Night Bulletfest

Bad things happened at two in the morning.

He could sense it in the air, that looming sensation of disaster ready to fall on them at any second. The two a.m. stretch always seemed to be the hour when righteous hell broke loose. That's why he'd left the dog in the truck. He wanted her safe when the shit rained down.

The tension buzzed all the way down to his fingertips, as if he held an electric razor instead of his submachine gun. No sign so far of the broodsire that Sergeant Drake had called in. The damn thing was supposed to be as big as a polar bear, but somehow it had vanished. No broodsire, but plenty of examples of its work. The place was filthy with ghouls.

Specter team had deployed around the half-built frame of unfinished apartment complex. They'd advanced from three sides after Richards locked the place down with silence wards. They'd shot down a ghoul on their initial approach, meaning the place was still hot, despite the missing primary target. The ghoul sprawled on a pile of cinderblocks, rebar, and discarded two-by-fours with a hole in its head from an MP10.

Chris had caught bodyguard detail, assigned to protect Richards as he played boy wizard. It was work Roth always referred to as diaper duty with his usual sneer. Richards stood on a four-foot by four-foot steel plate thrown on the dirt, crushing the weeds along the edges. A perfect circle had been drawn on the metal square in silver paint, with runes curving around the inside rim, and lines radiating from an intricate symbol in the exact center. A shimmer of light hovered a few inches above the circle's diameter, bright as a neon sign in the darkness. Because he was supposed to protect the guy, Chris had to stand close enough to the mage and his woo-woo lightshow that he felt the hair on his arms lifting, trembling as if in a breeze, and there was no breeze.

Another good reason for leaving the dog in the SUV, despite the sad eyes she'd loosed on him. He couldn't risk her prancing into the middle of Richard's spell-slinging and getting her tail burned off. That, and he didn't want her hurt when the shit went down.

Which it would any minute now, judging from the heavy charge in the air, that ominous feeling that bad things were on the verge of breaking hard.

At least one of them should stay safe.

He keyed off his mike headset so it wasn't hot and glanced at Richards. "Can you tell if it's here?"

"Hey, Hill," Richards said, keeping his eyes closed. "I'm trying to keep the wards up. You mind?"

The mage was tricked out in the same gear as the rest of the squad—Kevlar body armor reinforced with alumina ceramic plates and a tactical helmet—but he also wore a dark blue cloak with a deep hood. And then there was the requisite five and a half foot long wooden quarterstaff he gripped in both hands. He held it in front of him with the silver butt cap placed in the center of the pentacle, the staff's top end glowing with a thin wire of green light that reminded Chris of a light bulb filament or strand of fiber optic cable twisting around it. Magicslingers. Never without their stupid oversized magic cane, showing off.

"You guys are all flash, no fire, you know that?" Chris flipped down his night vision goggles and scanned the construction site again. Mounds of sand and gravel sat near a backhoe. Pipe trenches crisscrossed the ground in dark slashes, patiently waiting to break someone's ankle. Weeds sprouted everywhere—a damn forest of them. More dingy brick tenements off to his left and right flanks. This new complex they were building would probably look just as seedy within a year.

He hadn't seen any sign of the rest of the Specter teams since they'd breached the building with a full on dynamic assault. There'd been some shooting at first, radio chatter about the contact with ghouls, but nothing for minutes now. Chris didn't like the quiet.

Just as he was getting antsy, Captain Garcia's voice crackled over the radio. "This is Specter One Actual. Give me status, over."

Sergeant Drake checked in first for his assault team. "Specter Two-Zero, no visual. Heading to third level, over."

"Specter Three-Zero, no contact, no visual on primary, over." That was Karen Cox, from the sound of her voice.

"Specter Charlie-Three, silence maintained, over." Specter C3 was the command and control center for the unit. Bowen had taken over running the computers in the command vehicle since the captain was on the line. Specter One, Two, and Three were on active hunt. Specter Four consisted of one mage and one dedicated mage nose-wiper, also known as Chris Hill, today's sorry sack.

Chris keyed his mike on. "Specter Four, we're tight. Wards good. No visual on hostile, over."

"Copy that, all. Keep sharp."

Chris returned to his scan of the weeds and piles of half-rotted wood planks. The tense boredom of waiting for something violent to happen made him edgy. His long sword hung on his back, snug in its modified harness and sheath. The heft of the MP7 was an even more reassuring weight in his hands. Someday he might have the chance to pop off rounds from the submachine gun, firing one-handed like a pistol while hacking away at monsters with his sword. On second thought, if something got that close, he'd be in some serious shit.

"How many HKRs you been on, Hill?" Richards asked, startling him with the sudden question. "You seem over-torqued."

"How about you put your shiny stick between your ass cheeks and pogo? I thought you needed quiet."

"I'm serious, man. How many?"

HKR was an acronym for Hunt-Kill-Run—a search and destroy mission targeting any threat to humanity. Vampires. Psychotic Fae. Monsters of every shape and creed. The Thorn didn't discriminate.

"Millions. I got my monster card punched, so don't wet your wizard panties."

Richards closed his eyes again. A sour smirk twisted his lips. "What's your problem anyway?"

"Babysitting." But it was more than that. He didn't like working with guys he didn't know. You never could tell until it was too late if they were motivated to save your ass or just focused on saving their own.

"Just keep the bad things off me while I keep things locked down," Richards said. "All I expect."

"Yeah, my goddamn fun meter's pegged."

Richards had been tasked with sealing the area off so the teams could cut loose without pulling the attention every cop in Providence. Explosions and rifle fire tended to do exactly that. The wards would maintain the silence, cloak the operation, and keep civilians from straying into the combat zone. It was important, yeah, but he only wished someone else had caught the guard duty. He wanted to be inside on active hunt, adding to his monster tally. He resettled his grip on the MP7 and put his eyes back on the creepy apartment complex. Half-finished buildings always made him think of rotting corpses. He couldn't shake that feeling that bad shit was set to go down fast.

Gunfire erupted, shattering the stillness. Chris lifted the submachine gun, his heart lurching in his chest then falling into a rhythm of quick thuds. Bursts of muzzle flash lit up the third floor of the apartment complex, matching up with the gunshots that rattled over the radio and cracked in the air.

"Multiple targets! Hostiles! Hostiles!" someone— he thought it was Chen—shouted over the radio so loudly that the words distorted through the headset.

"This is Specter Actual, identify yourself and position!"

More gunfire. So damn loud over the headset speaker that Chris gritted his teeth. A grenade went off with a crashing *ka-bang*. The explosion blew out a chunk of half-finished wall and sent a hail of debris raining down. He felt the unpleasant push of the concussion wave even this far away. Smoke billowed out in a black-gray cloud.

Sergeant Drake's voice broke over the radio, sounding as calm as if he were having a beer on a fishing boat. "Specter Two-Zero engaging multiple hostiles on third floor. Secure all exits and check your targets."

Ghouls were screeching and screaming now. Sounded like dozens of them at least. Chris kept his weapon trained on the third floor, trying to keep the barrel steady, his index finger resting alongside the trigger guard. All he could see were occasional flashes of light from shooters inside.

"Watch the walls! Watch the walls!" That was Tashelle's voice.

More gunfire in sharp staccato bursts followed by the occasional shotgun roar. Gibbering wails and shrieks echoed from the windows, seeming to come from all directions. His heart hammered and all his muscles felt twitchy as he waited for something to happen in his area of responsibility, wanting to get a shot, not wanting to get a shot.

"They're breaking! They're rabbiting. Get that—" A swell of gunfire drowned out the words.

"Keep formation." That was Captain Garcia's voice, sharp with command. "Clear those rooms. Watch your corners."

Wood crunched and splintered as ghouls ripped their way through the framework, clawing and struggling to get outside. Their gray-skinned bodies were horribly disfigured with scar-patterns. They smashed through the planks and plywood, shredding their own bodies, and hurled themselves from the third floor. Christ, there were so many of them. A good dozen or so plummeted to the ground, shrieking as debris fell all around them.

"Tangoes in the open!" someone shouted.

Chris trained his MP7 on the first ghoul as it scrambled to its feet. It shook itself and began to lope toward him. The flayed mouth made it look as if it were grinning madly.

"Specter Three, ghouls incoming my position! Need support now!" he yelled into the mike, then opened up on it.

The flat pop of his shots sang out. His first three shots went wide and high—fear and adrenaline dump to blame. He resettled the butt stock against his shoulder and sighted in again. The ghoul began to howl as it ran. His next shot caught it in the forehead, blew through its skull and into the building behind. It went limp and collapsed—a puppet with its strings cut.

The other ghouls had spotted them now. They charged straight for him. Their gibbering shrieks echoed from the buildings. Their eyes flashed and slaver dripped from their slashed-wide mouths.

Behind him, Richards said, "Fuck me," in a whoosh of breath and began to rapidly whisper strange syllables.

Chris ignored him and took aim on the closest ghoul, knowing there was no way he could drop them all in time. Adrenaline sizzled through his veins in a white-hot flood, and his breathing came hard and fast. Everything seemed sharper. Louder. Even the distant traffic noises sounded clearer, his own breath whooshed in and out of his mouth in hurricane gusts, the smells of dirt and oil and green weeds flooded everything, and the resounding thud of the ghoul's legs driving into the ground as it ran echoed in his ears like kettledrum strikes.

He opened up on semi-auto, pumping out high velocity rounds that cracked through the air. Headshots on running targets were damn hard.

Frantic chatter sounded over the radio. Captain Garcia demanding a status update and breathing hard as if he were full-on sprinting. Someone else speaking too fast, with too much excitement. The words buzzed through Chris's mind but meant nothing.

The ghouls bore down on them with happy hunger in their eyes, sharpened teeth gleaming, the tall weeds whipping against their thighs as they ran. He continued to pump out bullets, biting down so hard it felt as if his jaw muscles would break his teeth. Two more ghouls dropped. A third staggered and shrieked, but was back in motion again a moment later.

The assault teams opened fire from the third floor. They were firing toward his position, but he couldn't call them off. He needed the fire support. And if one of his buddies ended up putting a bullet in him, that was going to be a bitch. Several ghouls immediately lurched and went down in flailing tangles of limbs under the second assault. The rest kept right on coming.

Shit, shit, shit. Chris squeezed off three more rounds pointblank, killing another, but they were on him now. There was no space to retreat. He had to keep them from reaching Richards. If they got to the mage, the silence and cloaking wards would drop. Then holy hell would bust loose.

A ragged female ghoul grabbed at him. She snapped her sharpened teeth and brayed laughter. Chris was already half twisting, half falling out of her reach. Some bastard shot her from behind. Her skull exploded, and the bullet buzzed past Chris's helmet like an angry bee before it finally buried itself in the dirt.

Weeds slashed at him as he fell to the ground. The impact drove the edge of his night vision device into his face and knocked it off. First one ghoul, then all the remaining ones threw back their heads and screamed high, keening cries. The closest one moved on Richards. A gray tongue peeked from between its teeth, tasted the air, then vanished.

Richards stood his ground, not moving from the circle drawn on the steel plate. His lips drew back from his teeth in a snarl as he swung his staff. The glowing wire of energy twisting around the staff left streaks of green afterimage in Chris's eyes. Two-by-fours and four-by-fours flew out of the weeds and smashed into the ghoul. The sound of its bones breaking was like snapping branches. It went down in a pile of debris. But more were already closing in.

Chris scrambled to his feet. He had no time for radio calls for help or to wait on support. He didn't even feel fear, only a pristine clarity, a laser-tight focus that made everything around him seem to be moving a second slower than he moved. He ripped his long sword free of its sheath. The blade was silver-plated steel, the edge was ultra-high carbon steel, wicked sharp.

A big ghoul with buckshot holes in its belly snatched at Richards with one wide, thick hand, its knuckles as big as walnuts.

Chris brought his sword slashing down on its bulging forearm. The blade sheared through flesh, muscle, and bone. The ghoul's hand went flying, fingers twitching, and landed in a pipe trench. It shrieked in outrage, not pain, then wheeled on him, sending a gust of reeking carrion breath into his face. He swung at its head, but it flinched aside enough that he only sliced a thin wound in its throat. He immediately followed with another slash and the blade hacked into its upper thigh.

The damn ghoul fell over. The sword went with it, ripped out of his hands and still buried deep in the bone. Dimly, he heard another flurry of radio chatter over his headset, but his ears were still ringing from his gunfire and the ghoul's screams and the words seemed nothing more than static-laced, disconnected sounds.

He hesitated, not sure if he should try the MP7 again at this range or pull his sidearm. The clarity he'd had only an instant before began to smoke rapidly away.

Another ghoul, flayed more elaborately than the others, turned and marked him with cold, dead eyes. It surged forward, jaws gaping, spike-sharpened teeth seeming as big as arrowheads.

He stiff-armed the ghoul in the chest as he yanked at his pistol. The ghoul was strong. It rocked him back on his heels and lunged at his throat. Its teeth barely missed. They scraped his helmet strap. He couldn't get the pistol free of the holster.

"Fucker," he grunted and shoved the ghoul as hard as he could. No fancy judo takedowns. No throws or finesse. Raw strength boosted by adrenaline sent the ghoul staggering backward.

Mage Richards cut loose with a spell sculpture. Cords of white-blue energy formed in a nimbus around his outthrust hand, spiraling there in between the miniscule wormholes that fed the spell its mystigen fuel across a spacetime bridge. The cords shot out and wrapped around the ghoul's legs and arms, jerking tight and cutting into the scarified flesh as it struggled to rip free. Finally it gave a gurgling cry and toppled over, crashing to the ground. The ghoul thrashed against the spell's energy cords but couldn't break loose. It howled in frustrated rage.

Chris realized he was standing there, empty-handed. His sword was still lodged in another ghoul's leg. He spotted it struggling to crawl its way to Richards, jaws snapping shut with those *clacks* that sent a shiver down his spine. His blade gouged shallow trenches in the earth with the crossguard. Blood beaded in the dirt and smeared on the weeds. He finally drew his pistol free of the holster. It came out smoothly, without a hitch. He shot the ghoul in the head.

There were no more ghouls standing. He blinked around at the carnage. Thorn knights swarmed around him now, guns locked on the fallen ghouls. Captain Garcia kept yelling orders to hold fire. Richards collapsed to one knee. He leaned on his staff, his face pale and strained. His hair was soaked with sweat.

On autopilot, Chris ejected the submachine gun's magazine and switched it out with a fresh one. He'd lost track of how many shots he'd fired. His hands didn't even tremble as he reloaded. He stared at them. His fingertips were cold, yeah, but he didn't see even the slightest tremor. Everything seemed almost unreal, but at the same time, filled with so much detail it threatened to overwhelm him.

Captain Garcia moved past him in a shooting stance, holding his assault rifle against his shoulder, its silver-plated bayonet gleaming. He gave Chris a nod before stopping near the bound ghoul. It hissed and filled the air with surreal curses. This close, Chris could see the incredible intricacy and detail to the patterns of scars all over its body, and it made him uneasy. Something very twisted had carved those wounds to ornament the maggot-colored flesh.

"Specter Actual, this is Specter Four," Bowen said over the radio from the van's command terminal. "Silence maintained. Negative police or emergency rescue activity, over."

"Copy that." Captain Garcia stared down into the ghoul's frenzied eyes as it strained against the spell cords binding it. "Maintain overwatch positions."

Sergeant Drake ambled up to stand beside the captain. He was taller, with a jutting lower lip and a jaw bristling with blond stubble, but his eyes were just as hard. His scarred-up M4 carbine looked as though it had been through a major offensive campaign and kept its owner alive. Drake glanced at the ghoul then turned his attention back to the surrounding buildings. He spat chew and wiped his lip with the back of his glove. "Big bad boy's gone."

Chris figured he was damn lucky the broodsire had run off. If that thing had gone for him or for Richards, he wasn't sure either of them would still be standing here right now. A broodsire was a nasty piece of work, huge, tough as a tank, as hostile as they came. They'd probably need the whole team to bring it down, including Pin with her boom-lance.

Captain Garcia glared at the sergeant. "How the hell did that happen?"

"Needed more men to lock down the area. He must've caught wind of us scouting, blitzed us with his little dogs to keep us busy, bugged out through the back." Drake shrugged. "Maybe this wasn't the main nest. Sometimes those fuckers have two, three places to hole up."

The captain grunted, then squatted down beside the ghoul, cradling his rifle in his lap. He cocked his head and stared at it. The ghoul tried to inch its way across the ground to his boot like a worm, gnashing its teeth the entire time.

"Where's your broodsire?" he finally asked it.

The ghoul ignored him. It continued to try and squirm its body close enough to bite him. The captain stood and put a boot on its neck, stopping it from moving. It tried to bite the tread but couldn't get the right angle.

"Is this your nest?" Captain Garcia asked. From the conversational tone of his voice, he might've been asking who would be the Yankee's relief pitcher instead of grilling a monster in the middle of carnage and gun smoke. "Where is your broodsire?"

The ghoul groaned and loosed a wavering whine. Its tongue drooped from its mouth and stirred in the dirt, leaving thick ropes of saliva behind.

"Tell me where the broodsire is and I'll give you mercy."

The ghoul strained against the cords again. They cut into its flesh but didn't break. It screamed one last time, then began to spit out words. "The father feeds his children. He would've given us your flesh. We are always hungry. We are remade and we are hungry."

Sergeant Drake spat a stream of brown chew across the ghoul's leg and sneered. "Meaningless babbling bullshit. Do better."

"The father will carve you!" the ghoul shrieked and began to thrash frantically. "Flay you, sculpt you, pierce you. *Decorate* you forever."

The captain's face twisted with disgust. He pointed his rifle at the ghoul, the bayonet blade near its face. "Your nest. Where is it? Are the people you kidnapped still alive? How many are left?"

The ghoul only wheezed laughter. Its tongue lashed out and trembled in the air under the bayonet. It licked along the blade, the knife edge cutting slowly into its tongue. Yeah, and there went Chris's appetite for the rest of the year.

The captain slapped the tongue aside with the flat of the blade. "Tell me, goddamn it."

"God gives His flesh to eat." A giggle bubbled from its throat. The ghoul sounded like a four-year old kid. "And so do you."

"Just kill it, captain," Sergeant Drake said. "Bastard wants to die."

Captain Garcia stared down at the ghoul but didn't reply. Many of the other Thorn knights watched it through their weapon sights. Chris kept glancing from the ghoul to the dark windows of the half-finished apartment complex. He felt sick to his stomach. All this, and if the broodsire had escaped, they were right back at square one.

"Last chance." The captain moved the rifle barrel, pointing it at one brown, bloodshot eye, the bayonet tip only inches from the monster's flesh.

"Too late for mercy." A thick gurgle came from its shredded mouth. "We took a little boy tonight. Such a tiny boy. His face will haunt—"

Garcia drew his rifle back and drove the bayonet

deep into the ghoul's chest. The blade rasped as it glanced along bone. The ghoul groaned and coughed out a mist of blood. Everyone was staring at it now, dread and loathing on every face. A little boy...

"Tell me where he is." Captain Garcia yanked the bayonet free and again set the bloody tip below the ghoul's right eye. His voice was cold, every word stabbing like an icicle. "Tell me or I swear to Jesus I will hurt you until you do."

But the ghoul cackled and drew its head away, arching its back off the ground. Then it reversed itself, shoving its head forward and driving its skull into the captain's bayonet. The blade pierced its eye, punched through to its brain before the captain could react. The ghoul shuddered and went limp. Blood ran from its flayed mouth. During the ghoul's thrashing, its limbs had been sliced to the bone by the spell cords and wept blood.

The captain cursed. He stepped on the ghoul's forehead with his boot heel and wrenched his bayonet free. But it was far too late. The ghoul was toast. Chris's hands began shaking with delayed reaction, so he clenched them tighter. That poor kid, trapped with monsters like this. Christ.

Sergeant Drake stared at the ghoul, his eyes bright with loathing. He spat a stream of brown chew across the ghoul's face.

It was Pin, the team's lancer, who finally put her hand on Captain Garcia's shoulder and asked what they were all thinking. "What now, Captain?"

He didn't look at her. He wiped the rifle bayonet clean on the ghoul's shredded clothing. When he spoke, his voice was low and fierce. "We're gonna save that kid. No matter what. We get him back."

Captain Garcia looked up and moved his gaze from face to face. Chris almost flinched when the captain turned that electric gaze on him. It was all he could do to meet the man's eyes. Commanders were supposed to be detached, cool-headed, but the captain was the farthest from objective he'd ever seen. No one spoke. Every face was grim. Chris felt as if he'd been kicked in the gut by a skittish horse. A missing kid. The only thing worse would be a dead kid, and that would happen soon enough if they didn't find him fast.

The captain shook his head and swiped a hand across his face, breaking the spell. "All right, clear the area for incendiaries. Get the corpses in the building and burn it. We move out in ten." He waved a hand at the dead ghoul that still had Chris's sword buried in its thigh. "Hill, get your sword out of that filthy piece of shit."

His sword was so embedded in the bone that

Weeger had to come over and help him lever the blade free. Chris cleaned the blade with a rag that he left on the dead body, then sheathed the sword and walked over to Richards. They stared at each other. Then Richards smiled a little and jerked his chin. Chris nodded back because he could think of nothing to say that wouldn't sound stupid and trite and absolutely irrelevant. Everything still held a disconcerting unreal, super-real cast. His thoughts felt bright but chaotic, zigzagging through his mind in random lightning bolts.

He slung his MP7 and walked away as the others prepped the site to burn. He didn't want anyone else to see combat reaction setting in. He didn't want a beer anymore, didn't want baseball or pizza, couldn't give a damn about how the war story tonight would spotlight him and Richards, front and center. He kept thinking about the kid—the faceless little boy the ghoul had taunted them about. He just wanted to find that kid, bring him home to his parents or whoever was missing him right now. Maybe see a little joy for once in a long fucking while.

He went to the tactical van and opened the door. The dog was there to greet him. He smiled at her. She sniffed his hand and licked his fingers. He patted her on the head until her tail wagged.

They loaded up the gear in the two SUVs and the

tactical van. Weeger spread accelerant throughout the half-built apartment complex and over the dead ghouls, then Tashelle and Chen tossed incendiary grenades and sprinted back to the van even as Sergeant Drake called in the fire to 911. Thermate burned hot enough to fuse metal, so with the accelerant it'd be enough to consume the freakish ghoul bodies. The civvies would know it was arson, there was no avoiding that. Sergeant Drake had called in the fire, skirting the Silence protocols, because nobody wanted the flanking tenements to catch fire and innocent people to die or lose their homes.

Innocent people...

That a fucking abomination like a broodsire had stolen a little kid for its nest of ghouls... All his bitching earlier—who gave a shit now? The kid was out there somewhere, scared, alone. The cops would have no idea what was in store for him.

Chris knew. He knew and it burned his heart inside him.

CHAPTER FOUR

Down Time

The fluorescent track light buzzed in the kitchen of the safe house. The sound reminded Chris of flies swarming a dead body. Shit, what an image, second time tonight that something had pulled corpses to mind. He really needed to work on his positive visualization.

The other distracting sound was his dog scarfing down the two hamburgers he'd cooked her after they'd rolled back to their base of operations. She was an enthusiastic eater, he'd give her that. He didn't have much appetite anymore.

Chris took a long pull from his beer. Sam Adams. He'd hidden the last bottle way in the back of the fridge. He'd set it on its side behind two Tupperware containers holding food decorated with fuzzy coats of mold. He'd had to hide it so none of the others would snag it. Fridge food and drink was pretty much fair game, first come first served. Besides, only one beer was allowed tonight because they'd be up at dawn, searching for the kid, so he wanted it to be a good beer. Sure that ugly son of a bitch ghoul might've been lying, bluffing about the boy, but no knight worthy of the title would take a chance on something like that. No way.

He was exhausted, but too wired to sleep, even though the After Action Report had seemed to drag on for hours instead of minutes. It was a bit of a cherished cliché that soldiers could sleep any time and through anything, but he couldn't stop thinking about the kid. No sleep would come with his brain racing like this, unable to turn itself off. The faceless boy—he didn't even know the kid's name yet. The captain, Sergeant Drake, and Bowen were on it, trying to verify if a child had gone missing recently, most likely in the last few hours because otherwise it'd be splashed all over the news already.

He sat on the tile kitchen counter, leaning back against the cabinets. He stared at the dog eating and wondered if the boy liked dogs. The kitchen still had ugly black appliances that looked as if they'd rolled straight out of the 1980s. Now that he thought about it, they probably had. The Thorn owned safe houses in every major city in the States. They served as both a center of operations and a secure place to crash for a while off base, outside the wire and in red zones. None of the safe houses he'd seen had been very well kept, but it wasn't as if Thorn knights were promised stays in the Biltmore Hotel. A roof was a roof.

Tashelle walked into the kitchen. She'd changed back into civvies—jeans and a T-shirt—and had her black hair pulled back in clips. She opened the fridge and scanned the shelves. "Where'd you get that? All I see's Bud Light."

He only smiled mysteriously.

She gave his bottle one last look, sighed, and grabbed a Bud Light. She twisted off the top and leaned against the counter. She glanced at his dog and then gave him a look.

"Really? Hamburgers? For the dog?"

He shrugged. "She was hungry. Haven't had time to buy dog food."

"You figure out a name for her yet?"

"I was thinking…Boomstick."

This time even the dog looked at him, although she took it one step further by letting out a whine. Tashelle only shook her head slowly.

"All right," he said. "I'll keep working on it. Names are hard."

"Only if you're brain-impaired." She took a long

swig of her beer then looked at him, her face now guarded. "So what do you think?"

"I think you're lucky my ego is diamond-plated. You try thinking up a good name for a dog that hasn't been used a million times."

She lowered her voice. "No. About Drake's people."

He frowned and glanced at the doorway, checking that they were alone. "I was going to ask you that earlier but we got interrupted."

"Yeah, and I didn't want to jinx our first big field op. You know the rules. Don't jinx stuff talking about it ahead of time."

"They seem to know their shit." He took a drink. "That girl, Pin, from Drake's team is *muy caliente*, though. You know, the lancer chick, whatever her real name is."

"I'm gonna forgive you, Hill, because you're brain-damaged and can't remember. But try to sear it into your brain that I'm not just one of the guys."

"Guess I won't talk about how much I want to smack that ass, then."

"Being a dick on purpose. Brilliant strategy."

"Saw an opportunity to be funny and seized the initiative. You hear why they call her Pin?"

She gave him an impatient look. "Her real

name's Something Deering. Maybe Jessica or Jessie. Her lance uses safety lock pins in the explosives, so they call her Pin. Don't make me break out the hand puppets."

He grunted. The dark-haired lancer had caught his eye from the first. She was a hard charger, but pretty cold. That ice-in-the-veins type. She was also crazy. All lancers were crazy. They ran up to monsters and rammed them with lances tipped with shaped-charges. That was pretty damn unhinged. In the field she wore modified heavy-duty bomb squad armor that made her look like an awkward spacewoman. He was surprised anyone could move in all that gear.

"Yeah, well, I was just asking," he said, hiding behind another swig.

Tashelle smirked. "Just asking. You're a fool *and* a horn dog." But she smiled at him. Tashelle was also a hard charger, but she had a charming smile. Probably charming because she showed it so rarely. "But I guess you're all right." She squatted down to pet his dog. "You and your mutt."

The dog's tail wagged wildly and she licked Tashelle's face.

"Careful," he said. "That tongue is loaded."

Tashelle stood and turned back to him. All good humor had left her face. "The captain's pretty pissed," she said after a long pause. "The broodsire getting past us. That ghoul offing itself on his knife. Not the way things should've gone down."

He didn't answer. He'd never seen Captain Garcia slip up like that, making a stupid mistake that had cost them intel when someone's life was at stake. Unnerving. But he didn't want to talk about that either. Everybody fucked up eventually.

She took another drink and very pointedly didn't look at him. "Wonder what Sarge's people thought."

"Who cares?"

Now she looked at him. "What's that?"

"Who cares what they thought. There's a *kid* out there. Captain let it get under his skin, let his blade get a little close maybe, and the monster offed itself. Good riddance. I'm not gonna piss on him 'cause he's human."

"Yeah? I'm not pissing on him either, but you know the deal. We aren't supposed to let it get to us, make us sloppy. You start letting it get inside…"

Chris didn't mention her freezing up on the ghoul. He couldn't. He was her friend. "I don't give a damn what Drake's people thought. We been with the captain for long enough, you know he's righteous."

"Bad way to start a new team is all. And that little boy out there…"

"I know." He went for another swig, but his beer

was empty. He flung it at the trash bin. The bottle hit the rim and bounced off. It didn't break, though. There was that.

"How many beers you have?" Tashelle asked, trying on a hesitant smile. "Miss a shot like that?"

"Just that one."

"So white boys can't jump and they can't shoot either."

He made an effort, because she was making an effort. "Don't make me remind you my beer was better than yours. Because it was."

She made a face like she thought he was a fool. Well, she was probably right. He called the dog to him, and she trotted over and yawned. He understood that well enough. He headed toward the hall, thinking about his bunk and wondering if he'd ever manage any sleep. And what were the chances his dog didn't have fleas?

"Good job out there, Hill," Tashelle called after him.

He glanced back and shrugged, uncomfortable with the praise. "Tomorrow's what counts."

CHAPTER FIVE

Early Morning Bleak

The briefing was the worst kind: early, while the coffee had barely started seeping into Chris's veins, and with jack shit for info. The entire team had pressed into the safe house's den, a room with pale blue wallpaper and pastel pink carpet and smelled faintly of mildew. Chris found himself a good seat while his dog laid down at his boots and put her head on her paws. Captain Garcia kicked the briefing off.

"Two watchers are scanning Providence, trying to pinpoint the location of the main broodsire nest and our primary target." The captain's black hair was in disarray, sagging skin bunched under his eyes, and his uniform was as rumpled as newspaper used for packing. He'd been out all night with Sergeant Drake trying to gather intel. "We confirmed that a five-year-old boy was kidnapped from his room last night, his abduction reported this morning. It's all over the news now. Amber alerts. Press conferences. We're certain it's the boy the ghoul taunted us about."

Sergeant Drake held up a color photocopy photo and slowly swept his arm around the room so they could all see the picture of a grinning boy with wide, green eyes. The boy wore a shirt with Batman on it, a red cowboy hat, and flip-flops. He leaned over the bars of his tricycle as if racing. The room was silent. Only eyes moved to track the boy's picture as Drake turned it.

"His name's Michael Cantwell," Captain Garcia continued. "His mother called it in an hour ago. She found his room empty this morning, the window open, screen slashed, Michael gone. I don't think I need to tell you how out of her mind with panic she was. We got the 911 call recording and we got access to all police databases. But they're looking for a human kidnapper, and we know different."

Chris stared at the photo. He kept his face absolutely blank, but god*damn* he wanted to find some fucking monster and carve it up. A kid. Part of him didn't even want to think about it anymore; it was too horrible. But he had to anyway because it was his damn job, and the boy deserved better than that. A little kid...and now he had a face to put on the boy.

"How long you think we got, Captain?" Weeger asked softly.

"That's an unknown, but time ain't on our side. When we get a location from the watchers, we roll out full force and take these bastards down. The broodsire's still out there, not to mention a shitload of ghouls we haven't engaged. We got people at Command pouring over missing persons data and recent unsolved murders, trying to triangulate high-probability locations where the ghouls might be holed up. A lot of search and destroy, but I'm confident we can pin them down, rescue the boy, and purge the threat. So I want everybody ready to go at a moment's notice."

Sergeant Drake glared around the room. "Killing these motherfuckers is top priority—"

"Saving the kid is top priority," Captain Garcia interrupted, throwing the sergeant a dark glance. "After we get the kid safe and clear, we don't leave anything standing."

Drake only nodded and barked out, "Boots on, all weapons clean and good to go. We'll feed out updates as they come in. Stay sharp."

With the briefing over, everyone started to disperse to check gear and weapons. Chris called his dog and started for the kitchen, hoping for another cup of coffee before he saw to his gear. He didn't even care if the coffee resembled sewer sludge, he just needed the caffeine.

"Hill," Captain Garcia called. "Hold back a sec."

Shit. Never good to be singled out. He turned back and waited as everyone, including Sergeant Drake, filed out. Drake gave him a long, considering look as he walked past. Chris kept his thousand-yard stare and tried not to shift under the scrutiny.

After the room finally emptied, the captain glanced his way, frowning. He rubbed his face, his hand rasping against the stubble. Exhaustion had deepened the lines around his eyes, turned his expression haunted. But when he spoke, voice was still whip-sharp. "Good work out there last night."

"Thanks, Captain."

"I know nobody likes to stay off the line to protect the mages, but you see what can happen when we leave the spellslingers with their asses in the wind."

Chris only nodded. He'd been lucky, nothing more. A few more ghouls or a few more misses and he'd have been monster food. No reason to be proud. He should've been better prepared, taken the task more seriously. But he wasn't going to admit that to the captain.

"You'll go in with us when we find these bastards," Captain Garcia continued. "I promise you that."

"Sounds good, sir."

The captain glanced at an ugly, spiky monstrosity of a sun-shaped clock hanging on the blue wallpaper. "We don't have a lot of time."

Chris didn't know what to say, so again he only nodded kept his peace. An image came back to him. Last night, the ghoul licking the knife-edge of the captain's bayonet, then driving its skull into the blade, impaling itself.

Captain Garcia turned back to him and tried on a smile, but it was a tired, half-hearted thing. The smile deepened, though, when his gaze shifted to the dog. "Got a name for your mutt yet?"

"I'm still thinking on it."

"Be certain she doesn't get in our way. If she's a problem, then she goes."

"Understood, sir."

"Better see to your gear, knight. You know what's at stake."

Chris bowed and walked out, feeling like his insides were tangled up knots of electrical cord. He was afraid he'd be seeing that kid's face in his dreams for a very long time if they didn't find him soon.

CHAPTER SIX

Shot Down

Six hours and nothing. No word on the missing boy. No strike location on the ghoul nest from the watchers. Nothing. And waiting was the worst.

Chris sat in the kitchen, eating a bowl of clam chowder from a batch Weeger had made. From time to time he tossed clams to the dog. She snapped them out of the air and licked her chops after every one. Weeger was a bit of a wingnut, but he sure could cook.

Richards sat across from him at the wobbly table with the mismatched plastic chairs and crumpled saltines into his bowl of chowder. Jessica, a.k.a. Pin, stood by the sink, eating quietly and staring at the vinyl floor as if lost in thought. Chris shoveled in chowder fast as he could work the spoon. He'd cleaned his MP7 again an hour ago, then moved on to his M9 Beretta, and after that his sword blade, combat knife, boots, and armor. Eating at least took his mind off the waiting and didn't require him to disassemble and reassemble things.

A steady stream of solemn words drifted from the TV in the other room, turned to a twenty-four hour cable news station. News had gone out across the country about missing Michael Cantwell. Cops had set up roadblocks in surrounding neighborhoods and were asking for help and any information people might have on suspicious persons in South Providence neighborhoods last night.

"This isn't very good chowder," Richards said, breaking Chris's train of thought. He stirred the cracker crumbs into the soup with both hands on the spoon, as if he were a witch brewing in a cauldron.

Chris eyed him. "What the hell are you talking about? This is great. Even the dog likes it."

"The dog likes it and that's a compliment?" He shook his head. "It's not thick enough."

"What do you know about chowder anyway? You're from Vermont. They don't even have any ocean." He turned to Jessica. "Hey Pin, you like this chowder?"

She glanced at him and frowned. She was trim and cut—not grotesque, not like a bodybuilder or anything, but tromping around in all that heavy armor gave a girl muscles, and he could appreciate it. Dark hair, blue eyes, those lips...she'd be downright stunning if she ever smiled.

"It was good," she finally said.

"See, Richards? She knows."

"Taste is taste," Richards replied with a shrug. "I never apologize for mine." He set his bowl on the floor next to the dog and patted her as she scrambled over and went to town on his leftovers.

Chris pushed down a twinge of protective jealousy, seeing Richards touching his dog. Instead he smiled at Jessica. That had been the first time she'd responded to anything he'd said that wasn't mission-related. Time to see if he could exploit the breakthrough.

"So Jessica...you like being called Pin better or Jess or what?"

She set her bowl in the sink and walked out of the kitchen without responding. Without even looking his way again. Ouch.

"Maybe she doesn't like any of those names," he said, trying to pull out of his nosedive.

"Maybe she just doesn't like you. Maybe she likes professionals. You know, people who act older than thirteen."

"Nah, that's not it. She's probably allergic to

dogs."

Richards stared at him and methodically ate soup crackers. He chewed for a bit, then said, "How come you're never serious?"

"I'm serious when I'm pulling the trigger. What are you? My girlfriend?"

"You're not exactly scoring with Jessica."

Chris grinned. "And after we shared that moment last night, you go and kick a man when he's down."

"And you're reading way too much into last night, Hill."

"Yeah? Well, I don't have to babysit you this go round. I'm sure you're happy to hear it after our difficult break up."

Richards grunted.

"Gonna headshot some ghouls instead."

The mage stared at him. "Just find that kid."

"Yeah, no shit." He took a breath, biting off an angry reply. He didn't want to get into it with Richards right now. Blessed were the peacemakers and all that crap. "So what do you think about the captain?"

"You ran with him. I don't know him."

"He's a hundred percent righteous. A quiet professional to the core."

"Suck his dick, why don't you?" Richards said,

then shrugged and looked away. "Heard he's high-strung."

"Yeah? You lose your kid, then find out some fucking monster stole another kid, and you got the gonads to sit there and say 'high-strung?'"

"That true? About him losing his kid?"

Chris didn't answer, furious at himself for letting it slip to begin with. It wasn't his place to talk about stuff like that. The captain deserved better. But the high-strung comment had pissed him right the hell off, yanked the words out of his mouth before he'd realized what he was going to say.

He couldn't imagine losing a child. Couldn't even imagine it.

Instead, he grabbed a dishtowel and went to clean the dog. She'd snarfled all the chowder in Richard's bowl and coated her muzzle in clams and white sauce. Try as she might, she couldn't quite manage to lick her dog face spotless. She looked so silly that he could only take pity on her and lend a hand.

"All right," Richards said slowly after it must've become clear Chris wasn't going to answer his question. "Guess that explains things." But he frowned, as if he didn't like something, as if a bad taste lingered in his mouth.

Chris wasn't hungry any more. He was tired of

Richards. He was damn well tired of waiting. He dumped his bowl into the sink. As he headed out to check his gear for the hundredth time, he stopped in front of Richards and looked him in the eye.

"One more thing, boy wizard. Don't touch my dog."

"That how it is now?"

"That's how it is."

CHAPTER SEVEN
Saddle Up

Captain Garcia walked into the bunkroom wearing a well-cut dark suit like a CEO or banker. He didn't seem to notice or care about the odd looks some of Drake's people threw his way. He scanned the bunks and the ready gear as he made his way to Chris's bunk. He even stopped to pet the dog as Chris scrambled to his feet.

"Hill, meet me at the SUV in ten. No weapons. No gear."

The captain walked out again just as abruptly, leaving Chris to blurt a quick, "Yes, sir."

Tashelle snorted. "Your ass is in trouble now. Always bad when they single you out."

"Don't sound so damned pleased." He glanced at the doorway the captain had left through. "Why's he dressed like that?"

"Covert ops. You're going to be a secret squirrel, spying in the vanilla world. Congrats."

"You serious?"

"You are an idiot, Hill. That's why I love you. I'll watch your dog though."

"Don't let her on your bunk," he said, grinning. "I think she has fleas."

"So do you, so I'm used to it. Better not keep the captain waiting."

He hurried through the safe house, unable to shake how weird it felt, heading street-side without any gear or weapons but in uniform. He caught a few looks from the other knights as he headed out. Definitely not feeling the love today. Still, it would be nice to get out of the damn house for awhile. Do something, even though he had an uneasy feeling about the whole thing.

The captain sat at the wheel of the idling Suburban. Chris climbed in the passenger side and shut the door.

"I don't have a suit, Captain." He wore mission-standard black fatigues and combat boots. Nothing with a Thorn insignia on it for a civilian or cop to see and remember, but he knew he looked military.

"Don't worry. What you got is fine. Anyone asks, you're FBI Hostage Rescue Team, along to observe. I'm FBI agent Darrel Rodriguez." He put the SUV in gear and backed out of the driveway. "We're going to talk with Michael Cantwell's mother. One of the watchers just gave me a heads up that the detectives are gone. Only one uniform's left on watch, in a cruiser outside her house. Time will never be better to find out what happened."

Chris knew better than to ask why he was being included instead of Sergeant Drake or Karen Cox or any of the knights with more mission time or who might be better qualified. This had to be some kind of test. Or maybe Captain Garcia wanted one of his own people riding shotgun instead of someone from Drake's crew. Either way, he wasn't looking forward to this—hell, he was already full-on dreading it—but he wouldn't let the captain down.

They drove in silence for a few blocks, without even the radio to cover the monotonous hum of the tires on asphalt. Chris had trouble finding something to do with his hands. He wanted to fiddle, to pop his knuckles, something, anything. His fingers itched to hold a gun. Even a knife would work. Instead he balled them into fists and kept them on his thighs.

"You know why I brought you along, Hill?" the captain asked, not looking away from the road. "Instead of Sergeant Drake?"

"No, Captain."

The captain drove on, not replying right away. They passed three-deckers, Colonials, and old Victorian-style houses, many of them well kept, others indifferently maintained. Garcia stopped for a red light and finally continued. "What's most important about this mission?"

"Maintaining the Silence, destroying threats to human—"

"Spare me the textbook bullshit. What's *most important* about this mission?"

"Saving that kid."

Captain Garcia stared at him, face expressionless, his brown eyes giving nothing away, before he finally turned back to the road. "Sergeant Drake would say killing the broodsire was top priority. Waste it before it can make more ghouls, start a new brood, kill more innocent people."

"I want to see it dead, too, Captain."

"Yeah, but the kid comes first. His safety. You said it, and that's why you're with me. You saved that dog. We'll be looking this woman in the eyes. I want you to see."

Chris nodded, but kept his mouth shut. He didn't know what to say and wasn't exactly sure what the hell the captain was getting at. Of course everybody on the team wanted the kid back safe with his mom.

Why would meeting the kid's mother even matter? In fact, he didn't want to see her. That would make it hands-down impossible to forget should something go wrong with the mission. If the kid got hurt, or worse. Make it impossible to forgive himself for failing them.

And shit always went wrong.

They finally rolled up to a white Cape Cod-style cottage with dark shutters, cracked steps and iron railings, and a brown lawn bisected by a concrete path. Lots of flowerpots, but no living flowers, only husks. A Big Wheel sat tipped on its side like brightly colored plastic wreckage from a movie car crash.

A Providence police cruiser sat at the curb. Garcia parked directly behind it and climbed out of the SUV. Chris followed a moment later, stepping down to the weed-choked swath of lawn beyond the gutter. The cop behind the wheel watched them in the rearview mirror and spoke into his radio. The captain strode over to him with his ID badge in his hand. He tapped it against the cop's window so the cop could see the ID — fake FBI credentials done by the best of the Thorn's counterfeiters.

The cop frowned and rolled down his window. "They said the Feds wouldn't be here until later."

Captain Garcia put the badge back in his coat pocket. "The mother inside?"

"Yeah..."

"This is preliminary. We'll be done quickly." He turned and motioned Chris toward the house. They walked up the path to the front door. Faded and smeared chalk drawings decorated the walkway—something that might've been a dragon, a bunch of numbers, something that might've been a sword and maybe a castle.

The captain gave him a sidelong look. "Always expect the blues to do what you say. When you're playing FBI, believe you're better than the cops. They'll hate you, but they'll respond and fall in line. It's like a dog pack. You're a Fed, you gotta be alpha."

Chris nodded, although a grunt like him wasn't likely to be playing FBI agent again anytime soon. They came to the front door. Neon toys and plastic robots were piled in a wicker basket at the top of the steps, along with a small pair of shoes and one Spiderman rain boot. He felt a moment of sharp, jagged pain for the mother. So many reminders of her son scattered everywhere... He couldn't imagine being in her shoes, sitting in that house, alone, acid-fear eating through her guts, and everywhere she looked another reminder of her boy.

Honest to God, he didn't know if he could take it, if he were in her place.

The screen of the screen door was ripped at the bottom and hanging in places. Rusted screw ends stuck out at odd angles from the metal frame. Garcia pushed the doorbell, but it didn't chime. He knocked. No answer. He knocked again, louder.

The door opened a crack, and a woman's pale face peered out. Dull, sunken hazel eyes, and every line on her face seemed cut there by a sculpting knife, carved deep into the flesh. Her brown hair was pulled back from her face in a ponytail. She wore gray sweats and a shapeless, stained Notre Dame sweatshirt. He couldn't tell how old she was. Somewhere between thirty and fifty.

"Ms. Cantwell?" Captain Garcia brought out his ID again and held it up so she could see. "We're with the FBI."

She stared at them.

"May we come in?"

She moved back, but didn't swing the door open for them. The captain opened the screen and pushed the door wide enough to enter. Chris tagged along behind him, feeling ridiculously out of place in his boots and fatigues. He could feel the cop's gaze on his back, but he fought off the urge to glance behind him. Glancing back wasn't alpha.

The air inside the house had weight, he would've sworn it—a thickness, a heaviness of fear and ever-tightening tension. Hard to breathe, as if it pooled in the bottom of his lungs like sludge.

They followed Ms. Cantwell through the foyer into a living room. Mismatched furniture. A coffee table with crayon marks on the wood. An old couch that had done double duty as a scratching post. Ms. Cantwell sat on the couch and leaned forward with her hands folded between her knees. She stared at the coffee table.

The only other place to sit was a worn rocking chair, but neither of them moved toward it. They remained closer to the front door, near the television. A parade of bright images flashed on the screen, but the TV was muted. Chris stood to the side and a little behind Captain Garcia, trying not to stare at her, trying to breathe without smelling the choking fear.

"We're going to do all we can to get your son back to you," the captain said. "I want you to know that, Ms. Cantwell."

She started to cry, but never made a sound. It was like watching a statue weep.

Chris looked away, at the television, which showed shaky video of some riot somewhere, burning cars and rocks and police advancing behind a shield wall. The same shit. Everywhere you looked, it was the same fucking shit.

"Tell us what happened, Ms. Cantwell," Captain Garcia said, keeping his voice soft, calm.

She finally looked at him. Her look was empty, hollow, as if a taxidermist had replaced her eyes with glass.

The captain walked to her and sat on the coffee table. He gently took her hand into both of his. Chris watched, feeling useless and stupid and awkward seeing her this way, as if he'd shamed her and himself by witnessing pain this deep and not being able to set it right.

"Tell me," he urged again.

"I already told the police everything." Her voice wavered only a shade above a whisper.

"I know, Ms. Cantwell. Thank you. But I'd like to hear it again. From you."

She stayed silent for so long that Chris began to think she'd never answer. He glanced out one of the front windows and could see the dark shape of the cop in his cruiser. Bright hate for the cop flashed inside him for a moment, because the guy was out there, and Chris was in here, where he couldn't even breathe.

Damn it. Time for him to man up, stop being so goddamn selfish. This woman deserved better. Little

Michael Cantwell sure as hell deserved better. He closed his eyes, and when he opened them again he had himself back under control.

"I worked late," Ms. Cantwell finally said. "I work two jobs. Dunkin' Donuts in the morning, three days. Waitress at Roslyn's Diner at night, six days. So Mrs. Johanna babysits Michael until I get home, but he's awake most times. Doesn't like to go to sleep without me here."

She stopped. Swallowed. She pulled her hand free of Captain Garcia's and slowly lifted it to touch her throat, as if swallowing hurt her. The captain never looked away from her face. Chris stood there, still feeling like useless ass. Still feeling like a voyeur for seeing all the hurt twisting inside her.

"I came home, went to Michael. I was still wearing my uniform. I'm always wearing my uniform..." She swallowed again. "He sat up in bed. Said, 'Hello, Mommy,' and there's something...some kind of little joy all packed into his words when he says it. Like just seeing his mommy made him happy."

Captain Garcia nodded, solemn.

"I kissed him goodnight. He rolled over on his side. He always likes to sleep on his side. And I shut his door and went to take a shower. I always stink like fried meat and grease after working. The smell gets in your hair, you know? I watched TV and went to bed. When I came in to wake him up, he was gone." She shuddered, but those silent tears continued, harder now. "The window was shoved open. The screen ripped off. Someone broke the lock."

"Any strange noises last night?"

"I sleep too heavy." She clasped her hands together so tightly her knuckles were white knobs of bone.

"Ms. Cantwell, this wasn't your fault. You're not to blame."

She looked down at her hands and said nothing. Tears formed drips on her chin and fell to splash on her lap, but she didn't wipe them away.

"I'm going to find your son," Captain Garcia said. "I swear that to you. I'll bring Michael home safe."

Chris fought to keep his face blank. Promises like that... Hell, with the monsters they hunted, it'd be a miracle to find the boy safe. And even if they rescued him, he would be haunted. Scarred. It was ugly. Just goddamn ugly and he wanted to kill something to stop the ugliness. He wanted that broodsire in front of him again so he could run his sword straight through one of its eyes. But that was only more ugliness, and all the ugliness and horror and pain stayed locked together, eating its own tail like the damn serpent of infinity.

Jesus Christ. He wished he'd never come. That the captain had never brought him. And he hated himself for feeling that way.

She shuddered again, but wouldn't look up, as if she feared to see some insincerity in the captain's eyes. "The other detectives…they said…the more time that goes by… They wanted to know about his father. Other things. Strange people hanging around. Vans. I told them his father ran out on us when Michael was just eight months. They're trying to find him. In Texas, I think. And no vans." She closed her eyes. "I didn't see any vans."

"Okay, Ms. Cantwell, thank you for speaking with us. May we see Michael's bedroom?"

She nodded. "Down the hall. On the left."

Captain Garcia stood and walked toward the hall. Chris followed behind like a dutiful dog. He glanced at Ms. Cantwell. She stared out the window. He wanted to say something to comfort her, but every imagined word sounded stupid and trite. So he kept his mouth shut.

Michael's bedroom sported Mario and Spiderman posters on the walls and copy paper decorated with wild scribbles in tons of colors, people with lumpy heads and stick arms, hands and feet with too many fingers and toes, all taped to the wall. A battered trunk seeped toys in a plastic lava flow.

The window was opposite the bed. It had been dusted for fingerprints, and more dark fingerprint dust covered almost everything in the room, bed, dresser, toy box, walls. The window was still open, the wood frame splintered where the simple swivel latch had broken. A ghoul would be strong enough to do something like that, easy. He could see the screen on the lawn outside, bent into a rhombus shape.

Captain Garcia walked the room while Chris stood in the doorway. He looked at all the fingerprints outlined by the dark dust—most of them were tiny, a child's fingerprints. There were gouges in the wood window frame that had been marked with a little square of paper pinned to the wall. A place where the ghoul's claws had scored the wood, gouges the cops would probably mistake for tool damage...maybe a crowbar or something.

He looked at the bed. The cartoon character sheets lay half off to the side. He could still see the rumpled impression where the kid had slept. He looked away, back at the window. Looking at the bed was too hard.

Captain Garcia walked to him, slapped a hand on his shoulder and jerked his chin toward the door.

They headed back into the living room. Ms. Cantwell hadn't moved. She still stared out the window. The muted television flashed its parade of woe and turmoil, but in silence, which made it seem worse.

"Wait outside," the captain told him. Then he went to Ms. Cantwell again.

Chris waited outside on the front step, standing there, ignoring the cop who was watching him, trying to look as if he weren't gulping in air, grateful to be out of the house.

Captain Garcia came out a few moments later. They headed back to the street. The captain walked to the cruiser and tapped the glass until the cop rolled the window down. "We're done here. For now."

The cop nodded. He rubbed the bridge of his nose and glanced at the house. "I hate things like this."

"You and me both."

The cop looked at them and his eyes narrowed. "Think you guys can find that kid?"

"We'll bring him home."

The cop didn't say anything. His face stayed carefully impassive.

They climbed back into the SUV. Chris stared at the house. Something about it seemed tired, violated...profaned. It made him want to do something

—to fix things somehow, make them right again. It was wrong for a house to look like that.

"Goddamn," Chris said, very softly.

"I know." Captain Garcia shifted into drive and pulled out into the street.

CHAPTER EIGHT

The Other Side

C hris collected the dog and grabbed something to eat as soon as he and the captain arrived back at the safe house, though he sure as hell wasn't hungry. Something he'd learned on his very first op was to always eat when he had the chance. He could never be sure how long he'd have to go before another plate of food found its way in front of him. Energy bars helped, but they didn't fill a guy up worth shit. Nothing worse than a dynamic entry and full-on assault with your stomach growling.

The dog was hungry enough for the both of them. So he snagged a couple frozen chicken patties from the fridge and a last lone hotdog, microwaved the hell out of them, piled it all on bread with mustard and grabbed a soda. They ate together out on the backyard stoop where they could be alone, sitting on weather-damaged wood and keeping company with the weeds. Thirteen wasn't a lot of people, until you crammed them all into a small house for a few days, waiting for the green light on a mission.

He fed the dog a chicken patty and tried to eat his own, chewing and staring at the rusty swing set. It leaned drunkenly near the back fence, missing one swing. The sun cut a slow arc toward the horizon, spilling red, purple, and orange across shreds of cloud. He watched it stretch the shadows long and paint them darker. He kept thinking about Michael. Kept thinking about the boy's mother—that wounded face. His own mother had looked that way sometimes, when she'd thought Chris couldn't see.

The screen door swung open behind him with a rusty screech, startling his dog. He took a swig of soda and glanced back, expecting Tashelle or Weeger or, if he were super lucky, Jessica the cute lancer. None of the above though. Sergeant Drake stood there with a bag of chips in his hands, staring down at him and chewing.

"What's up, Sarge?" He petted his dog to calm her, then took a bite of chicken patty-hot dog sandwich. He hoped Drake didn't have some stupid busy work for him.

"Heard you went on a little field trip with the captain today." Drake smiled, but he was one of those guys where the smile could appear a hundred percent righteous and never touch his eyes. His hair was buzzed so short it was little more than blond fuzz. Acne scars dotted his cheeks. Tallest man on the squad, and buffed out—not a crazy muscle-head, but big enough to rock and roll. Sergeants had to be hard-asses anyway, and Drake seemed made to order for the job.

"Yeah," Chris said. "Talked to the kid's mother."

"Surprised he brought you." He crunched a handful of chips, smiling, chewing with his mouth open. "What'd you think?"

Dammit, and he'd come out here to catch a break. Today it seemed everybody was tailing him around, wanting something from him. "I think the whole thing's fucked up."

"True enough. But you can't let yourself take this personal. You see people hurting, you want to go out and wreak some big time vengeance. Kick ass. Carve notches on your sword hilt. I know the feeling." He stared down at Chris. "You feeling that?"

Chris shrugged. Drake looming over him was starting to grate on his nerves, but there wasn't anything he could do about it without tipping the sergeant off to the fact. Instead, he took a big bite of his sandwich. The mouthful was sawdust dry and hard to swallow.

"Because if you were feeling that," Drake continued, "my *official* response would be to tell you to get over it. We need professionals out there, yadda, yadda. You a professional, Hill?"

"Yeah, Sarge, I'm as pro as they go."

Sergeant Drake stared at him, smiling and chewing. "We'll see about that. Hey, maybe you are, maybe you aren't. Wasn't my bright idea to throw two teams together, patch 'em up with duct tape and a prayer, send them back out again. Be nice to get everybody accustomed to my expectations in the field."

Chris ate the last of his sandwich, chewing without enjoyment, washing it all down with soda. Why was Drake telling him this shit? He'd only wanted to eat in peace.

No such luck, though. The sergeant started in again.

"Like I said, that would be my *official* response. Truth is, I love killing ghouls. Nothing needs killing more than a ghoul. Not the bloodsuckers, not the weres. Maybe the Nassid—they're degenerate motherfuckers too..." Drake tossed a chip to his dog, who snatched it out of the air, tail wagging. He smirked and looked back at Chris. "So what I'm saying is this: we go in, killing shit is top priority. Easy for everyone to get all bent about a kid missing, and I wish to God he wasn't, wish to God he was home safe in his mama's arms, but we go in there without the right mindset, one of those things gets away and it'll be another kid gets it. And another. Or someone else. A goddamn librarian. Somebody's granny. Who knows? Point is, you don't let the monsters go for any reason. You take your collateral damage, you do what needs to be done, and you lay the blood of innocents at God's feet. Because, end of the day, who the fuck else is responsible?"

He wants you to agree with him, Chris thought. So just nod and make some agreement noises and he'll leave you alone. Easy.

Instead he said, "I don't know, Sarge. I mean, I joined up to save people."

"Everybody has that idea at first. Superman ideas. What've you done—one, maybe two missions? Just wait, see if I'm right."

More like four missions, but he didn't contradict. "All right, I'll wait and see."

Drake snorted. He stared at the swing set for a moment, tossed his chip bag into an empty flowerpot, and then went back inside.

The dog looked at Chris with her head cocked, as if asking what the hell that had been about.

"Everybody's crazy," Chris told her.

CHAPTER NINE

Cracks

Still nothing from the watchers. No sign of the ghouls or broodsire or the boy. The mood in the house was dark.

Chris couldn't shake his uneasiness, couldn't stop his thoughts from racing through his mind at a million miles an hour. If only the safe house had a shooting range, he'd be there right now, finding solace in putting lead exactly where he wanted on the target. The waiting was killing him. He wanted to punch something.

Restless, he paced the house with the dog trailing at his heels. He walked to the bedroom he was crashing in, but he only stood in the doorway, staring at the bunks. The air in here reeked of body odor and onions, so he went to the window and yanked it open. He paused for a moment, staring at the sky as it finished bleeding down to black.

A memory slipped to the front of his mind. Standing at the open window of his parents' house after his father's funeral, staring at the sky as it faded blue to black. Remembering the creeping silence within the house, the emptiness, the hollow way the sounds had echoed off the ceilings. He'd gone to the garage, where his father had his workbenches and tools, and he'd stood on the cement step near the washer and stared at the empty space where his father had been not even a week ago. A dusty row of tiny plastic collector's baseball helmets sat on a metal shelf near his father's circular saw. He remembered, quite clearly, staring at those helmets. His dad had put tons of quarters into a vending machine trying to get the Yankees helmet for him.

He shunted the memory aside and turned away from the window. Past was past—he couldn't let it drag him down. All that mattered was the now and the future. The now was nothing but endless frustration with all the damn waiting, but the future, yeah, he'd be bringing that boy home to his mom.

He went to find Tashelle and see if he could give her a hard time about something, maybe pull himself out of this black mood. First he came across Peralta cleaning his M21 rifle at the table, holding the disassembled barrel up and inspecting the bore. Peralta was a short, stocky Portuguese guy with graying hair. He'd served with Hill as a sharpshooter in Captain Garcia's unit before their unit had been ripped up in Baltimore and had to be up-strengthed by Sergeant Drake's squad. He'd seen Peralta's shot groupings on the firing range, and the guy was scary-good.

This time the dog wandered off first, and he followed her into the living room. She found her way to a bowl of popcorn on the table and started eating it. A bunch of Drake's people were clustered around the video game system and playing Madden football. Tyson and Roth were going at it, playing the Cowboys against the Ravens. Bowen sprawled in a threadbare recliner with a soda. Weeger was the only grunt in the room Chris knew well. The rest of them might as well have been strangers.

"Hey, Hill," Bowen said, glancing away from the screen and smirking at the dog. "Your mutt's all about the people-food, looks like. Can I get her a beer or something?"

"No, but you can get me a beer. And a sandwich."

"Still full of shit, I see. So you want to play next? I'll take you, Chargers versus any team you pick. Twenty down. I'll even spot you three points."

Chris tried a smile that felt fake. "Football? Don't

you know God created baseball on the sixth day and rested, because the game was too awesome, even for Him."

Weeger glanced up from his book and shook his head, looking for all the world like one of the wise men from the classic nativity scene but tricked out in fatigues and boots. Something about the beard, no, the eyes, that gave off a certain vibe...

"Every little word of blasphemy is another hour in purgatory." Weeger smiled as if to show he was kidding, but with Weeger a guy could never be a hundred percent sure.

"Purgatory? Yeah right," Tyson said, "He's goin' straight to Hell like the rest of us. That's where the best strippers are." He grinned at Weeger. Tyson had on a blue Cowboys beanie and a huge sweatshirt only a shade darker than his skin. "Weeger, you're pretty enough to do the stripper thing. Rock it, man, rock it. Think there's a pole at the fire station down the road."

Weeger only laughed and returned to his book, some kind of Scandinavian philosophy thing. Chris had read somewhere that Scandinavians were the happiest people in the world. Maybe this Nordic self help book by some dude with the mouthful name of Kierkegaard would let Weeger find his happy place.

"You guys seen Tashelle?" Chris asked, wanting

an excuse to get gone.

"Nope," Roth replied. He looked like one of those lightweight boxers or mixed martial arts guys — some scarred-up dude with a shaved head who seemed like he should be missing teeth and speaking with a Liverpool accent. Instead, a hint of Minnesota lingered in his voice. "So, Hill, you went out with the captain. What the hell was that all about?"

Chris shrugged and looked away. He wasn't going to spill that scene out here for them to rag on. No way he wanted the boy's mother getting any disrespect. He didn't think they would, hell, they were knights after all, but he wouldn't risk it. If anyone threw out any disrespect to her then he'd have to start throwing down, and there were problems enough without one of the captain's crew going after one of Drake's crew. Even if they kept their mouths shut, it didn't belong to them. They didn't get to know because they weren't there, seeing her face, trying to breathe in that house when it felt like drowning.

"Secret mission, right?" Tyson said when he didn't answer. "Super commando stuff."

Bowen laughed and jerked his chin in Chris's direction. "No worries if you don't want to say. I know this is our virgin voyage and all that, but don't sweat it. You newbies are in good hands. Sarge raised us right."

He made a pistol with his thumb and pointer finger. "I don't miss."

"Don't rub it in on him." Tyson's laughter was a deep rumble. "That boy must've missed half his shots last night."

"Yeah, fuck you, Tyson," Chris said, smirking despite himself. "You guys let about a million ghouls through your perimeter. Our mage almost got eaten."

Tyson grinned wider. "Good thing he had a babysitter. You like taking care of things, right? You got that poochity-pooch. You got your caster girlfriend's nose to wipe. You a real nurturing son of a bitch, you realize?"

"The real question is," Roth broke in before Chris could respond, "whether the captain can keep it together. Things being what they are."

"So what the hell are you saying?" Chris stood very still. Richards had said something, spilled the beans about the captain. Goddammit.

All the playful back-and-forth vanished, burned up to nothing in an instant. Tyson shifted and frowned at the TV screen. Weeger stared down at his book, but it was clear his eyes weren't tracking the words, and Bowen's expression was too carefully blank.

Roth set his game controller down. His eyes were half-lidded, his lip curled. "I'm saying I want to know what I'm getting into. I need to know I'm with people I can trust, following orders that aren't all crazy with emotion. That's it. That's all."

"The captain's righteous, don't worry. He wants the boy back safe."

"Yeah? Don't we all? But what's he willing to do to make it happen?"

"Whatever it takes. Same as me. I'd say same as you, but maybe I'd be wrong."

Roth gave him a bitter smile. "You got it. Because I ain't keen to jump into the meat grinder."

"You can sit in the fuckin' truck then. Guard the caster. Diaper detail for a pussy."

Roth held up a hand. "You get a freebie because we don't know each other. I'm just saying, I've seen knights and commanders and lords and ladies come and go. Some of them have shining ideals. Some of them are trench fighters, willing to do whatever it takes to get the job done. Some float above the high road, others think no blood's too red to shed." He shrugged. "But that's all bullshit. Me, I'm simple. All I want to know is if I'm gonna get back with my head still on my shoulders, my balls still dangling below my dick, and my mama's first-born son living to see another day."

"That ain't the oath you swore," Chris said.

Roth shrugged. "You better believe the same or

I'll be seeing your name up on the Lists. I'll lift a glass, though. To the memory of all the bright-eyed fools who didn't realize, at the end of the day, you only win if you come back alive."

Chris stared at Roth and Roth stared right back. It was very quiet except for the electronic cheering roar from the stadium crowd in the videogame running on an endless loop.

"Thanks for letting me know," Chris said. "I like to be a hundred percent certain of the guy next to me. And you can stay the hell out of my foxhole with a shitty attitude like that."

"I'm honest. What can I say? I only wanted to know what kind of man the captain was, and hear it straight from a guy who goes running off with him and does things he won't talk about to the rest of the grunts. Just wanted everybody to know where everybody stood."

"The captain cares. That's all you gotta know."

"Sounds like something you write on a tombstone to me."

Chen walked in the room, straight into the tightening silence while chomping away on an energy bar. He glanced around at them and raised his eyebrows. "Whoa. What the hell, guys. Who burned your marshmallows and pissed in your soup?"

Roth turned back to his game. "Just talking football with someone who likes baseball. Go fucking figure."

"Basketball kicks all their asses," Chen said.

Nobody answered. The words hung in the air like meat on a hook.

Then Sergeant Drake was yelling orders to assemble, everyone broke into a mad scramble, and that was the end of the waiting.

They'd found the ghouls.

CHAPTER TEN

Go Time

Twenty-one hundred hours. Green light. Time to rock and roll.

Chris gathered with the rest of the squad in the den. It was crowded and close, with most people standing and the rest crammed onto an old teal couch shoulder to shoulder. He chose to lurk near the doorway so he had enough space that his dog could stay with him. She settled down at his feet and rested her head on one of his boots. Sergeant Drake leaned against the wall opposite the door, walking a bullet through his fingers like a stage magician with a gun fetish. Captain Garcia stood next to a printed set of blueprints tacked to the drywall and a bunch of 8.5 X 11 sheets of paper taped together. Beside them hung a large street map of the greater Providence area with clusters of red dots in south Providence and north

Cranston, and a color satellite photo of a few blocks of street.

"We roll out in fifteen minutes," Captain Garcia said. "We just got a major break. A solid lead and location on Michael Cantwell."

"He okay, Captain?" Karen called out.

"He was when the watcher identified him, but it's critical we move fast."

A low, relieved murmur swept through the room. Chris nodded to no one in particular and took a deep breath. Still a chance. That was all they needed. Just one damn chance to bring the kid home.

The captain continued. "An analyst at Command narrowed down the recent attack locations and missing persons reports as radiating outward from two distinct locations in south Providence." He tapped a finger on the street map where the red dots were scattered. "One was the apartment complex we hit the other night." He traced his finger along the roads to another part of the map. "But Oakland Cemetery, where Hill and Parker took down a ghoul last night, is within walking distance, south of I-95. The oldest attacks and disturbances were clustered around the cemetery, but they've since moved northward to here." He circled the densest cluster of red with his finger.

"Michael's house is also within walking distance

of this area. Both watchers astral jumped there and began an intensive search. One of them came up with a lucky hit twenty minutes ago—a ghoul who'd been sniffing around the streets near Brightview Funeral Home. The watcher tailed it all the way back to a house on Norwich Avenue."

Watchers, God love 'em. Chris knew a bit about them for purely personal reasons. He'd tried to get one out on a date a couple times but had been shot down. Just the way it went sometimes. He'd been fascinated with them at the time, since they were mysterious and so far removed from the line animals, but with 20/20 hindsight it was probably pure idiocy to hook up with a woman who could warp around the country at will and see into a guy's dreams. Still, they were straight up angels on a grunt's shoulders in the field, just that there weren't enough of them to go around. Rumor had it there were less than thirty for the whole of the Order of the Thorn, spanning the entire globe. Someone had pulled some serious strings to score two for this mission.

"The good news," the captain continued. "Positive ID on Michael Cantwell. He appeared physically unharmed, but he's being held in a dog cage in the basement."

Restless shifting from the Thorn knights, soft

curses and lots of angry faces and hard stares. Tashelle, who'd evidently been in the garage with the SUV the whole time he'd been searching for her, looked ready to tear something apart barehanded, and he was right there with her. A kid in a damn dog cage...

Captain Garcia held up a hand for quiet. "The bad news: the broodsire's holed up inside with its entire remaining nest. The watcher counted seventeen ghouls."

Someone whistled. Seventeen hostiles plus a pissed off big daddy broodsire, who couldn't be happy about a bunch of knights hunting him through the city and wasting his progeny. Chris only hoped he was the one to paint the wall with its brains, just for taking a kid. If he closed his eyes for too long he could see Ms. Cantwell's weary, wounded face in his mind. He clamped his teeth together, popped his knuckles, and tried to lock his attention back on what the captain was saying.

"We go in weapons tight, no flashbangs, no frag grenades. We use a battering ram on the door; no Primacord or any other explosives. I don't want to risk Michael getting hurt with ordinance going off."

"Are there other hostages, Captain?" Tyson asked, his game face on.

"Our watcher reported one other living civilian

in addition to Michael Cantwell. Male. Thirties. Caucasian. In need of serious medical attention. Our last intel puts his location on the first floor of the house. But he was in the process of being changed into a ghoul, so he should be considered compromised." The captain glanced at Weeger, who sat on the arm of the couch, frowning and scratching at his brown beard. "Weeger will evaluate and give medical attention to any hostages once we have them secured."

Weeger nodded, but the rest of the room filled with grim silence. If the hostage was compromised, the only thing they could do for him was put him out of his misery. Like shooting an injured horse. Christ.

"Specter One's mission priority is Michael Cantwell. Specter Two clears and secures the first floor. Specter Three maintains the Silence and holds the perimeter. Once Michael and any surviving civilians are secured, we neutralize all threats and burn the house.

"Teams are as follows. Specter One is me, Deering, Weeger, Hill, and Chen. Specter Two is Sergeant Drake, Cox, Tyson, and Roth. Specter Three is Richards, Parker, with Bowen and Peralta on sharpshooter duty. Richards sets the wards and maintains them from inside the van with Parker tasked for guard duty."

Chen was sitting next to Tashelle on the couch

and nudged her with his shoulder. "Babysitting, eh? Looks like you miss the fun."

Tashelle gave a snort that was either disgusted or amused, but mage Richards fixed Chen with a nasty look. "Hey monster-chow, I'd watch what you say. Pissing off magicslingers reduces life expectancy."

"Enough." Captain Garcia glared from one knight to the other. "This isn't the time." He waited until he got chagrinned nods and then continued. "Standard dynamic entry. All hostiles are kill on sight unless a hostage is endangered."

"Study this layout." Sergeant Drake pointed to the house floor plan with the bullet he held. "These are the floor plans on file with the city. Our techies came across intel that the place was a crack house at some point. There may be hidden rooms, crawlspaces, and other assorted bullshit that aren't on these floor plans, so be on the lookout for hinky shit when you run the walls."

The captain drew their attention to the satellite photo of the neighborhood. "A bunch of these houses right on the street are boarded up, but our target house is the anomaly. City records indicate the house was built much later, after the original burned. Set back from the street, has a front yard, such as it is. Different architectural style, front and back porch, fenced backyard. There's an overgrown lot to the west, an empty concrete lot to the east. The house across the street is boarded up, condemned. Likely, the broodsire chose this place to give him and his ghouls maximum access, concealment, and freedom of movement in a built up urban environment."

"In other words, a real nice hood," Drake said with an exaggerated drawl. "Downright reasonable rent."

The captain ignored him. "Here's the deal. I'll run the van into the yard, near the porch and deploy Specter One. Chen on the ram. Weeger and Hill through the funnel first. We're assaulting from one direction to avoid blue-on-blue fire. The first floor windows are all covered, either boarded up, painted over, or covered in tin foil, so they won't see us coming. Command also promised a watcher to scout." He locked gazes with Weeger and then Chris. "Some ugly shit is waiting for us inside. Be ready."

Sergeant Drake twirled his bullet through his fingers. "Because broodsires aren't just content to eat people like your normal vanilla monster. These motherfuckers like to carve people up, re-shape them, cut patterns on their bodies like some kind of psycho artist, then send them out like zombie worker ants to gather more human meat. These things are big and nasty and hungry."

"We know the profile, Sarge," Chen said, surprising Chris with the annoyance in his tone. Never wise to spout off to a sergeant unless you wanted your life to turn into an active hell. "We aren't noobies."

"Do you 'know the profile?'" Sergeant Drake leaned over and stared Chen in the face from less than a foot away. "I want us all clear on the stakes. Because you can add a righteous mind-fucking to go along with all the carving. He'll shove tentacles up your nose, in your ears, all the way into your brain. What, you think that's funny, Chen? Yeah, real cute when he scrambles your gray matter with neurotoxins. Messes up the synapses. Kill the victim, reanimate the corpse with its mind all fucked-up weird. So we don't show these pusbag scrotes any mercy." He grinned. "Not that we ever do, but hey."

Captain Garcia let the sergeant talk without interrupting, but his mouth had tightened into a slash across his face. When he paused, the captain jumped back in. "Confirm all targets before firing. I can't stress that enough." He looked at Jessica. "Pin. Keep the safeties and shield on your lance until we secure the boy. I don't want Michael hit by shrapnel or concussion blasts. If we encounter the broodsire before we get to Michael, we take it down the hard way."

Jessica had her dark hair pulled back in a ponytail, and it bobbed when she nodded. Chris would say one thing about her. She was all business. She was one of Drake's team, but so far she'd showed zero problem working with the captain. Of course, taking down a monster as big as a broodsire the hard way—without the use of explosives or heavy ordinance—was going to be a pure nightmare. Nobody said anything about that either.

They'd do what had to be done.

Captain Garcia slowly scanned the room, making eye contact with each of them. "Michael Cantwell is our highest priority. We secure him first. Questions? No? You know the drill. Grab your gear and load up. We're bringing that kid home."

CHAPTER ELEVEN
Dynamic Entry

Chris and his dog rode in the tactical van with the rest of Specter One—Captain Garcia at the wheel, Jessica in all her heavy armor with her explosive lance capped and laying along the length of the floor, Weeger and Chen with him in the back. The black Chevy Suburban behind them carried Specter Three, tasked with securing the perimeter and setting down the silence wards. Bringing up the rear in the other SUV was Specter Two, the beta assault squad.

"Almost there," Captain Garcia called back to them. "Stay sharp."

The radio played alt rock from WBRU with the volume turned low, and a police scanner occasionally spat out short streams of cop code. Chris stared out the van's tinted back windows, his hand on his dog's side. She was so quiet that the captain hadn't even noticed she'd jumped in the van with him when they'd been loading up. Jessica had given him a dark look, but no one else had seemed to care. He allowed the dog along because he wanted something to give comfort to Michael when they got him free, and what boy didn't love dogs? The rescue would be terrifying enough for the kid as it was.

The electric dread of pre-combat arced and hummed in his chest and guts. He was juiced to finally do something, but afraid they'd be too late—wanting to do his job, but chased by the fear he'd make a mistake, fail his team, fail the kid. These thoughts turned in a never-ending spiral inside his mind.

They drove through south Providence, down Broad Street, past markets and a gothic-looking church with a huge tower and spire. They turned down a residential street, swung around and came down Norwich Avenue from the east. The neighborhood had long since descended into decay: painted-over graffiti, lots of chain link, and very little greenery except for the weeds growing through the cracks in the cement. Old cars huddled on the street. A line of rusting appliances had been quarantined along a driveway like a row of lepers. The paint on the two-story houses had faded and flaked, other houses were boarded up entirely, and litter lay scattered about in soggy drifts of paper and brittle plastic.

Captain Garcia pulled the van to the curb, idling in front of a house down the street from their target. The two SUVs pulled in behind the van and did the same. A man sitting on the steps outside his front door jumped up and darted inside, making Chris smirk. Guy probably thought they were cops on a raid. The rest of the street appeared empty and quiet, with few lights on and long stretches of darkness between streetlamps.

"Specter Actual, this is Specter Two," Roth said over the radio. "We've been seen by civvies, over."

"Can't be helped yet, so sit tight," Captain Garcia radioed back. "Com and weapons check."

Everyone checked in with a flurry of affirmatives and copies. Chris was good-to-go on his gear. He had his MP7, suppressor, and a flashlight mounted on the rails. His long sword hung in the sheath harness on his back, silvered combat knife in a quick-draw sheath on the front. M9 Beretta strapped to his thigh. Flashbang grenade. Fresh batteries in his NVD. Armed and armored and ready to get it on.

"This is Specter One Actual, all teams sit tight. Checking on a situation update." Captain Garcia keyed off his mike and turned in his seat to look into the back of the cargo van. He spotted the dog, but his face remained impassive when he spoke. "Clear space for the watcher."

There wasn't much room, but Chris and the rest of Specter One cleared a spot dead center of the van, above the rune-decorated steel panel on the floor and its inactive caster-square. Nobody grumbled about having to move for a ghost image astral projection that couldn't even touch anyone. For soldiers not to be bitching, it could only mean they were all locked dead-on getting this mission done. A warm burst of pride spread through his chest, a heat as if he'd just thrown down a serious shot of whiskey. He felt close to all of them, connected to each one like a vital gear in the machine, because this was what they did, what they stood for. Saving people, paying out vengeance for the fallen, making the world safer one bullet at a time.

This would make a difference, to Michael, to his mother, and to every future victim they saved from a horrific fate, and he was fiercely proud to be a part of it, no matter what. Of course, he couldn't tell anyone his thoughts without sounding like an over-wrought asshole, so he kept his mouth shut and waited for the watcher like everyone else.

A tiny ember of brilliant white light appeared in the middle of the air as the watcher astral jumped inside. The spark spread out horizontally into a line three or so feet long, and then sliced downward, forming a glowing two-dimensional rectangle whose surface swirled with smoky illumination. A woman's form pushed out of the rectangle, featureless, like someone draped in a wet sheet, distorting the door out of shape and warping it into three dimensions. The smoky white light resolved itself into a woman's body, but with less detail than could be seen on a mannequin. A second later the doorway was gone, having transformed completely into the female shape. The light cut out, and the details filled in on the woman's body, freezing into place all at once, as if her image had just finished uploading into this slice of reality.

A form-fitting green and black Psi-jump suit covered the watcher's astral projection from neck to toes. Her head was shaved clean, with even her eyebrows gone. He thought her name was Winters, but wasn't a hundred percent on it. She was middle-aged, with brown eyes that seemed to be seeing through several layers of reality at once, something he'd always found unnerving—hell, *creepy*—but fascinating. Her astral form wasn't affected by the yellow light from the streetlamp shining through the van windows. When she moved she made no sound and didn't even disturb the air.

She looked at Captain Garcia. Her mouth moved, but no sound filled the van—still, he could hear her voice inside his mind where it held a strange, flat echo, as if her words were as insubstantial as the rest of her. *"The boy's still alive, but the ghouls are moving around. The broodsire's up to something."*

"He still in the basement?" The captain asked.

"He was, just minutes ago. But you need to hurry."

Garcia nodded, his face grim. "What kind of opposition are we facing at the front door?"

"Five or six ghouls. The number is fluid. The broodsire's on the second floor. The north-facing room off the staircase landing."

"What's the status on the other hostage?"

"He's gone. The broodsire carved him up and destroyed his mind with neurotoxins."

"Get back in the house and stay with the boy. We go hot in two minutes."

Winters nodded and closed her eyes. Her form reversed itself exactly from her arrival, losing detail, turning into white solid blaze of woman-shape whose surface was smoky and indistinct, then flattening back into a glowing rectangle. The rectangle collapsed to a pinpoint spark and disappeared as she astral jumped. She wouldn't need to worry about the ghouls or broodsire seeing her. They had no access to the astral plane. Chris could only see her astral form and share her telepathy because the binding Oaths of knighthood had seared a spell sculpture into his synapses and bones. It had been one of the most painful things he'd ever endured.

"Somebody needs to teach me how to do that," Chen quipped. "No more cover charges at the club, and I mean *ever*."

Nobody else said anything. They were all looking to Captain Garcia. Waiting.

The captain keyed his radio. "Specter One, Two, and Three, stand to. Prepare for fast deploy. All right people, this is it."

"Specter Two good to go," Sergeant Drake radioed back. "Weapons tight. On your lead."

"Specter Three good to go. On your lead."

Chris grabbed one of the van's sweat-stained roof straps bolted to the ceiling and held on tight, his heart beating harder, feeling the spike of energy, the sharpening focus, knowing it was go time. He bent over enough to wrap an arm around the dog to keep her steady.

Captain Garcia pulled the van away from the curb back into the narrow one-way street. The engine roared as he accelerated toward the target house. Out the back window, Chris saw the black SUVs tailing close behind them.

The van bounced as it swung into the empty

driveway and rocked wildly on its springs. He gripped the strap hard to keep from being tossed around and managed to keep the dog from going flying.

"Stay here, girl," he murmured to her. "That's no place for a pretty, fur-face lady. We'll be done quick."

The dog craned her neck to peer up at him and licked his arm.

He caught his first glimpse of the house through the windshield as they raced toward it. The paint had peeled enough in places to show dark patches beneath, turning the walls and porch columns splotchy and diseased. The moonlight fell in sharp angles, carving black folds and crevasses of shadows along the clapboard siding, eaves, gables, and the porch. The house looked vaguely Victorian, but had so many small additions and haphazard modifications that now it only gave the impression of ugly rot, splintered decay, and the weariness of decades of neglect.

The captain spun the steering wheel hard. The van cut onto the grass and the tires tore grooves in the weeds as the van's backend swung around in a sliding stop. The brake lights painted the house in crimson, dousing the porch in blood-light.

"Go! Go! *Go!*" Captain Garcia yelled. Chris shoved open both back doors and cleared the way.

Weeger jumped out and ran for the house,

covering the front porch with his M4. Chris leaped out next, breathing fast, heart pounding, off and running as soon as his boot heels hit the dead grass.

Weeds poked through the slats in the sagging porch steps. Half way to the stairs, vertigo blindsided him, and the two-story house seemed to lean over him, giving the impression it was falling toward him. Instead of him storming the house, for one crazed moment he was certain the house charged at him.

He gritted his teeth and pounded up the steps behind Weeger, shaking the sensation off. They stacked on either side of the front door. Chen followed and stopped behind Weeger near one of the tin-foil covered windows, carrying the battering ram in two hands.

Specter One was in place. Now they only needed the silence ward up before they could continue. Chris flipped down his night vision device and glanced back toward the street as adrenaline rocked and rolled in his veins.

Specter Two had spread out and was hauling ass toward the house in a wave of heavily armed soldiers. Roth and Bowen drove in the metal ward spikes at opposite ends of the yard with rubber-encased hammers to help Richards cycle his spell sculpture around the property, bending light and suppressing sound so anyone who looked toward the house wouldn't see or hear anything.

Hurry, hurry, hurry. He felt dangerously exposed here on the porch, waiting for the wards to go up.

Tyson and Karen sprinted along the side of the house toward the backyard, guarding Roth and Bowen and the last two ward spikes. They moved quickly, but throwing down the spikes always seemed to take too damn long.

Mage Richards jumped into the cargo van and knelt on his caster-square, leaning his staff against his shoulder. Tashelle crouched near the van's fender with her semi-auto shotgun raised as she scanned for hostiles. His dog scrambled out of the van, starting toward him, but Tashelle spotted her and grabbed her before she could get far. She heaved the dog back into the van and slammed the doors, God bless her.

Chris's grip was so tight on the handles of his submachine gun that he had to force his fingers to release a little or he'd never hit anything once he started shooting. He tried to keep focused on the moment. He tried not to think about charging into the house with no flashbangs to stun and disorient, no simultaneous breeching assault to distract hostiles. He and Weeger could be forcing their way into a funnel straight to hell.

"Ward spikes three and four in place," Tyson finally called over the radio. "Securing sector two now, over."

"Roger that," Captain Garcia replied. "All teams stand by. Richards, charge up the wards."

Chris looked away quickly when the end of Richards's staff flared bright green through the van's open back doors, the eldritch light burning bright as a star and dazzling the optics of his NVD. Dammit. He turned back to the door, breathing fast, impatience gnawing all his thoughts.

"Wards are go!" Richards yelled over the comm. "You are green!"

"Copy that, wards in place." Captain Garcia signaled Chen. "Execute, execute! Go, go, *go!*"

Chen stepped out in front of the door and swung the battering ram back. He slammed it into the door directly above the knob. One swing was all it took. The door flew inward with a crash and the sharp crack of breaking wood. Long splinters rained to the floorboards.

Chen spun to the side, out of the line of fire and out of their way. Chris and Weeger charged across the threshold into the darkness.

His heart slammed fresh adrenaline through his body. Every detail and sound and smell around him vibrated with preternatural clarity. Time seemed both slow and fast, an impossibility that still felt true.

Weeger opened fire, his muzzle flash a lightning flare in the dark, the crack of his M4 very loud, even with ear protection. Chris had only an instant to see what Weeger was shooting at—a hunched, disfigured shape loping toward the door. It fell to the wood floorboards and began to thrash and squeal.

Chris pushed to the right. He cleared the doorway and swung the barrel of his MP7 to cover his area of responsibility. The air stank of blood and shit and rot, all intermixed and overwhelming in a house with every window shut. The room glowed green through his goggles, scarred wood floors, empty walls, and little furniture.

A ghoul crouched on the floor near one of the covered-over windows. It was naked and very pale, its flesh marked all over with elaborate patterns— scarification taken to an insane level. It grinned at him with cheeks flayed back along the jaw to show rows of sharpened teeth. Drool ran between its teeth and dribbled from its chin. Its eyes blazed with hunger as it lurched to its feet.

He put the gun sights on its head and squeezed the trigger. The suppressor didn't silence the shot, but it cut the heart out of the noise. The round took the ghoul just over its right eye and blew a chunk of its head onto the tinfoil-covered window behind it. He sighted in again after the recoil and squeezed off another round. This one caught the ghoul just to the left of its nose as it started to collapse. The ghoul slumped to the floor, fingers twitching, claw tips ticking against the wood.

More Thorn knights pushed through the front door, moving in tight pairs behind him. He hurried forward, running the wall and searching for new targets to engage.

"Hostile!" Chen yelled. "Eleven o'clock, hostile, hostile!" His words were followed by the rapid suppressed chatter of his MP10 and punctuated by a shotgun roar.

Chris started to turn in that direction. Then he saw the couch with the body of an old man sprawled across it and he froze. Stains covered the cushions, appearing black in the ghostly night vision world. Flies crawled across the old man's face, buzzing lazily as if complaining about the commotion. One of the man's arms dangled over the side of the couch, red from shoulder to elbow, the muscles gnawed down to bone. His chest cavity had been ripped open and hollowed out. His gray, filmy eyes stared at the fly-specked ceiling.

A kneeling ghoul hunched over the old man's thigh, biting deep into the meat and paying no attention to Chris or the other knights, despite the gunfire and shouting. A female ghoul, scarified like the one he'd capped seconds ago, but with a completely different, fractal-like pattern. She ripped off a chunk of flesh and gulped it back like a goddamn shark, gnashing and snapping and making little contented grunts deep in her throat.

He lit that fucker up. The first bullet vaporized her ear, getting her attention, but making him feel like an ass for pulling his shot. But he was already shifting, already firing again, putting two rounds in her head, dropping the sights and sending another into the base of her throat. The ghoul flopped forward onto the old man's body, then slid to the floorboards with a thud.

He hurried to the couch and kicked over the ghoul to make sure the threat was neutralized. The bullets had turned much of her head to shredded gristle. The stink of rotting meat and split intestines turned his stomach.

A ghoul bounded down the staircase at the far end of the house, past the kitchen where the main room emptied into an open dining area. The ghoul swung around the banister and loosed a keening wail through its deformed, gaping mouth. Half the team opened up on it with shotguns, assault rifles, and small machineguns. The ghoul crashed to the floor, riddled with holes.

"Clear!" Weeger shouted.

Chris swung past a half-destroyed bay window covered with plywood planks. "Clear!"

The walls seemed to hold the echo of the gunfire—a *neeeeeeeee* sound that rang in his ears. Or maybe that was just the result of so many gunshots in an enclosed space, despite his hearing protection designed to dampen anything over eighty decibels.

"Specter Two, hold this room," the captain ordered. "Specter One, form up on me."

Tyson and Karen Cox took positions at the bottom of the stairwell, weapons aimed up toward the second floor darkness. Furtive footsteps sounded overhead. Floorboards creaking and groaning. Drake and Roth took up positions covering their rear and flank, facing the west hallway that stretched deeper into the house.

Chris broke from his AOR to form up, but stopped cold when he spotted the man's corpse dangling from the opposite wall. The drywall had been ripped out in a seven-foot swath exposing the studs. He'd missed seeing the body until now because he'd swept to the right after clearing the threshold, and now he wished he'd been spared the sight completely.

The corpse was held upright by electrical cords, but the dead weight strained at the bindings and made the cords saw into the flesh, leaving it purple and distended. Drywall dust, stained and splattered with red, covered the floorboards. Blood beaded in the strands of the man's hair. His skin had been carved up, though it was so streaked with a mix of fresh and dried blood that Chris couldn't tell much more than the body was a seeping mess of wounds. More lacerations clustered on the man's face around the nose and ears, slowly weeping blood.

Captain Garcia glanced at Weeger, who stood nearest the corpse. "Weeger, put that poor bastard out of his misery."

Weeger hesitated, confusion on his face. He seemed reluctant to move closer to the body.

Chris's stomach felt as if it had executed a slow roll down into his guts. "That guy's gotta be dead already, Captain."

Sergeant Drake answered. "He ain't dead. The broodsire was working on him, fucking up his brains and playing paint-by-numbers. So you heard the captain. Unless you want a brand new ghoulie on our six, then give that guy some fucking peace and do it *now*."

Weeger pushed his NVD goggles up, yanked away his Kevlar mask, and swiped a gloved hand across his lips. He moved in front of the corpse, brought his M4 up to his shoulder, and took aim. The man groaned and shifted. Weeger flinched and so did Chris. Weeger's finger jerked on the trigger and he sent a bullet skating along the wounded man's scalp, peeling back the flesh and filthy hair.

The man let out a shriek like a train whistle. His head jerked up, and he thrashed in his bindings, causing them to saw deeper into his skin. His eyes were wide, but they were blank, devoid of anything save blinding pain and suffering. Through it all, that train whistle scream never stopped.

Weeger staggered backward. "Fuck!"

"Fucking shoot him again!" Chen yelled. "*Again!*"

Weeger fumbled the rifle back to his shoulder, aimed, and fired twice. The man went rigid for an instant then slumped in the bindings, motionless, a red hole where his left eye had been.

"Jesus Christ," Chris whispered.

"Amen," Pin said, just as softly. He looked at her. She stood near the captain, staring at the hanging corpse, her explosive-tipped lance resting against her shoulder. He could barely see her face behind the blast shield and all her bulky armor.

"Specter One rally on me!" Captain Garcia said again. He wasn't wearing a facemask, and his eyes were cold and his mouth set in a grim line just past the curve of the headset mike.

Something moved in the kitchen. A soft *click, click, click, click* that made Chris think of a dog walking across linoleum.

He swung his MP7 toward the kitchen archway, careful not to sweep anyone's head with the barrel. He could just see part of the counter and cupboards from where they stood clustered at the far end of the living room. A breathy, gurgling sound bubbled out of the darkness.

Captain Garcia raised a hand, pointed to Chris and to Chen, then to his eyes, and back to the kitchen. *Check it out.*

Chris nodded and he and Chen stalked forward. They started to stack against the wall on the near side of the door, Chen in the lead, when a huge ghoul leaped through the archway. It lunged and grabbed for Chen.

Chen cried out and opened fire pointblank, sending 10mm rounds ripping into its chest. The ghoul pushed him backward, falling on him, biting and gouging with its ragged claws, and knocking his NVD goggles off.

Chris staggered backward trying to get room to fire. Chen shoved a hand under the ghoul's chin to push its jaws away. It bit into his hand. The blood splashed bright red on the ghoul's flayed lips and filed teeth. Chen screamed jagged, brittle curses. The captain yelled for them to *suppress that fucker now!* The smell of dead flesh and corruption and mildew in the walls fell around Chris in a suffocating blanket. He was still too damn close.

He let his submachine gun drop, the weapon dangling from its sling. He couldn't shoot into the ghoul's head from this angle with Chen trapped underneath it. His rounds would travel through its skull and hit Chen.

He darted clear of the wall, giving himself space. With one fast sweep he drew his long sword from the sheath on his back. He swung it hard. The carbon-steel edge whispered as it divided the air. The blade cut deep into the ghoul's neck. The blade was heavy enough, and his swing strong enough, to shear through its spine.

The ghoul's head toppled from its neck, bounced off Chen's helmet and rolled to a stop. The head gnashed its teeth and snapped at the floorboards as if it wanted to chew through the wood. It stopped biting and started to lick the planks with a blackened tongue, lapping at the drops of Chen's blood that had spattered on the floor.

He reversed the sword, putting two hands on the grip, and drove the point down into the ghoul's skull so hard the tip punched through and pinned it to the wood.

Chen shoved the ghoul's body off him. He clutched his injured hand to his chest and cursed non-stop. Chris glanced at him, then found himself staring at the ghoul's filthy bare feet. The clicking sound had been made by the misshapen nails—closer to claws—on its toes. Disgusting.

"How bad, Chen?" Captain Garcia asked.

"Fucker bit off my *fucking pinkie finger*! Motherfuckin-cocksuckin-sonuva*bitch*!"

"Roth, get over here and patch him up, I need Weeger with me." The captain glanced at Chris and nodded. Chris frowned, put a boot on the ghoul's head and yanked his sword free. He left a bloody boot print on the thing's face. God, he hated monsters.

Captain Garcia turned back to the squad. "Chen will stay with Specter Two. Specter One form up on me again. Clear the kitchen, clear the basement."

"Captain," Sergeant Drake said. "Specter Two's down to three guns until Roth's done and Chen's back in action. If the tangos push, we could be neck-deep in a river of shit real fast."

The captain paused, scowling. Chris noted the impatience in his eyes and felt the same. They needed to get to the kid and *now*. But Drake was right. Not enough firepower left in Specter Two if Garcia led the rest of the squad into the basement before Roth was done with Chen. There were still a lot of ghouls in the house somewhere, not to mention the broodsire, which hadn't shown its ugly face yet.

"All teams hold position," the captain said, his tone all business, the only hint of his frustration evident in his eyes.

Roth worked fast and bound Chen's pinkie stump tightly. He secured the bandage with medical tape and stood. "He's good to go"

"All right," the captain said. "Get back in position."

Roth hurried to his position covering the hallway. Chen followed after and crouched near him. He was still pale and shaking, his hand held against his chest, sweat on his face and pain in his eyes, but he pulled a 9-mil and covered the hall with the pistol.

Still nothing from upstairs except those occasional footsteps and creaking floorboards. Chris looked back to the kitchen archway. This was taking too much time. They had to move, dammit. Had to press the assault.

"I'm on point," the captain said. "Hill next. Jessica on the lance, Weeger on our six." He glanced at Jessica. "We see the broodsire, you take Hill's support position and shove that lance down its throat, but only after the boy's clear. Hear me?"

Jessica nodded, resettling her hold on the lance's dual grips and triggers. Her lance was a type of modified lunge mine—six feet long and tipped with a directed explosive shaped-charge and two secondary charges filled with steel pellets the size of gumballs. A circular steel plate and recoil suppression system helped shield her from back-blast and shrapnel, though the shaped charge was designed to channel its explosive force away from her and into the target. Even though she might be easy on the eyes, anyone who ran around shoving explosives into angry monsters qualified as a few clowns short of a circus in his book.

Captain Garcia lifted his assault rifle and advanced toward the kitchen archway. "All teams, Specter One on the move."

They pushed into the kitchen. Cheap Formica countertops followed the wall in an L-shape. Lumpy and cracked linoleum rolled in a hideous green and yellow pattern beneath their feet. The oven gaped open, and a scattering of red drops dotted the cracked glass. More flies, but not moving much, as if they were asleep, their bodies ugly and iridescent in the green-black light amplification world. The door to the basement stood closed, just beyond the oven and an ancient refrigerator with smears of blood on the handle. They fanned out as much as possible and advanced toward the door.

The dishwasher was missing from under the counter, leaving a gaping black hole. A ghoul crawled out of the space on all fours, scrabbling straight for Captain Garcia. The captain opened up with his SG 553 on semi auto, pumping bullets into it. It shook as each round hit and finally collapsed. But a second later it lunged and grabbed for his boot, jaws snapping. Garcia raised his leg and stomped its hand, then drove the bayonet into its eye and pulled the trigger.

He yanked the bayonet free and kicked the ghoul's body out of the way. He signaled for them to follow. They stacked outside the basement door. The captain reached for the doorknob, and the watcher came straight through the door, her form ghosting out of the wood and startling Chris so badly he almost opened fire by reflex.

"Dammit, Winters," Captain Garcia snarled. "A warning would be nice."

Winters's face was as frantic as her telepathic speak. *"They moved the boy!"*

"What?"

"They just moved him. When they heard you break down the door and start shooting. You have to hurry."

"There's only one way out of the basement—"

"They're moving him up through the walls, up a passage inside the wall," she said. "Lifting him up to the second floor. Hurry!"

Captain Garcia kicked in the door.

CHAPTER TWELVE

Basement Black

The darkness down the basement stairs seemed to defeat their night vision devices, as if they peered down the throat of a massive, crouching beast into an emptiness where all light had been swallowed.

"Switch to flashlights," the captain ordered. There wasn't enough ambient light in the basement for good images in the NVDs, and they didn't have infrared illuminators, so Chris turned on the gun light mounted on his MP7's rail. Weeger turned one on as well, and Jessica flipped on a small flashlight mounted on the side of her blast helmet.

The light beams pierced down the stairs. He would've tossed his flashbang if there hadn't been standing orders from the captain forbidding it. The kid complicated things, forced them to take risks to keep him safe. He didn't have to like it. How could he live with himself if a little boy got hurt because he didn't have the balls to go down just on guns?

Captain Garcia advanced down wooden steps worn smooth and bowed in the middle. The bayonet on his SIG carbine still dripped blood. It made Chris uneasy—having the captain on point, headed down into the darkness where anything might spring on him before he had time to react. Chris followed on his heels, covering his flank, but careful not to bump him. Weeger and Jessica tailed behind him, and he tried hard not to think about her explosive-tipped lance so close at his back and what would happen if she fell on him with the safeties off.

While the first floor had been nearly empty, the basement overflowed with junk. He scanned for targets, traversing his gun barrel and flashlight beam over benches, boxes splotched with mold, and tumbling stacks of black plastic trash bags. Pieces of an old bed and an upside down table leaned against the mildew-spotted cinderblock wall. The stink of mildew and wet cardboard hung in the air.

"I got visual on the cage," Captain Garcia said.

All their lights swung to line up with the captain's and flooded the big dog kennel cage with white light. The wire door gaped open. A dirty sheet inside sat crumpled in one corner, but nothing else.

"They kept him in that?" Weeger whispered with pure loathing in his voice.

"That's why they call 'em monsters, Weeg." Chris spread out along the captain's flank, tracking his light over the south side of the basement. He wanted to shoot something. It was the weirdest damn thing because he'd seen that guy upstairs, half turned into a ghoul, and the old man hollowed out like a green pepper, and neither sight had really put the fire in his blood. But seeing the dog kennel they'd kept Michael in made him yearn to open up full-auto into some ghoul's skull.

The watcher flowed past them. The flashlight beams, when they hit her green-and-black suit, went right through her without lighting her up, but he was still able to see her form move around as if she were a life-size cut-out of a person sliding across the concrete basement floor.

"Over here," she called. "They took him up the wall."

A hole opened in the wall near the far corner where there was wood paneling and not cinderblock, as if someone had once harbored hopes of finishing over the basement. The hole was square, maybe three and a half or four feet in width and the same in height. The studs had been sawed away, and the interior was thicker than normal, as if it had been expanded on purpose. Built as some kind of half-assed secret passage maybe? In the briefing, the captain had said this had been a drug house before the broodsire and ghouls moved in. Maybe the druggies had used the walls to hide product from DEA agents, moved it around like a dumbwaiter.

Something moved in the hole. A ghoul slowly leaned out of the shadows. Its eyes flashed silver in the flashlight glare. Chris took aim at its forehead, and his finger tightened on the trigger.

"Hold your fire!" Captain Garcia said, raising a hand in warning. "Don't hit the wall. Michael might be inside."

The ghoul crawled beyond the protection of the hole and unfolded from its hunched crouch. The captain moved toward it, keeping it in his sights. Chris and the rest of the team advanced behind him in a staggered V formation across the dirty basement floor.

"Where's the boy?" the captain shouted.

The ghoul cocked its head and blinked at him.

"Where's the kid, you ugly bastard?"

The ghoul squealed and clawed at the half-healed scars patterned across its body, ripping them open again. "We have him. We'll *eat* him—"

Captain Garcia's rifle cracked. The muzzle flash painted an explosion in the darkness. A single brass casing jumped out and *tinged* across the cement. The ghoul went down with a hole in its forehead, mouth agape, bloody drool running from between its sharpened teeth.

Weeger advanced toward the hole, moving in a wide arc. Chris hurried forward to cover him, weaving in and out of the boxes and old junk, past a partially burned mattress so filthy he wouldn't have slept on it for the promise of his own jet boat and a hundred thousand dollars.

Gunfire erupted upstairs, a rapid chatter and a shotgun boom, followed by deep quiet.

"Specter Two this is Specter Actual," Captain Garcia said. "What's your status, over?"

"Engaged two hostiles advancing down the stairs. Holding position, over."

"Roger that, Specter Two." The captain wheeled on the watcher. "Get upstairs and find that boy."

The watcher nodded. She looked up at the exposed beams and wood supports of the basement ceiling and her body smeared upward, becoming an afterimage of bright light lingering in his eyes, and then she was gone.

Weeger reached the ghoul corpse and kicked it

over, covering it with his M4. He shoved the barrel of the carbine in its eye, hard into the socket, making sure the damn thing wasn't playing possum. Then he squatted down next to it.

Chris moved closer, uneasy. "Hey careful, man—"

A ghoul dropped down from the wall passage. It scrabbled out of the hole right at Weeger, quick as a rat. It grabbed for him. Weeger swung the rifle around, but another ghoul lunged out and seized his leg. They yanked him toward the hole.

Chris had no shot. Their heads were too close to Weeger's body. He ran toward Weeger, shoving a stack of moldering boxes out of his way. "Ghouls at the hole! Hostiles! Hostiles!"

Weeger lost his M4, but he pulled his knife and started to stab and slash at the arms holding him. The ghouls shrieked and gibbered but didn't let him go. They dragged him into the hole and started hauling him up the interior wall.

He wasn't going to reach Weeger in time, and if the ghouls got him up the wall he was as good as dead. Chris had no choice but to drop into a crouch and open fire and risk hitting him.

His shots hit one of the ghouls, he saw it jerk with the impacts, but he didn't score a headshot so it kept its hold on Weeger. His shots grew wild as a frantic desperation sank its teeth into his mind. He had to stop them from tearing at his buddy. He had to make them let him go.

Another set of pale, scarred arms reached down from inside the wall and grabbed Weeger. The ghouls hauled Weeger up the narrow crawlspace between the wood planks and the cinderblocks.

Chris ran for him, but most of Weeger had already disappeared. Only his boots dangled there, kicking and thrashing. He heard grunts and curses— heard the wet tearing of a blade plunging into muscle, and the grating rasp of the edge stuttering against bone. Then Weeger screamed.

Chris's mind spun its wheels, throwing thoughts around like mud. He couldn't randomly open fire into the wall. He sure as hell couldn't climb into the hole and risk being pulled up by ghouls crawling around in the walls like cockroaches. But he had to do *something* because time burned away and Weeger was screaming and now there was blood splattering on the cement floor.

He had to something now.

He grabbed the flashbang from his assault harness, pulled the pin and underhand-tossed it into the hole. It hit the cinderblock and spun for a moment on the cement like a slowing top. "Fire in the hole!"

Everyone scattered. He ducked away, but not in time. He was too close to ground zero when the flashbang went off with a crashing boom—smoke and light and a concussion wave that hammered him to his knees. Something slammed into his cheek near his temple, just missing the rim of his helmet. Pain shot through his face, up his skull and down his jaw. White light filled his vision, blinding him. His ears were ringing—a never-ending *reeeeeeeee* like a deranged cricket trapped in his ear.

He couldn't breathe. It felt as if all the air had been sucked from his lungs. His balance was crazy, his head swimming. The world flared white.

Someone was yelling, but he couldn't make out the words, couldn't tell who it was. It came to him as if through a padded wall, drowned in the insane cricket *reeeeeee!* and a flood of pain.

The world was locked in white, a snowstorm without depth or definition. He lost everything in the blank embrace.

CHAPTER THIRTEEN

Snowstorm's Eye

"Your name Chris Hill?"

"Yeah." He eyed the man who'd approached him in the grocery store, carrying a gallon of milk in one scarred-up hand. A hard-faced guy, looked like a Marine or something. Jeans and a button down shirt. Work boots. Gray eyes that made Chris think of the flat head of a nail. "I know you?"

"You shopping for your mom?"

Chris didn't answer, just stared at the guy, suspicion twisting in his guts. His mother was home with one of her migraines—pain so sharp and drilling that all his mother could do was curl up on sweaty sheets with every blind in the house closed and cry. He could hear her sobs through the door and her whispered prayers for God to let her finally sleep and escape the agony. They'd had no food in the house, so Chris had borrowed the car and some money out of his mom's purse and headed to the market, thinking maybe he'd make her something to eat. As if that would help. He only had his driving permit, so if he got pulled over without an adult in the car, he'd be in some serious shit. So he'd driven to the store like an old woman. Cops never went after old ladies unless they ran over somebody or backed into a bank.

The man kept looking at him, waiting for an answer. What the hell did he want anyway? Chris sure as hell wasn't going to tell the guy about his mom.

"Your father's dead," the man finally said. It wasn't a question, just a statement. Like commenting on how windy it had been last night.

"How the fuck you know that?" Angry now. Angry and scared. Because the more he looked at this guy, the more he knew he'd never seen him before. The guy wasn't some friend of the family he'd forgotten. Not some friend of his dead father either. He was sure of it. This guy was different.

"You know what happened to your dad?"

"Leave me alone." He started to swing the grocery cart around, but the man stuck one boot in front of the wheel and stopped it so fast that Chris banged his gut on the push handle. "What's your problem, asshole?"

The man smiled, but there wasn't an ounce of humor in the curve of teeth. "You know what happened to your dad?"

"Some piece of shit stabbed him. *Okay*, you asshole? Stabbed him when he was waiting for the bus. Now can you get the fuck away from me?"

"He wasn't stabbed. He was ripped up, sliced six ways to Sunday by something that crawled out of a scrap yard and attacked your dad as he waited for the bus. Gnawed off the end of his bones and sucked out the marrow."

"*Fuck* you. You're fucking crazy."

The man nodded. Nodded, but Chris couldn't tell if he was agreeing that he was indeed crazy, or agreeing that he could see how somebody might think so. "There was enough to bury, but it was closed casket. How old were you? Seven? Eight?"

"You..." It was hard to talk. His heart slammed away. His anger so huge and massive he couldn't compress it into words. "You—"

"I feel for you. I really do." The man shifted the milk to his other hand and reached into his pocket. He pulled out a piece of paper and handed it over. "We got to the thing that killed him a week later. This is what we left. I'm sorry about your dad."

Chris took the paper with numb hands. He fumbled with it, finally unfolded it, and stared at a photocopy of a photograph, dark and grainy and hard to make out. Something...something vaguely humanoid, but with jaws more like a shark's, its arms twisted, one forearm sticking up from its body at a ninety degree angle, fingers curled and deformed, the whole thing looking as if it had been charred black by fire.

"What's that supposed to be?"

"The thing that killed your dad." He took the paper back and shoved it into a pocket. "It killed some other people too. So we killed it back."

"Who the hell are you?"

The man shoved the paper into his pocket, shifted the milk, and pulled a business card. He held it out to Chris.

This is some kind of weird joke. The card will say something stupid—Ghostbusters, or monster hunters, or Candid Camera or something. He took the card and turned it over. It was blank except for a phone number printed in black numbers. He stared at it. The slanting numbers seemed threatening somehow, a guilty verdict in code.

"When your mom is gone," the man said, "call that number. But only if you want to start dealing out some payback to the things that gutted your life."

The man walked past him, swinging his milk jug back and forth by the handle. Condensation had beaded on the plastic. Chris watched him round the corner at the end of the aisle and disappear from view. His heart beat a slow, solemn rhythm.

When his mom was gone? What the hell did that mean? He had no idea. It only poured him full of a frenetic, directionless terror. It was hard to breathe. He had to concentrate on it, sucking in air, forcing it out again. A woman pushing a cart overflowing with frozen food moved past him, one wheel squealing and wobbling as it spun. She glanced at him with concern on her broad face.

He started pushing his own carriage again, barely paying attention to what he was doing. Rolling on autopilot. Thinking about his mom and her migraine headaches and how she only left the house when she had to and how quiet she always was. Very quiet. And his father's closed casket.

Then the black slammed down like a guillotine, the memory disappeared, and for a moment there was nothing. No time. No thought. Only black.

The blackness vanished when someone pulled off his hood. Chris knelt on a floor set with a mosaic of knights on horseback and foot soldiers, all carrying banners and flags. At the top of the mosaic sat a tile image of a large black rose, curled about with a stem sprouting wicked thorns. He blinked rapidly, trying to adjust to the sunlight streaming in through long, narrow windows in the stone walls.

His mother was dead. She'd swallowed her entire prescription of Valium and chased it with aspirin, vodka, and Xanax two weeks after his nineteenth birthday. He'd been the one to find her. Hurrying to see her, to drop something off before he had to get back to his apartment, get cleaned up for a hot date with Allison, and when he said hot date he meant it because she was most aggressive girl he'd ever been with and he loved the hell out of it. When his mom hadn't answered her door or her phone, he'd used his key and found her. He'd cried, sitting on the edge of the bed, hollow inside as if she'd taken him and emptied him when she'd left. A week later he'd broken up with Allison. A month and a half after that, he'd called the number on that card. The card he'd kept ever since that day in the grocery store.

A sword blade pressed against his throat. The sword was real. He could feel its edge held a fraction from slicing into his skin. He tried not to move, not even to swallow, and fought to dampen down the fear that wanted to firecracker through his muscles. This was what he wanted. Knighthood. The Order of the

Thorn. The only way he could see to do some good in a universe that watched people die without either a frown or smile but with blank indifference. Same old story, but he wanted to change that story if he could, and he believed he could. If he were strong enough. If he were brave enough.

"Do you, Christopher David Hill, swear upon your life and soul to serve and protect humanity? To save the innocent. To stand against the darkness?"

"I do," he said, and his voice rasped and nearly broke.

"Do you, Christopher David Hill, swear upon your life and soul to serve the Thorn?"

"I do."

"Do you, Christopher David Hill, swear upon your blood and faith and hope of redemption to keep the Silence?"

"Yes, I swear it."

"Rise, squire, and begin your new life with us as a knight of the Order of the Thorn."

He'd stood and turned to look at the man holding the sword, who was the hard-eyed man from the grocery store all those years ago, whose real title was Thorn Lord Maddox. Maddox smiled, and then the magic had hit—a spell sculpture that ate right through Chris's skin and fused itself into his marrow, etched itself on the muscle of his heart. The pain was freezing, an icy burn that swept his body. Even as he realized he could never go back to how things were before, back to the mundane world, he also realized he would never want to.

And then someone yelled into his ear and the words rolled and echoed in his mind. "Hill! Can you hear me? I need you on your boots, soldier!"

CHAPTER FOURTEEN

Reload, Shoot Again

"Hill! Goddammit! Chris! You hear me?" Someone shouting. Someone shaking him. His head flopped around on his shoulders and jagged bolts of pain ripped through his brain and down from his temple to his jaw. He raised his hands, trying to get them up to protect himself. Disoriented. The white had faded back into darkness when he opened his eyes. A dark shape loomed over him, helmet, armor, and a bright light stabbed into his eyes, making him squint and look away. His night vision goggles weren't on his face anymore—why? He couldn't remember. The shadows pooled in the basement ceiling beams. The air reeked of mildew and shit and a lingering sweet chemical stink. He finally realized it was Captain Garcia leaning over him, shaking him, committing small murder on his head.

"Yeah, Captain, I hear you." He tried to roll away and had to stop as nausea rippled through him. "Give a kid a break."

The captain stopped shaking him. Chris had fallen over on his back at some point, and now he lifted his head, blinking at the bright flashlight beams. The ringing in his ears had subsided a little. Thank God for his hearing-protection or he'd probably have heard that sound for the next year.

Captain Garcia and Jessica helped him to his feet. Jessica had her helmet's blast shield visor up. A streak of grime ran down her face, dusting her dark eyebrow with gray. He wanted to touch it, wipe it clean, and shook the feeling away. Stupid and weird thing to want. He must have a concussion or something.

"How many fingers I got up?" The captain waved a hand in his face. Chris tried to focus on it.

"Fourteen."

"Damn it, Hill, I don't need another smart ass," the captain said, both his face and voice grim. "The fuse blew off the flashbang and hit you in the face. You got a bruise the size of New York."

"Lucky bastard, that's me. Saving my helmet with blows to my face." He still felt sick to his stomach, and everything around him stank of burned magnesium. Then he remembered. Oh, shit, Weeger...

"You guys get Weeger? Where's he at?"

"Dead."

Chris closed his eyes. A fresh wave of dizziness washed through him and it was hard to keep standing. He opened his eyes again and saw the trashed remains of his night vision goggles. He must've fallen on them.

"They opened him up in the wall after you set off the flashbang," the captain continued. His eyes were hard, bright. "I gave orders not to use them, because of the kid, and you disobeyed."

"I had to try and save Weeger."

"That right? And what if that goddamn fuse had hit the kid instead of your hard head? Or what if you set the damn place on fire?"

"I couldn't think, I just had to save him. To do something. Get them to drop him. Something..."

Captain Garcia shoved a finger in his face. "Weeger got sloppy and that got him killed. You obey orders. Understand?"

Chris started to nod but immediately stopped as his stomach did a queasy flop. Did the captain think he'd just let a buddy get ripped apart without doing anything to try and stop it? The boy hadn't been in the basement anymore, and the fuse blowing off the flashbang grenade had been a freak accident. Something that probably wouldn't have happened if

Chris hadn't been holding his balls right at ground zero...but still, what if he had hurt the kid? Started a fire, like the captain said? Jesus, there didn't seem to be any right answers.

"C'mon," the captain said. "We're gonna push to the second floor. Finish this."

First Chen hurt, now Weeger dead, and too much time had burned away already. Successful dynamic entry and assault depended on speed and overwhelming force. They'd lost the initiative. The monsters had outmaneuvered them. He tried to fight back the dejection dragging at him and refocus on the task at hand. The boy. Michael still needed him.

Chris picked up his MP7 and wiped off some of the dust. He noticed two battery-powered electronic eyes mounted on small tripods and set near the hole in the wall. Proximity sensors.

Captain Garcia saw him looking and held up the remote alarm, which looked like a small, folded-up cell phone. "So we know if they come back down again. Can't use claymores. Now let's move out."

He headed for the stairs. Chris and Jessica followed him out. For a moment Chris thought he heard whispering in the walls, echoing out through the hole, but the ringing in his ears made him uncertain, and when he paused to listen, it faded away to nothing.

CHAPTER FIFTEEN

Deals

C hris and the rest of Specter One had just
entered the living room when a deep, inhuman
voice bellowed down the staircase, startling
them all.

"Come no further or the boy is meat for the
table."

Chris hurried to a support position against the
wall. He hadn't had time to sort himself out after the
basement fiasco. He still felt shaky, nauseous, but he
wasn't about to abandon the rest of the team or the boy.
The knights of Specter Two already knew what had
happened to Weeger. Every face he could see was a
mask of grim determination. They all had blood in the
game now.

Captain Garcia moved to the stair banister, and
both Chris and Jessica followed. Tyson crouched at the

foot of the stairs, aiming up into the darkness on the second floor with his Steyr-AUG, backed up by Karen on shotgun. A ghoul sprawled halfway down the stairs, leaking sap-like blood onto threadbare carpet tacked to the steps. Another ghoul body lay unmoving near the landing.

"I want to know the boy's safe," the captain yelled back.

There was a long moment of ominous quiet. Then the deep voice said, "Speak, boy. Tell them how safe you are."

Silence.

"Speak," the broodsire rumbled. They heard a child sob, but no words, and the broodsire roared. "*Talk*, sniveling meat puppet!"

Chris's hand tightened on his weapon's grip and a jolt of pain told him he'd clamped his jaw down hard. Filthy, dishonorable sonuvabitching monster. God, he wanted a chance at it. Just one chance to shove his sword in its eye.

"All right! All right!" Captain Garcia called out quickly. "Calm down. Don't hurt the boy."

"Then withdraw. It's your presence which endangers him, child-killer."

"We don't kill children."

"You kill mine."

The captain stared for a moment at the scratched and damaged wainscoting across from the stairs, then peered back up into the darkness. "We won't let you leave here with the boy. And if he's hurt, you die."

"And I won't let the boy free until I leave. And if you try and slay me, *he* dies." Deep laughter echoed down the staircase. "It seems we have a standoff, but time is on my side."

Captain Garcia paused again. "I need some time to clear things with Command."

Now the voice sounded blackly amused. "Don't wait too long, poppet. I'm hungry."

* * *

A short while later, Captain Garcia crouched with Sergeant Drake in the living room, talking in low voices. Tension ran high. The two teams had taken up defensive positions on the first floor in the areas they controlled. The rest of the house belonged to the monsters.

Chris covered the hallway that led into the unsecured bedroom and bathroom areas on the first floor. The ringing in his ears had dialed down to a faint but constant whine, and his head had cleared a bit. His stomach was still queasy though. The stink of blood made him want to puke, but there was no escaping it. Bloody smears trailed along the floorboards where they'd dragged the ghoul corpses into the kitchen and piled them against the basement door. A makeshift meat barricade, half-assed at best, because the basement door opened inward. Hopefully the proximity alarms and the improvised barricade would be enough to warn them of any threat moving up from the basement and slow them from charging out into the kitchen. It was a bad scene though, any way they cut it.

"Specter Three, this is Specter Actual," Captain Garcia said quietly over the encrypted radio. "What's the containment status outside the house?"

"Specter Actual, this is rifle one." Chris recognized Bowen's voice, one of the team's two designated sharpshooters armed with M21 rifles. "I got movement upstairs but no sign of primary target or the hostage. Hostiles have made no attempt to escape out the windows or onto the roof, over."

"Specter Actual, this is rifle two." Peralta this time. "No movement, north side backyard. No sign of tangos, over."

"Rifle one and two, have they identified your positions?"

"Affirmative, Specter Actual," Bowen said. "I'm being watched. I have a shot—"

"Hold your fire, rifle one. Sit tight and hold position. Let me know if they try and bug out, but do not engage without authorization."

"Roger that, Specter Actual. Rifle one, out."

Chris wondered how the hell the broodsire planned on escaping out any of the top windows without ripping out half the frames. He'd never run up against one in real life, but the gun and helmet camera footage he'd seen had shown a monster as big as a Kodiak bear reared up on its hind legs. Judging from the bass-heavy blast of the broodsire's voice from upstairs, the camera hadn't exaggerated.

"We push these bastards, Captain," Drake said in a low voice. He didn't speak over the comm, but Chris crouched close enough to overhear him. "Dynamic assault, clear the second floor in seconds. They'll fold if we go in hard."

Captain Garcia shook his head. "I want a report from the watcher first."

"If we wait—"

"Upstairs could be a nightmare, charging up through only one assault vector. I don't want a lot of wild firing until we know exactly where the kid is and what kind of immediate threat he faces."

"They already got Weeger. You heard that freak—time's on their side. Richards can't hold up the wards forever, and this goddamn house's a rat's nest. They're in the walls. The first floor's not even secure. Our asses are in the wind here, sir."

"I'll take Specter One and clear the rest of the bottom floor." Captain Garcia glanced toward the hallway. "We'll secure it, dig in, and if we can't get to the boy in a way that keeps him alive, I'll bring in more support. We'll lock this whole area down until they get here if we have to."

"We should've cleared the entire shithole at once. Two-pronged assault back when we had surprise on our side. The longer we sit holding our dicks, the worse things'll get."

"Saving Michael Cantwell is our primary objective," Captain Garcia said. "This mission will be a failure unless we get him back in one piece. We clear?"

Chris tried to read Sergeant Drake's face without being obvious about it. What he saw at a glance told him enough. Angry eyes, sweat beading along a clenched jaw, everything about the sergeant screamed tension. Chris quickly looked back to the hallway he covered and focused on running the flashlight beam along the walls and ceiling, just in case something came crawling along up there like a spider.

Drake tried again, his voice fierce but so low that Chris had to strain to make out the words against the ringing in his ears. "We can't keep areas secured if they have rat holes and they can move up and down the load-bearing walls. We don't have enough boots to pull it off."

Captain Garcia motioned Chen over. Chen carefully got up from where he crouched with his back to the wall. His injured hand was bandaged up and held against his chest, and he gripped his 9mm pistol in the other. "Yeah, Captain?"

"Switch places with Parker in Specter Three and keep watch on Richards. Send her in here."

A good call. They could use Tashelle's shotgun in here. Chen was not quite combat ineffective, but close enough, still shivering and maybe in mild shock from the bite. He'd be better off sitting tight in the van, watching Richards's back while the mage maintained the wards that locked this place down. Also, the dog would cheer him up. In fact, Chris wished his dog was here with him now. He could use some cheering himself.

Chen nodded and hurried to the front door, which was closed but so damaged by the battering ram that it would never latch again. He flipped down his night vision device and nudged the door open, peering out into the darkness. After a slow scan, he shouldered his way outside and headed for the van, trying to look everywhere at once. Roth moved to the window to give him cover and tore away the tinfoil so he could see outside.

The captain's voice broadcast over the radio. "Specter Three, this is Specter One Actual. Knight incoming to your position. Cover him, over."

"Copy that, Specter One Actual."

They waited in tense silence until the door finally swung open again and Tashelle moved inside in a combat crouch, her shotgun up and ready. She'd strapped her falchion's leather sheath to her thigh, balanced on the other leg with her 9-mil sidearm. Her falchion was a nasty piece of work that reminded him of a machete, and machetes were a hundred-ten percent vicious business.

She nodded to Chris and took up a covering position nearby.

"How's my pooch?" he whispered. "She okay in the van?"

"Your girlfriend misses you. I swear to God she'd be in here with you if I let her." She must've seen something in his expression because she smirked. "Relax. Chen's watching her."

He nodded, feeling a little better. He didn't want his crazy dog anywhere near this dangerous hell pit.

Captain Garcia turned to the stairwell again, his

face weary and his eyes grim. Chris tried to guess at what was going through the man's mind. He would've bet even money the captain was thinking about how they'd missed the kid and lost Weeger. Both had felt like a double kick in the balls with a steel-toed boot.

"Even with Tashelle on shotgun," Drake said to Captain Garcia, "there's more than seventeen ghouls here, sir. The watcher did a fuck-all job counting."

"*You try counting a nest like this, all those ugly things looking the same, some of them inside the walls,*" the watcher interjected before the captain could reply. She appeared in the center of the room, smearing down from the ceiling like running watercolor paints until her image stood complete before them. She too looked exhausted. Her form flickered, started to blur and smear around the edges again, making him think of a kid coloring outside the lines.

"What's the situation upstairs?" Captain Garcia demanded. "The kid okay? Where is he?"

"*He's not okay, but he's not injured. The broodsire's using him as a human shield. They're in the big room directly off the staircase.*" Her astral projection flickered again and she frowned. "*I don't have much time. I've been in the tank for nine hours. Three past protocol.*"

"How much more time can you give us?"

"*I'm losing cohesion. I won't last long...and the down*

time... They're prepping Cindy to take my place, but you have a three hour gap with no watcher coverage."

Chris shifted and looked back down the hallway, where the darkness seemed to push back against the narrow beam of his gun's flashlight. More bad news. No watcher meant they'd be vulnerable, lose priceless intel for awhile. Although so far the intel hadn't saved Weeger's ass, and news about the kid being moved had come too damn late to be of any good.

Still, he found himself glancing back to the captain and the watcher again, unable to look away for long. So he caught the look of frustration and anger on Captain Garcia's face before the captain locked it down again and took a deep breath. "All right. Tell them to get me as many watchers as they can spare. This is a delicate situation here, and I need more eyes."

The watcher's form flickered and smeared so badly she hardly looked human any more. Her voice wavered, becoming soft and indistinct on some words. *"Only one available...other watchers searching...Eastern Europe...High priority. Hunting...vamp and a traitor..."*

"Jesus Christos," the captain snarled. "This is a kid we're talking about here. *Fuck* the vampires."

Winters started to say something, but her voice slowed, deepened and dragged out like distorted audio. Her body flickered rapidly and vanished.

For a long time no one spoke. Chris could see little Michael Cantwell's face in his mind from that picture, his brown eyes, one of those smiles beaming fun around the room like a searchlight. He saw the guy with the gallon of milk in his hand, the man whose name and title he knew but who'd always be the Milk Jug Guy in some dark part of his mind, swinging it back and forth, looking at him, telling him when he was ready for payback, give him a call.

A long moment of silence spun out after the watcher vanished. Captain Garcia stood up and looked around at the room. His gaze fell on Chris. "Hill, you combat effective?"

"I'm good to go, Captain."

Ninety percent true. He wasn't about to admit to being anything else, even if his head still pounded and the side of his face throbbed. Though why the captain had such a hard on for him recently he had no idea. He'd been second on the entry team, gone with the captain to see Michael's mother, and now here was something else. The trust boosted his ego, but damn he was a little tired of being singled out.

"Maybe Hill should hang back, Captain," Sergeant Drake said. "Get his head back on straight. Roth or Tyson can watch your six easy enough."

Captain Garcia glanced at him and keyed his

radio. "Parker, you're with me and Hill. Deering, I want lancer support for Specter Two. Specter Two hold position. Specter Three sit tight." He ejected his magazine, checked the rounds remaining, and seated it again. "I think I made myself clear, sergeant. You just concentrate on keeping this area secure."

Drake didn't reply. The clenched jaw was reply enough.

They stacked up along the wall beside entrance to the hallway, the captain on point, Chris next, followed by Tashelle. The captain flipped down his night vision device and eased into a combat crouch. He slowly swung out from the edge of the entranceway, back far enough to avoid striking the wall with his bayonet, and then advanced into the hall. Chris swung out behind him, sweeping the hall with his gun's flashlight beam but careful not to dazzle the captain's NVD with a flood of light. Tashelle moved into position beside him, using the light on her assault shotgun.

Three doors opened off the hallway, the door on the left and one on the right stood closed, the farthest one on the right-hand side yawned like a dark mouth. Dozens of tiny holes riddled the drywall where pictures had once hung, and cobwebs swayed in tiny currents of air he couldn't feel. The floorboards creaked under their boots as they moved. The only other sound was the intermittent buzzing of flies. He really hated flies.

He fought to settle his breathing—breathe in through the nose, out through the mouth—but it was useless with new adrenaline rushing through him and his heart slamming away. Nothing like humping down a dark corridor to really get the blood pumping. Hurrah.

Captain Garcia signaled—three nods, the go signal. He swung wide into the closest doorway on the left with his assault rifle up and aimed. He kicked the door near the knob and sent it crashing back into the wall. He pushed into the room, shouldering aside the rebounding door. Chris moved right behind him, swinging the opposite direction, barrel traversing to the left while the captain covered the right. He cleared the doorway fast to give Tashelle a clear line of fire.

A bed sat against the opposite wall, near a window covered with tinfoil and cardboard. The tarnished brass headboard had flaked and cracked along the metal arches and rods. A huge bloodstain marred the center of the bare mattress. Flies crawled on it, but there was no dead body in sight. Darkness pooled under the bed. An old dresser had been tipped over near the closet. Bare walls. The light fixture had been torn from the ceiling.

Chris moved toward the closet door. It was

closed. Tashelle came up beside him and stopped in front of the closet, shotgun covering the door. She gave him the three-nod go signal. He took one hand off his weapon, grabbed the crystal-cut knob, and yanked the door open, moving back out of Tashelle's line of fire.

"Clear," she said.

"Room clear," Captain Garcia said. "Form up."

They swept the bathroom next. The captain signaled Chris inside. Space was so tight that he had the most maneuverability with his MP7, suppressor or not.

Discolored and lumpy linoleum covered the floor, stained yellow around the bottom porcelain of the toilet. The top of the tank was off, and the float and water inside had turned green with algae. He caught sight of himself in the mirror out of the corner of his eye, but didn't glance that way. In dark, high-tension situations like this, it was easy to put a few rounds into your own reflection if you came across an unexpected mirror. Then you felt like a complete assclown, and nobody ever let you live it down.

He moved toward the claw-foot porcelain tub. Sunflowers dotted the shower curtain, but mildew stained the lower half in big black-and-green patches. The shower curtain had been left closed. He couldn't see inside.

He settled his finger on the trigger, feeling the

heavy beat of his heart as it lurched in his chest. He grabbed one edge of the curtain and ripped it aside.

The bathtub was empty. Water stains and soap scum and that was it. He turned back, careful not to sweep Tashelle with his gun barrel as she covered him from the doorway. He bent and checked the cheap wood cabinets under the sink. Nothing but old ant and roach traps, and way back in the dusty corner, a single tampon still in the wrapper.

"Clear," he said.

They formed up in the hall again. One last room to check. The one at the end of the hallway with its door gaping open and pitch darkness inside. They took up position and listened for a moment outside. Chris could hear nothing except the faint ringing in his ears, but he had a feeling there was something waiting in there. Hiding in the dark. Watching for them to cross the threshold.

Captain Garcia gave the go signal again and took point, rushing through the doorway. Chris followed on his heels, sweeping the cone of his AOR.

A completely empty room this time. The light fixture was shaped like a snow-frosted fishbowl and filled with dead bugs. One electrical outlet had been pulled from the wall and dangled on the end of the two wires. Both windows had been covered with tinfoil.

Captain Garcia pointed toward the closet. Chris nodded and moved toward it from one side of the room, while the captain closed in from the other, and Tashelle covered the door to the hall. Chris yanked the closet door open. Two wire hangers and nothing else. So much for his feeling that something lurked in here waiting for them.

"Room clear," Captain Garcia said. He keyed his radio. "This is Specter One Actual. First floor clear."

Chris blew out a long breath. After crap like this—the build up to violence and then...nothing—he always found himself with a weird feeling of hollow gratefulness. A kind of bitter and sweet mix of disappointment and relief.

They headed back down the hallway, maintaining assault formation. Chris left the last door open. The closed doors bothered him. Anything could be happening behind a closed door.

The sound of a soft scrape came from somewhere close. Muffled. Furtive. The three of them froze. A shuffling sound was followed by a crack as the house either shifted or something heavy moved on the wood floor. The beams from their flashlights made the hall a murky tunnel of shadows. Chris held his breath, listening.

A thump. More scrapes.

Captain Garcia lifted his hand and pointed toward the first room they'd cleared, the one with the bed and all the blood. But how could anything be inside there? They'd found nothing when they'd cleared it.

Another scrape. Another thud. Footsteps—bare feet padding rapidly along the floorboards. Chris quite clearly heard sniffing as something smelled the air, searching out their scent. The tiny squeak of springs told him something was on or near the bed.

The captain started forward again, his rifle up and aimed. A ghoul slowly leaned out of the room's open doorway into the hall. They could see only its head and upper torso as it turned to peer at them. For a long moment they stared at it; it stared back. Then the ghoul began to laugh with the same braying, hysterical shriek heard in psych wards.

Captain Garcia was on point and the shot was his. The ghoul grinned its cheek-flayed grin as its laughter died down into giggles.

The ghoul leaned farther out, settling one clawed hand on the doorway trim. Its ragged nails gouged the paint. Captain Garcia shot it in the head. It crumpled, slumping forward into the hall. One of its hands twitched.

"Status! Status!" Sergeant Drake called over the radio.

"Specter One engaging hostiles," Captain Garcia said. "Hold your positions."

Chris moved to cover the first room doorway, his heart thundering away, blood rushing through his veins so fast he could feel the pulse in his neck. How the hell had the ghoul gotten into a cleared room? It was impossible. A second later he had it. They'd carved out another mouse hole—some way to move up and down from inside the walls. Had to be.

The upper half of the ghoul's body sprawled into the hallway. Its mouth gaped open; its blank eyes stared at the floor. The lower half was still in the bedroom, obscured from view by the door frame. The ghoul jerked backward suddenly, sliding on the wood.

Chris almost opened fire before he realized that something he couldn't see was pulling the corpse out of sight. Slowly, the body disappeared into the room, making a soft scraping sound as it dragged along the floorboards. The torso vanished, then head, and finally one outstretched arm covered with scar patterns and tipped with claws disappeared from view, leaving behind an uneven snail-trail of gore.

Captain Garcia took up a shooter's position against the wall and signaled to Chris. Chris moved past him in a crouch, his heart thudding, thudding. He tried not to think about how damn unnerving it'd been to witness that corpse slowly dragged out of view by something he couldn't see. He reached the edge of the doorway, MP7 good to go. His breathing was heavy, rasping in and out even though he was trying his hardest to be quiet.

He swung out wide past the doorway, gun barrel traversing the room in an arc as he moved. Nothing.

The scraping sound continued. The gore trail led out of his line of sight. He gritted his teeth and crossed into the room. His pulse hammered away hard enough to make the gun barrel tremble.

He entered in time to see the ghoul corpse pulled behind the half-open closet door. No visual on the creature doing the dragging. He almost opened fire on the closet door, knowing his rounds would punch through the faux wood paneling as if it were tissue paper. But he had clear orders to check his targets, so he held his fire. He heard Tashelle swing into the room behind him.

He couldn't get a clear line of sight into the closet unless he shifted closer to the bed. But no way in hell would he step next to that gaping darkness beneath the box spring and risk something grabbing his boots and dragging him under.

But it was either risk getting close to the bed and whatever might or might not be under it, or stalk up to the closet door and swing it fully open and find himself face-to-face with God-knew-what. Maybe a ghoul. Maybe the broodsire.

He chose the bed. He took two running steps and jumped on top of the bloodstained mattress. Tashelle cursed as he crossed her line of fire, but he'd had no time to warn her.

The springs squealed. His boots sank deep into the mattress. He leveled his weapon at the closet again. From this angle he could see a female ghoul hunched over the one the captain had shot from the hallway. Tracks of moisture glistened on its flayed cheeks when his flashlight lit its face. It pressed the dead ghoul's hand to its neck, cradling it between its face and shoulder, and rocked slowly back and forth.

He pulled the trigger four times. Hit with three shots. The ghoul jerked and slumped over and did not move again.

Something grabbed his ankle.

He looked down and saw a rail-thin arm reaching from beneath the bed. A filthy hand was clamped around his boot and tugging him toward the edge. The ghoul peeked out from beneath the bed. It looked entirely too eager as it grinned like a hungry man with his paws on a turkey drumstick.

Chris yanked his leg free and fell against the

wall. He swung the MP7 around, but didn't have a clear headshot. "Kill it!"

"Get clear!" Tashelle crouched with her shotgun aimed at the ghoul. The ghoul was flailing around, struggling to climb out from under the bed and get at him again.

"Fuckin' *shoot* it!"

She opened fire full-glory with the semi-auto shotgun. Twelve gauge buckshot erased the ghoul's head and part of its arm and transformed it into pinkish mist. She aimed low, trying not to clip him. He felt the bed shake beneath his boots. The walls echoed with the shotgun's furious roars.

"Hostile down." Tashelle swept under the rest of the bed frame with her gun's light. "Bed clear." She swung her shotgun back on the closet again.

Captain Garcia still covered the hallway, his face pale and grim. Chris pushed away from the wall and stumbled across the mattress, wondering if his unsteady knees would dump him onto the floor with the ghoul blood and bodies. His knees held out, but as he stepped off the bed he couldn't help but notice how the buckshot had ripped the hell out of the mattress sides. He had no idea why he wasn't picking pellets out of his shins. So damn lucky.

Tashelle covered him as he moved on the closet.

He swept his light beam over the dead ghouls and along the walls inside. His hands were shaking and the flashlight beam jittered. Something wet—not blood—dripped down from above to splatter on the floorboards. The black emptiness beyond the hole swallowed his flashlight beam. He could see the joists and beams and the jagged edges where the wood had been sawed away. A dark shape was moving up there.

"Captain," he called out. "They got a hole cut in the ceiling. They're moving between floors." He edged closer, keeping the gun light trained toward the closet ceiling and intending to shoot when he illuminated a target. Those sneaky freaks…

There was no warning when his dog ran into the room. He never heard any barking, just growls and the scrabbling claws on the floorboards as she ran past the captain and Tashelle.

"Shit!" Tashelle yelled. "Chris, grab her!"

Cold fear flooded through him at the sight of her in this nightmare house. She ran between him and the closet and skidded to a stop at the closet door. She was staring up into the closet, at the ceiling, and growling as if she were protecting him.

He let his weapon fall to dangle on its sling as he lunged after her, intending to pull her to safety. Dread iced every part of his insides. She was too close to that damn hole.

A ghoul dropped down from the ceiling. It nearly fell on his dog. It grabbed at her, but she twisted away, snarling and snapping.

Chris slammed his shoulder into the ghoul and drove it into the wallboard so hard its head left a dent. He pinned it against the wall with his forearm pressed against its neck. His crazy dog was still trying to get at the ghoul. He had to nudge-push her out of the closet with his leg. He reached for his pistol with his free hand but the angle was wrong. He couldn't pull the 9mm.

Tashelle grabbed the dog around the middle and dragged her away. "Clear! She's clear!"

The ghoul thrashed and battered at him. It was like trying to keep an enraged eel from sliding out of his grasp. Its sharpened teeth clacked shut inches from his face. He was staring right into its empty, soulless eyes. Smelling the dead-thing reek of its breath. It flailed and nearly broke free, its claws scraped on his body armor plates.

He gave up on the pistol and pulled his combat knife from his harness instead. The ghoul hissed and twisted, seconds from breaking free of his hold. From across the room, his dog loosed mournful *barooos* that echoed from the walls.

The ghoul got its feet under it and nearly sent

him flying as it pushed back against him. He shoved his knife up under its chin. The blade sank in with disturbing ease. Thick blackish-red blood seeped out. He yanked the knife free and then drove it into the ghoul's right eye.

It sagged in his arms with a trailing, pathetic moan. He stepped back quickly and let it fall.

A ferocious roar blasted from overhead. It was so loud and unexpected and close that he fumbled his knife and nearly tripped over his own feet backing out of the closet. He grabbed up his submachine gun again from where it dangled on its sling over his shoulder. He aimed at the hole in the ceiling.

The flashlight beam glinted off a massive, staring eye as big a car's headlight. The iris was amber with black, elliptical pupils. Not a ghoul. The goddamn broodsire.

It roared again, and he caught a glimpse of a huge mouth rimmed with curved teeth for ripping meat, black tongue, and rows of heavy molars that looked capable of crushing a femur.

He froze, his finger curled on the trigger, staggered by the size of the thing hiding in the darkness above. His dog still loosed those mournful "barrooos." Then he shattered through his brief paralysis and started pulling the trigger.

The broodsire reared back out of his gun light, vanishing in the shadows, safely out of his line of sight. Chris reached for a frag grenade, then remembered the rules of engagement and backed away instead.

"Captain, that son of a bitch was right there," he said, his voice low and over-torqued with all the adrenaline crashing through him.

Garcia rushed up beside him, peering along his gun sights up into the hole. Now their lights illuminated nothing, but they could hear plenty of ghouls hissing and gibbering in the darkness. And something heavy moving around, very close.

The captain cursed softly and signaled them to retreat. He keyed his radio as they edged away from the closet. "This is Specter One Actual. First floor is not secure. Repeat, first floor is *not* secure. Pulling back to primary position."

"Solid copy, Specter One Actual," Drake said over the comm. "All teams hold your fire. Friendlies inbound."

Slowly, the three of them backed to doorway leading to the hall not taking their weapons off the closet. His dog stayed by his side, circling back with him as they retreated.

"All right, listen up," Captain Garcia said. "We're in deep shit, so here's what we're gonna do."

CHAPTER SIXTEEN

Siege

S talemate.

So far there had been no further contact with the monsters since the foray down the hall. Chris could hear furtive footsteps and creaking boards overhead as things crept around on the second floor. Once something laughed. Another time something screeched in rage, and then a door slammed, startling them all.

Chris and his crazy basenji friend had taken up position in the dust where the couch had been, near the plywood-covered bay window. This close, he could see that the plywood on the window was only hung on bolts—balanced there and easy to remove and replace— making it the likely spot where something as big as the broodsire crawled in and out of the house. He fed his dog some of his beef jerky and she repaid him in face-licking.

"How'd you get in here, you *pero loco*?" he said, rubbing her behind the ears. "You about gave me a heart attack. Leave the killing to the professionals, would you?"

"You're perfect for each other." Tashelle crouched near them, cradling her shotgun and staring toward the barricaded hall, the strain on her face easy to see. "You're both too dumb to live."

"But too beautiful to kill," he finished for her. His dog seemed to grin back at him, so he kissed her on the top of the head. She really needed a bath. "How'd she get out of the van anyway?"

"Shit." Tashelle keyed her mic. "Chen, this is Parker. What's your status, over?"

"Copacetic," Chen replied over the radio. "I'm chowing on jerky and watching Richards and his light show. Oh, and I don't have a finger because a monster fucking ate it."

"You got eyes on the dog?"

"Nah, the dog escaped. She ran into the house like a boss, through that busted door. Why?"

"Because you were supposed to be watching her. How about a heads-up next time? I was worried something happened to you guys."

"Something *did* happen to me. A ghoul ate my

finger. Besides, I can only babysit one thing at a time and it's not even my dog. Out."

Tashelle shook her head. Chris wanted to get the dog the hell out of danger, but there was zero chance of him leaving his position until this goat-rope mess was finished. The captain was none too pleased with either of them, but at the moment they all had bigger shit on their plate.

"Close call back there," Chris said. He kept his tone offhand, the words an understatement. They'd almost ended up meat.

"Lucky."

Lucky was fickle bullshit and didn't cut it in this game. Still, shit happened. Hadn't he almost blown himself up earlier? At least no one had died this time.

"Nobody could've spotted that hole they ripped in the ceiling," he said. "Not in the dark. This house is messed up."

She only looked at him, then looked away, saying nothing.

Specter One had done the best with what they'd had on hand to fortify the small area they controlled. They'd set up more infrared-eye beam alarms. They'd barricaded closet door with the box spring and bed frame. Tyson and Roth had flipped the couch in the living room upside down and shoved it into the hall.

Captain Garcia and Chris had dragged the bloodstained mattress from the bedroom into the hallway as they retreated. They'd folded and pulled the reeking mattress against couch while Tashelle covered them, wedging it on top of the couch.

It was a chintzy, half-assed barricade at best. It wouldn't do much more than slow down a couple of ghouls for a few seconds. He would've loved to have rigged up some claymore mines from the tactical van and give those bastards a nasty surprise if they crawled through the ceiling again. Mission force protocol was against explosives though. So they were forced to hunker down and hold their own dicks. As big as that broodsire was, pissing on it would probably be more effective than shooting it with all these small arms. If Jessica couldn't use her lance, they were fucked.

Sergeant Drake wasn't impressed with the half-assed barricades either. He stood in the middle of the living room with his M4 in his hands and faced off with the captain. He didn't bother to keep his voice low.

"What's the plan now, sir? That piece of shit barricade ain't gonna hold anything back. And we don't have Weeger's body. We don't leave a fallen knight behind."

"We hold here until another watcher gets in," the captain replied, his voice calm. "We'll get Weeger back.

And the boy."

Sergeant Drake stared at him, his jaw slowly moving back and forth as if he ground something to dust between his teeth. The tension in the room twisted tighter than barbed wire. Finally, the sergeant turned on his boot heel and walked over to where Tyson and Karen held the line at the bottom of the stairs.

Captain Garcia eyed him for a long moment, then glanced around the room at the rest of the knights who silently watched the scene. "All right, Thornheads, listen up. I want two of you to haul in the gear from the trucks, generators, trouble lights, and flood lamps. If we're gonna be here for awhile, I want this place locked down."

* * *

Fifteen minutes of haul-ass later they had three portable floodlight stands set up, filling the living room and kitchen with harsh, stark light. They even hung a trouble light on the highest staircase banister railing they could safely reach. It threw jagged shadows against the second floor ceiling and upper walls. The decision to go from relying on night vision devices to flood lamps and trouble lights showed better than anything the mission had changed from assault to siege.

Both sharpshooters reported sighting movement upstairs. Captain Garcia kept Bowen and Peralta on standby at their firing positions, with orders to hold fire until authorized or the ghouls attempted a break out.

"Watcher won't be here for another hour and a half," Tashelle told him as they watched their sector. She was eating beef jerky. His dog watched her hopefully, but she didn't share.

"How the hell you know that?"

"Heard it from Chen. He was in the van when the captain made the calls. He also told me about his missing finger. Again."

"Yeah? So we getting reinforcements or what?"

"A watcher. Weren't you paying attention?"

"Not ghost eyes. Watchers can't kill anything real. I mean boots and swords."

Tashelle shrugged, and that was answer enough. They waited. Ninety percent of his life as a Thorn knight revolved around waiting. The other ten percent was the lightning-riding, jacked-up, terrifying, full-on snake-eater warfare that made all the waiting worth it.

Jessica caught his eye when she pulled off her heavy helmet and face shield and set it aside. She leaned back against the wall, close to the dried blood stains and the dangling wire where the ghoul corpse had hung until they'd cut it down and used it to help block the basement door. Her lance sat near her on the floor with its safety locks and metal shield in place over the explosive detonator tip. Her sweaty hair stuck out all over the place thanks to her helmet. He smiled at the sight. She carried a long, narrow knife on her hip, almost a stiletto, and had a small patch on her chest—a blue silhouette of a knight in full plate armor, charging on horseback, lance lowered. She stared off into space as she chewed on an energy bar, unaware he watched her.

He'd never been the pine-from-afar type, so he slung his weapon, called his dog, and headed over. She liked to keep to herself. Maybe she didn't fit in with Drake's crew. Maybe they thought she was certifiable, so everybody kept their distance.

That she was crazy, he had no doubt. Crazy in the fearless Geronimo once-more-into-the-breach style of insane. No one in their right mind would willingly get close enough to a monster to shove a pole mounted with explosives into its guts. Lancers, like a few other Thorn knight breeds, were hands-down crazy cowboys. Though Jessica didn't seem to have the same cocky, devil-may-care attitude. She didn't broadcast any vibe of better-than-the-grunts invulnerability he picked up in a lot of the others.

Maybe she was shy. He snorted a laugh, and she

glanced up at the noise. He smiled quickly to cover. "Mind if I sit?"

She looked away again, staring off toward the emptiness of the opposite side of the house. Nothing much to see over there except a broken beer bottle, a half-shattered crack pipe, and the requisite crumpled ball of aluminum foil. Charming.

She stayed quiet long enough for him to wonder if she would reply at all. Then she finally said, "I'm eating."

"You don't like people to talk to you when you eat?"

"I don't like people watching me eat."

He reached into his pocket and pulled out one of his energy bars. It was squished and half melted. "Here, I'll eat too. It'll be like a dinner date."

She didn't say anything. He'd hoped for a laugh, maybe a smile...or at least a couple good profanities. Even his dog wasn't helping break the ice, though she sat at his feet, wagging her curled tail and panting happily. She was also eyeing his energy bar. He tossed her a piece and she snapped it out of the air. He sat against the wall and leaned his head back because she hadn't told him to get lost.

"What do you think about all this?" he asked around a mouthful of energy bar.

Again with the dragged-out silence. This time he waited her out. She stared down at her lance. "I think it's wrong."

"What do you mean, wrong?"

She shook her head and took another bite. Didn't look at him. Didn't answer again. It was like trying to talk to a DMV employee when they were on break. It unnerved him, annoyed him, and so he filled the silence instead.

"I remember once, we were out trying to hunt down some degenerate piece of shit vampire killing women in Central Park. *The* park. So we had to be careful. Stake out, undercover." He waved a hand at her lance. "You couldn't have brought that thing. Even for Central Park it'd be too damn weird."

"This story have a point?"

"Whoever said war stories had to have a point?" But he didn't go on. She'd sapped the strength right out of his story. Seemed she didn't go for the whole blustery bravado thing. He couldn't figure her out. But he didn't leave either.

They sat in silence, chewing. She surprised him by speaking first.

"What you did was brave." She frowned at him as if he'd done something wrong and pissed her off.

"I didn't do jack shit."

"It was brave. Trying to save Weeger like that."

It was his turn not to say anything, his turn to look away. Maybe if he'd saved Weeger he'd have run with the praise a bit. But Weeger was dead. He cast around for something to say, anything to get them off the topic.

"Must be fucking hot in all that gear," he said, eyeing her heavy armor. "What's it weigh? Seventy pounds?"

She scowled and stared down at the last chunk of her energy bar. Damn. Keeping this girl engaged was about as easy as dog paddling through mud.

"You swear too much," she said.

"What?"

"It's crude. The mark of a stupid person without much vocabulary."

He nearly choked on his bite. "What the hell are you talking about? There's nothing wrong with my vocabulary."

"You swear all the time. Like diarrhea from your mouth."

"What are you? The goddamn swear word police?"

"Just shows you have no class."

"No class? Me? I *taught* the class. You hear me?"

She shrugged and popped the last piece of

energy bar in her mouth.

Her refusal to engage only irritated him more. "And who ever heard of a soldier who didn't swear? That's like a whore who doesn't fuck people."

Jessica stood. "The hole. You just keep digging it deeper."

"Yeah? And for digging holes, I'm the fucking man. Like a steam shovel that runs on awesome."

She bent over and picked up her lance. He wanted to say something else, somehow stop her from leaving, but everything in his mind sounded trite or stupid or weak. If she wanted to date some twinkly vocabulary dude then let her. No skin off his ass. No, make that: no skin off his posterior quadrant.

Jessica walked off, stopping near the barricaded hallway and prepping her lance for battle. Her body language told him if he followed, she might try shoving it down his throat. He continued to watch her anyway, part of him wishing she'd come back, most of him still pissed off. Riding him about cussing. Jesus Christ. When he was shooting monsters, he had to have freedom of speech, that was a given.

Tashelle walked over and stared down at him. "Why are men such idiots?"

"So you heard that?"

"Every word. You crashed and burned." She

squatted down beside him, pulled off her helmet and ran a hand along her corn-rowed hair. She sat on her helmet and leaned back against the wall next to him.

"It's because you won't date me, Tashelle. What is it? My taste in music? The fact that I'm a better shot than you?"

"It's your white-ass legs. See you in a bathing suit and I'm blinded for the next twenty minutes."

"Since you just broke my heart, think I have a chance with Jessica on the rebound?"

"Only if you stop acting like such an ass all the time."

"So…that's a no."

"Hey, you still have your fur-faced friend."

"She's all I need." He rubbed the dog behind her ears as she tried to lick his hand.

He grinned at Tashelle. She grinned back. Tashelle—a girl you could give a hard time, because she'd throw it right back at you, straight off. He felt a little better. Distracted for a few moments from all the darkness and pain suffocating everyone in this run-down house. But the moment he realized he was distracted—actually feeling halfway good for the first time in seventy-two hours—the feeling evaporated, and all the old shit flooded back.

Overhead, the floorboards creaked from time to

time driving his thoughts back to Michael Cantwell. Five years old and having to deal with this nightmare. He tried not to think about it, but couldn't get his mind to disengage. Couldn't get the image of the kid in the photo out of his brain. And the boy's mother. How the pain seemed to shimmer off her like heat distortion...

"The captain's wired pretty tight, this time." Tashelle's voice was little more than a whisper, but it startled him out of his thoughts.

He didn't look at her. "You know why."

"Sarge isn't happy."

Chris didn't know what to say about that, so he said nothing. He and Tashelle had served under Captain Garcia, but they'd known little about Sergeant Drake until the two under-strength teams had merged. Drake had always been known as a hard charger, a real devil dog when it came to full-fledged assaults against anything—vampires, Nassid, wolf packs. So far, Chris thought the sergeant was kind of an asshole. And what the hell had been up with that little interrogation back at the safe house when he'd been trying to eat? Drake spouting stuff about being professional, keeping things in perspective, not getting hung up on the fact that a kid was in danger.

Bullshit. Try as he might, he couldn't get over that fact. It'd be easier if he could. Simpler. Kill the monsters no matter the consequences, to hell with the collateral damage. But that was irresponsible bullshit. Being a knight had to mean something. Had to mean something more than just killing shit. He'd taken oaths to protect the innocent. He meant to keep them.

Tashelle finally shook her head and glanced at him. "Things don't feel right. You know what I'm saying?"

He opened his mouth to reply, but the words never got out. The broodsire's deep voice rumbled down the stairs from the second floor. "Meat puppets, have you contacted your masters? Me and mine grow weary of waiting."

All heads turned toward the stairwell. The broodsire's voice made him think of a dump truck's harsh, growling rumble, but woven through with nasty amusement.

Both Captain Garcia and Sergeant Drake hurried to the stairs where Tyson and Cox held position. The trouble light threw a blaze of harsh yellow glare along the banister and the nicked drywall. Chris stood and moved closer, leaving Tashelle to watch the hallway barricade with the others, but staying close enough to support her. He wanted to hear this.

"I contacted them," the captain shouted back. "But I need to know exactly what you want and how you want this to go down."

"Simple. As we are at an impasse, I beg parlay and temporary peace for negotiations."

"Is the boy safe?"

"Safe." Laughter rumbled like rocks breaking. "For now. But you've murdered so many of my little projects that I believe the word may soon lose its meaning for him."

Sergeant Drake took a step toward the first stair. "You won't get out of here alive, you filthy piece of shit."

Captain Garcia grabbed Drake by the shoulder harness. The sergeant looked back, throwing a glare, his lips skinned back in a snarl. The captain only shook his head, scowling. The sergeant retreated and his face dropped back into an impassive mask.

"Then it seems we don't have a deal," the broodsire said.

"I have command," Captain Garcia called. "I speak for the Thorn, and we can work a deal. What do you need?"

"Send one of your knights up here. Arm him only with the power to negotiate. I wish to discuss terms."

"Unarmed? What assurance do I have you'll hold to the peace of a parlay?"

There was a long pause. "Is my word not good enough, little meatsicle?"

"You follow no code of honor a Thorn knight would recognize," Captain Garcia said.

"Code of honor." More angry laughter. "If you don't negotiate, the boy will be ingested. He's too small to make into one of my flesh sculptures. Such a small canvas is too restrictive. Send someone to negotiate the boy's release and I'll even let you bring back your comrade's corpse. It's unmolested…to a point."

Nobody spoke. Nobody moved. The captain stared at the shadows stretching up the staircase where the trouble light threw its glow. Drake turned his head and spat on the floor.

"No takers?" the broodsire said in mock wonder. "I thought Thorn knights were renowned for bravery and honor." Thunderous, booming laughter followed, as loud as it was deranged. "You may have your negotiator keep his sword, if it makes you feel safer. But no guns. No explosives. You are warned."

Captain Garcia leaned his assault rifle against the wall and began to pull off his weapon harness.

"What are you doing, sir?" Sergeant Drake demanded.

"I'll go." The captain pulled the harness off and dropped it next to his rifle.

"You're in charge of this operation, Captain. You going up there alone—that's an unacceptable risk, and you know it."

"Who'll go then? You? Would you put the boy's safety first?"

"You going is a complete violation of protocol. Don't make me say it again, *sir*."

They stared at one another. Tension crackled in the air. No one moved.

"I'll do it," Chris said.

Both Captain Garcia and Sergeant Drake turned to look at him—Drake with anger in his eyes, the captain with something more like speculation.

"You want to be a hero, Hill?" Drake said after a long pause. "That it?"

"No, Sergeant. But I'll do it."

Captain Garcia's voice was softer. "Things go wrong, there's no guarantee we can get to you in time."

"I understand, sir."

"All right, then. Give me your gear and go see what it wants. Check on the boy. Bring back our honored dead. Don't agree to anything yet, but bring back its terms."

The sergeant shifted his weapon. "Captain, you aren't gonna negotiate with that fucking thing—"

"Enough." The captain didn't even look at him,

and Drake finally subsided. He smiled at Chris. "We'll keep your dog safe down here."

Chris handed off his gear piece by piece. His dog watched him and uttered a low whine as he offloaded his MP7, assault harness with all his ammo, his silver combat knife, and his 9mm Beretta M9. He left on his armor and drew his long sword. The light from the lamp stands flashed on the silvered blade, glancing along the twin fullers, making the etched crosses glint.

Captain Garcia slapped a hand on his shoulder and nodded. Chris nodded back. He walked to the stairs past Tyson and Karen and paused at the first riser.

"You want a flashlight?" Tyson asked, not looking away from the scope of his Steyr-AUG. Chris's flashlight was still mounted on his MP7's rail, back with the captain.

"No lights," the broodsire called down. "We live in darkness, and so shall you."

"That fool's a real dick," Tyson said.

Chris grinned at him. He glanced around once more, all those faces watching him, his buddies and his comrades, and the weight of what he was about to do pressed down on him, making it hard to lift his leg to take the first stair. But Michael Cantwell was counting on him.

He lifted his boot. Set it on the stair. Another step. Another step, all up into the darkness. And behind him only silence.

CHAPTER SEVENTEEN
Meet and Greet

His shadow stretched on the wall as he climbed, at first creeping behind him, then walking beside him, and finally striding eagerly before him, thrown there by the trouble light hanging on the banister railing.

The upstairs wasn't as dark as it could've been. Light filtered up from the first floor. Most of the second story windows hadn't been covered, which allowed a pale yellow glow to seep in from the streetlamps. He took the last step with his sword in hand, but kept the blade down at his side. The silver on his blade didn't matter. Ghouls couldn't heal themselves, not like vampires and werewolves who could repair damage almost immediately. Still, he'd be hacking off heads and cleaving skulls if the ghouls made a move on him. If it came to that... He prayed it wouldn't. The shit hitting the fan meant the boy was as good as gone.

He stepped onto the second floor landing and stopped. A ghoul crouched in the shadows at the far end, and another crawled along on all fours like a stalking cat, a dark shape seen through the banister slats.

Two rooms opened off the top floor, along with another bathroom. One door was shut, but the rest gaped open. He waited, wishing he hadn't broken his night vision goggles. Hell, wishing he had a rocket launcher.

Another ghoul appeared in the doorway leading directly off the stairs. Male. Bald. Head tilted downward so a long string of saliva hung from its lower lip, drawing attention to its jagged teeth. It stared sidelong at him—a dog wanting to bite, but waiting until his back was turned. It wore some kind of blue jumpsuit like a power line worker, though its feet were bare, and black claws curled out of misshapen toes. It gestured to Chris, waving him toward the room, and stepped back out of reach.

Chris walked forward slowly, breathing in through his nose, out through his mouth, fighting to keep his heart steady and his breathing slow and measured. He didn't need another adrenaline dump right now. He needed cool, calm, and laser-eyed.

The room's doorway had been broken wider, the frame shattered apart and the first studs smashed, as if someone had said *to hell with it* and rammed a tractor through, ripping out half the surrounding wall. His mind jumped back to what he'd glimpsed through the hole in the closet ceiling. How big the broodsire had to be. His grip tightened on the sword.

He entered the room. He knew from the blueprints that the room was large, but it still seemed grotesquely big, taking up the whole north side of the second floor. Strange, random junk was piled along the walls. An old trunk. A mini fridge with the door ripped off. An empty fish tank turned upside down. Dining room table chairs arranged in a half-assed pyramidal stack against the baseboard. Other crap that looked like boxes of women's clothing, scarves, and shoes and miscellaneous cast-offs.

Michael Cantwell huddled against the far wall, near a coat rack tipped so it fell at an angle above his head. He hugged his arms around his knees. His hair was dirty, his face smeared with grime, and those wide eyes—God, kids had such big eyes—stared back at Chris with a mix of terror and hope. He forced himself to meet the kid's gaze, to try and reassure him with a steady look. Let him know he was here to help. Holding that gaze was hard. Harder than meeting the captain's eyes, or staring back at Sergeant Drake. Harder than anything he remembered. Anything except meeting the kid's mother.

"Ah. The knight errant," the deep, amused voice said. "A knight of pentacles, no? Or are you a knight of swords? I can never keep them straight." Mocking laughter filled the air. "So brave with his sword, yet his armor no longer shines in the moonlight. Pity."

Chris spun toward the voice. The broodsire lounged in a pile of junk—shattered particleboard bookcases, shredded cardboard boxes, and scattered clothes. It levered itself to its feet, standing at least eight feet tall on heavily muscled legs, its shoulders at least twice as broad as his. The two thick black claws that curved out of its feet gouged the floorboards when it moved. Its skin was grub-like, glistening, veined and grayish-white. Its neck shoved forward from between its shoulders, more like a dinosaur's than anything humanoid. Translucent white eyelids flipped shut over its amber eyes for a second, then slowly drew back again. Its flattened nostrils opened, and it snorted. The nostrils flapped shut again. Large slabs of muscle shifted beneath that glistening skin as it moved. Its features contorted into something that might've been a smile, showing wicked predator teeth along the front of its jaw.

But it was the broodsire's long gray tongue that repulsed him the most. The tongue slipped past its black lips and rasped along its cheeks and jaw. Then it zipped back inside its mouth like measuring tape snapping home when the lock released.

Chris faced it, sword bared. "Where's our fallen knight?"

The broodsire made a noise like far off thunder and smiled. "Business first with you, eh, little marrow-bag? And you don't appreciate my descriptions of you, either? Fine. Your rotting friend is there." It pointed to a crumpled blue tarp beneath one of the windows. Blood stained the floorboards and seeped from beneath the tarp edge in a pool black as ink.

Chris walked to the tarp, moving within a dozen feet of the huge monster. He kept his pace steady, even though his heart rate spiked, his palms soaked his gloves with sweat, and it was a constant struggle not to keep glancing at the broodsire to make sure it didn't move. He had to play the superhero for the kid. Give him some hope.

The broodsire laughed as if it guessed what he was doing. Chris ignored the bastard.

The tarp crackled when he grabbed the edge and pulled it away. Nothing surprising, but he sighed out a slow exhale anyway. Weeger's legs were missing from the groin down, arms thrown back over his head, his eyes open but horribly blank. His armor had been ripped off and hung to the side like a huge flap of black skin, his abdomen had been hollowed out and was now an empty shell. A wide red mouth opened below his chin, his throat bitten open, blood in his beard, blood gathered in the hollow at the base of his neck.

He struggled to keep his face neutral. Show no emotion. Don't give the monster the satisfaction. Don't give Michael another reason to be afraid.

Weeger had made a mistake and now he was dead. Someday it would happen to him as well. Look. See. Remember. It was the life. He couldn't let it affect him—especially not now.

"I would've preferred to turn your friend into one of my little art projects." The broodsire raised its hand, and the strange, thin tentacles, tipped with hard blades of bone, pushed out of its palm. Chris fought the urge to hack them off.

Instead he bent down and grabbed Weeger by the harness and dragged him back to the damaged doorway. A ghoul lingered outside, blocking his path to the stairs. Chris stopped and looked back to the broodsire. "Where are his legs?"

"Consumed."

He said nothing for a moment. Finally he pointed

at the ghoul lurking in the hall. "Tell that thing to get out of my face or I'll throw it down the fucking stairs."

The broodsire grinned, which he found about as unnerving as seeing a shark smile. The broodsire grunted at the ghoul and it disappeared from view.

Chris turned back to Michael. The boy's eyes were still locked on him. Tear tracks had cut through the grime on his cheeks. Seeing the kid like that was like taking a hit to the gut with a sledgehammer. The urge to run at the broodsire and shove his blade through the top of its mouth into whatever stinking shitpile it called a brain made him clench his fists, his glove groaning on the sword grip, his teeth grinding in dull rage.

But rage wasn't what Michael needed now.

"Heya, Michael." He managed to keep his voice even, without the slightest tremor, but still very serious. "You like to be called Michael or Mike?"

For a long moment the boy only stared at him. The broodsire laughed again. Jesus, he was gonna cut that thing's tongue out just to stop the damned freakish basso hyena laughter.

"Michael," the boy finally whispered.

"Michael, then. I'm gonna get you out of here, Michael. Bring you back to your mom. You understand me?"

The boy nodded slowly, his eyes still wide, but

there'd been a slight change to his face. Hard to say exactly what had changed, but Chris could read hope there now. Dim, almost hidden behind all the fear, but there all the same. God, he had to come through for this kid. He made a promise like that and if he failed, he'd never live it down.

"Best not make vows to the piglet," the broodsire warned. "The fates have not decided whether you can keep your word."

His hand crushed even tighter on the sword hilt, so hard he could feel the grip biting back through the glove and digging into his palm. He still didn't acknowledge the monster though—wouldn't give it the satisfaction. "Just hang in there, Michael. Just a little longer. Can you do that for me?"

Michael stared at him. "You have a sword. Are you a knight?"

"I am a knight."

The broodsire yawned, a showy, disturbing spread of its wide jaws. "A knight tilting at windmills, ah?"

Chris had no idea what it was babbling about. Nothing worse than a piece of shit degenerate abomination puking out meaningless words as if anyone gave a fuck.

Michael unfolded a bit from his protective

huddle, but then he glanced at the broodsire and drew himself back into a ball. "Do you kill monsters?"

"I do."

The broodsire grunted and licked its nostrils clean of snot. Michael continued to stare at him with those pleading eyes.

Chris finally turned back to the broodsire. "You wanted to negotiate. Name your terms."

"You filthy maggot-bags have destroyed so many of my creations. My helpmeets. Progeny that I rely upon to ease my way."

"Those poor bastards you turned into ghouls deserved some mercy."

"Mercy. You know nothing of it." The broodsire blinked its amber eyes, the translucent eyelid shuttering down then slowly peeling back. "Ghouls. Your name for them, not mine. They are intricate parts of my creative being, slices of my DNA intermixed." The freakish tentacles that sprouted from its palm waved around, begging Chris to castrate the unnerving things. The broodsire stroked them with the fingers of its other hand. There was something so slyly profane in the gesture that Chris's mouth twisted in disgust. The broodsire noticed and laughed. "I rearranged their brain matter with *this* in a process more intimate than any lover's penetrations. I changed them. Decorated their flesh canvas. Opened their smiles, so they could eat freely and without shame."

Chris stared at it, saying nothing.

"I could give you the gift, if you wish. The freedom from despair, the sense of belonging to a group, to a father who broke the shackles of your unending self-loathing and sentience." The light in its strange amber eyes was crazed. The glint to its stare—as filthy as a sheen of oily water on cracked asphalt—made him uneasy.

It licked its lips again, then sucked its long tongue in. "When I change you, you'll hunger for flesh. Dead tissue, corrupted meat, rotting flesh—" It laughed. "*Fresh* flesh. Does not matter. The yearning is the same, and it will be as ecstasy to you. A release as blissful as a rain of endorphins." It laughed again, leaned closer, and reached out an arm toward him. The appendages from its palm weaved snake-like in the darkness.

He lifted his sword. "You bring those fucking things any closer, I'll cut them off and shove them down your goddamn giggling throat."

"So frightening and profane." It grinned, its fang-filled mouth spreading wider. "And in front of a child, ah? Where are the knights of old with their silver civil tongues?"

Control. He couldn't let his hate and loathing for this monster deep-six his chance to get the boy away safe. "You wanted to negotiate. Speak your terms."

"Terms, messenger boy? Simple. You fear for the child's safety or you little maggot-bags would've already charged up here, spraying your bullets, hacking and slashing and undoing the beautiful creations I've given the world. Your taste for slaughter is profane. The truth of it is in your face. You cannot conceive my rage—"

"I didn't come here to listen to you bitch. We have something to talk about or not?"

The broodsire blinked slowly, that translucent eyelid flicking up over the amber iris before the heavier eyelid dropped down and flared wide again. It drew itself up as if it would charge at him, muscles bunching in its shoulders and thighs, black talons scraping the floor.

Michael scooted away from it, pressing deeper into the corner. Chris stood very still. Watching it. Not moving. Not letting himself be afraid. Not allowing himself to think that his bravado might've destroyed the chance to save the boy. The sword was a heavy weight in his hand. The blade seemed insignificant against something so powerful and hideous.

The broodsire hesitated and finally settled back

into its throne of junk. Even seated, the monster seemed huge.

"Bold," it said. "Brave and foolish and utterly without nuance. Somehow I think you are no true negotiator. Was your leader afraid to face me?"

Chris didn't answer.

"Ah very well, silent negotiator. Tell your master my terms. Tell him he must give me assurances, sworn on chivalry, sworn on his Order and his God and any other hallowed thing he can think of. Tell him to allow me and mine safe passage from this den and we shall let the boy go, free of harm." The broodsire glanced out the window. "We'll leave this city. Find another."

"Where you'll start eating people again? That it?"

"What if we promise to restrain ourselves once more, feasting only upon corpse meat, as your ghouls of lore?"

"A promise. From you."

"Your derision is misplaced, but that's because you're lost and unadorned and know nothing of which you speak. But I wouldn't waste my gift on a Thorn monster who sees only in blood-red and bone-white when the best meat is always pink."

"I'll take your terms and pass them on." He lifted his sword, staring along its blade right into the broodsire's huge eyes. "But you hurt that kid, I'll carve you up."

The broodsire only grinned at him. Chris lowered the sword to his side again, feeling stupid and impotent and hating it. He grabbed Weeger by the harness and dragged him away, leaving smears of blood behind, as stark as slashes of finger paint trailing red across paper. He couldn't carry Weeger's body, not and keep his sword free, so he silently apologized to his buddy for the disrespect as he pulled him into the hall. The ghouls stayed well out of range. He dragged Weeger to the stairs and hauled his body down behind him, smelling the stench of blood and bile and opened intestines. He struggled with the weight, trying not to let his comrade's remains tumble down the steps while still easing him downward. Weeger's head thudded on every step, but there was nothing he could do about it.

Tyson moved up the stairs and covered Chris with his rifle as he brought Weeger the rest of the way down. Other knights hurried to relieve him of his burden, and he finally didn't have to drag his dead buddy across the ground anymore.

CHAPTER EIGHTEEN

No One Goes

"We can't let those freaks stroll out of here," Sergeant Drake said. "That ain't gonna happen."

Chris looked up from his dog and glanced at Captain Garcia, expecting fireworks. The three of them had headed outside to discuss the broodsire's terms. The captain didn't want to run the risk of some ghoul hiding in one of the hollow walls, overhearing them, and then tipping off the broodsire. Better yet, it gave Chris a chance to see his dog again. After that scene on the second floor, he definitely needed some pooch love. The rest of the assault team was sitting tight inside, holding position.

The captain didn't respond to Drake. He only continued to lean against the side of the van parked haphazardly on the lawn as he stared at the house.

Long scars cut across the grass where the tires had ripped up tracks. Inside the van, Richards sat in the middle of his spell-sculpture circle, cycling energy into the wards that kept them from being heard or seen from the street. Chen stood nearby, pistol in his uninjured hand as he protected Richards. Bowen had a shooting position on the roof of one of the SUVs and never moved the scope on his rifle from the front of the house. Light from a three quarters full moon made the yard bright, even without night optics. The neighborhood was quiet, the other houses dark and silent. Dead houses all in a row. No people. No cars.

Drake shifted his weight and spat. "We were sent to eliminate a threat, Captain. They move on, we've solved nothing. Failed the mission. And there's no guarantee they'll let the boy go."

The captain turned to Chris. "How'd the boy look? He injured?"

"Scared to death." Chris peeled off his bloodstained gloves and wiped his hands on his fatigues as the dog watched him and gave a plaintive whine. Weeger's blood had seeped through one glove and worked its way deep into the lines of his palm, turned his fingernails into red crescents. "I didn't see any wounds."

"Give me a rundown on the broodsire. We make

a deal, will it honor the terms?"

Drake answered before Chris could speak. "It's a fucking monster, Captain. It won't honor jack shit."

Captain Garcia ignored him, staring at Chris, waiting for an answer.

"I don't know, sir," he said. "It sure had a fucked up way of talking."

"Will it keep its end of the deal?"

"I don't know." He looked at his hand. Shook his head.

"I want this boy safe, same as you," Drake said. "But we got other people to think about. We got a duty to see this finished and done."

"I know our duty, sergeant." The captain still didn't look at him. He kept his eyes on Chris.

"Then letting something like that walk free ain't an option. Let's make sure Weeger didn't die for nothing."

Captain Garcia finally turned on him. "Knight Jason Weeger died trying to save that kid. Same as any of us would."

They locked stares. Drake looked away first and spat chew on the ground. He wiped his lip with the back of his hand.

Captain Garcia returned his attention to Chris. "How many hostiles you count up there, Hill?"

"I only had visual on four ghouls and the broodsire. But I'm sure there's more."

"Location on Michael?"

He looked at the house. "In the room off the top of the stairs. The one facing out to the back yard."

"There's a porch roof back there. We could reach the second floor using it. You said the windows aren't covered over?"

"No, sir."

"Any chance we might create a diversion, smash in from outside and snatch the boy?"

He hesitated, very aware his next words might cost Michael his life. "It might work, Captain, but it'd be real touch and go."

"We could lose half the squad pulling a stunt like that," Drake said.

"I already know your objections, Sergeant. You've made them crystal-clear. So let me make myself clear. Again. The boy comes first. Over your life. Over my life. We understand each other?"

"All due respect, Command won't like this—" Sergeant Drake slashed the air with his hand. "This shift in priorities. We should call in. Get their clearance before we strike any crazy deal."

"Let me worry about Command. You just do your damn job, Sergeant."

"Yes, sir." A jaw muscle twitched in Drake's cheek. Chris suspected that was a reprimand the sergeant wouldn't soon forgive, especially one handed out in front of a grunt like him.

The captain turned to stare at the house again. Then he yanked off his chinstrap, pushed his helmet off his head and let it fall to the dead grass. It hit the ground with a dull a thump. He ran a hand into his matted black hair, scratched his scalp hard, gritting his teeth, and then sighed. Chris sure as hell didn't envy him. Decisions like this were one of the reasons he wasn't chomping at the bit to be the big dog in the squad. Fucking weight of responsibility would kill you young.

His dog moved over to the captain and licked his hand while staring up at him with soulful doggy eyes. The captain snorted, then his mouth quirked in a half smile as he reached down and petted the dog.

"All right," Captain Garcia finally said. "Hill, it looks like you're up to bat again, since you and the broodsire have a little bond." He glared at the second floor windows, his smile gone. "Tell that piece of shit we'll allow it safe passage, provided it lets the boy go unharmed. All the ghouls must leave the city. And tell that bastard it'd better keep his word about feeding on corpses, or we'll be right back on its ass."

Drake leaned toward Garcia. "We don't negotiate with monsters. You need to contact Command before we make a move like this."

"No. This is a call made by the boots on the ground. You have a problem with that, Sergeant, you stay in the goddamn van." He turned and walked back to the house. Chris followed him. He felt the weight of a gaze burning into his back. When he glanced behind him, he saw Drake watching him go.

He didn't like the look on the sergeant's face. Not at all.

* * *

Chris climbed the stairs again, this time with less fear. After all, no one killed the messenger these days, right? His sword still felt damn near useless. A stupid joke for facing off against the broodsire, like attacking a tiger with a steak knife, but he kept it out anyway. He felt steadier with something in his hand.

He could see nothing at the top of the stairs except the slanting, distorted shadows of the banister rails and slats thrown against the walls by the trouble light. No noise. He glanced back to check that his people were covering his ass. Tyson and Karen crouched at the bottom of the staircase, their weapons aimed up the stairs. Of course, he didn't exactly want them opening up with his ass stranded in the middle of the staircase either. Karen gave him a thumbs-up, and then Sergeant Drake moved into view.

Chris hesitated, but Drake never even glanced his way. Instead, he knelt down and spoke first to Karen, then to Tyson, with his radio off and talking low enough that Chris couldn't hear what he said. Drake moved out of view again. Chris had nothing to do but continue up to the second floor.

A wave of dizziness hit him the moment he set his foot on the last stair. He had to grab the handrail to steady himself. He felt as if he might vomit, but he fought back the urge. Sweat dampened his upper lip and made wet patches under his arms. After a long moment, he finally felt steady enough to let go of the handrail and swipe the back of his fist across his mouth. Some lingering affect from the flashbang, or maybe he had a concussion. Good fucking deal.

A ghoul squatted in the damaged doorway, rocking back and forth on its heels and humming tunelessly to itself. It fled when he approached, scrambling off on all fours along the landing into a room on his left. Another ghoul watched him from the bathroom door, peeking around the doorjamb, half its flayed face visible. Its eye shone in the moonlight that poured in from the uncovered window at the end of the landing. A female ghoul. Maybe in her twenties when she'd been human. What he could see of her long hair was tangled into rat's nests, the wounds around her nose and ears flared like burns, the flesh sealed over and seared shut where the broodsire had tinkered. She sang under her breath. "Jesus loves the little children...all the children of the world."

That line. Over and over again.

He walked across the landing and through the damaged doorway. The broodsire knelt by one of the windows as if at prayer. It turned its strange thrust-forward head to watch him with those large amber eyes. "The knight who slays monsters, now returned. What's your answer?"

He didn't reply until he spotted Michael huddled in a different corner, half hidden behind a box, and as far from the broodsire as he could get. The tentative hope was back in his eyes, but his face remained pinched and afraid.

"Let the boy go," Chris said. "We'll let you leave."

"Only to be hunted down and murdered as soon as you have the child, ah?" It laughed.

"Leave the city. Go somewhere far away. And this time, stick to eating corpses. Otherwise, deal's off."

The broodsire closed its eyes. "Seems we have a bargain. Tell your fearless leader I agree. I'll gather my work and go."

"The kid?"

"When I breathe night air, I'll let him run to you. Unharmed of body. His mind I cannot account for."

The dirty bastard. He'd never wanted to hack a monster down so badly as he did right then. "How long?"

It ran a thick finger along its lips. "Imminent."

Chris looked at the boy again. "Michael. It'll be over soon."

The boy stared at him and didn't answer.

CHAPTER NINETEEN
Deal Goes Down

"All right, listen up, people," Captain Garcia said over the radio. "I want you to hold your fire. Repeat, *hold your fire.* Do not engage hostiles, is that clear?"

"Roger that," Chris said, adding his voice to the chorus of affirmatives. He ejected the magazine from the MP7 and checked the round count, then switched it out with a fresh magazine. It was good to have a firearm in his hands again. His sword was righteous and all, but there were few things as reassuring as having forty rounds at his fingertips, ready to burn off into some monster's face.

He felt jittery, as if he'd chased energy drinks with tons of sugar. Soon this shit would be over. All he *wanted* was for it to be over, with the kid safe at home. It was ironic. Sitting around, cleaning weapons and drilling, all he wanted was to be out in the field, rocking and rolling. Then, ten minutes of this shit and all he wanted was to be back in barracks, bored and cleaning weapons and drilling.

Captain Garcia's voice broke into his thoughts, crackling across his headset speaker. "We have a ceasefire agreement in force until I say otherwise. Hostiles will proceed down the main stairs, hand over the boy, and leave this location. I repeat, we are *not* to engage. Hostage safety is highest priority."

The captain had redeployed them through the secured section of the house. Sergeant Drake, Tyson and Roth had positions on the west side of the room, near the kitchen and dining room, Jessica and Tashelle had the kitchen. The hall remained barricaded off. Karen and Chris were positioned on the right, out of the line of fire and on the same side as the busted out bay window frame covered with plywood. The damaged front door was propped open. Through it he could see Chen chugging water from a plastic bottle. His dog was in the van to prevent any problems when the monsters came down.

Captain Garcia and Chris were tasked with taking custody of the boy from the broodsire. The captain was still outside, doing a last minute check on Specter Three and the perimeter before the hand off. He still didn't know why the captain was keeping him on such a short leash on this mission, or why he'd become the captain's go-to guy. The others were starting to give him sidelong glances. Roth had muttered something about him being the "captain's little bitch." Surprisingly, Sergeant Drake had been the one to come down hard on Roth for the comment.

He heard thumping and bumping and creaking floorboards overhead. Still no sign of the ghouls or broodsire yet. It had been at least fifteen minutes since Chris had come down the stairs and informed the captain that the broodsire had accepted the terms. He glanced at the door again. What was taking the captain so long? Damn it. He didn't want to do the hand off alone.

Sergeant Drake crossed the room. He had his helmet off and his mike headset dangled down around the neck guard on his armor. A silver necklace hung down to his chest plate armor, weighted with several holy symbols from various religions. He stopped next to Chris. Outside, the captain was talking with Bowen, who still maintained his firing position on top the van's roof.

"Turn your mike off," Drake said.

He frowned and obeyed. "It's off, sergeant."

"You saw what those bastards did to Weeger.

You had to drag what was left of him down the stairs. Now he's wrapped in plastic, doesn't have any legs to bury. Weeger had a kid, you know that? What about *his* kid?"

Chris didn't answer. Jesus. Yeah, he'd known about Weeger's kid. The guy would show off pictures of his family any chance he had, grinning the entire time. He'd been married to a girl in one of the support arms of the Thorn. They'd adopted a kid from the Ukraine whose parents had been killed by monsters—shadowlings or vampires or slin, he couldn't remember. Chris couldn't think about Jason Weeger and his family right now or his brain would start bleeding, lock him up, make him useless.

What the hell did Drake want from him? What did all these people fucking *want* from him? He just wanted to do the right thing. He took a deep breath and forced his hand to relax on the grip of his weapon, where it had crushed down, cutting creases into his still faintly bloody hands. He kept his expression neutral and stared fixedly at the stairs.

Drake leaned in, his face only inches away. "This ain't right, and you know it."

"What am I supposed to do about it? We gotta save that kid. He didn't do anything to anybody. And it sure as hell isn't his fault about Weeger."

Drake rubbed at his face, his palm scratching against his stubble. Dark shadows made half-moons beneath his eyes. "We let these things go free, you think they'll stick to digging up graves and eating rotting bodies? Now that they got the taste of fresher meat? And that monster up there. Now maybe you understand a little about a broodsire's fucked-up proclivities. So you think they're really gonna go their happy way and keep their assholes sparkly winter-fresh from here on out?"

"No."

"Nobody does. Which is why this is bullshit. We let them out now, we'll have a helluva time running them down again, and that's if we're not pulled off to deal with some other shit. In the meantime, more people die. Maybe other kids."

Chris stared at the stairwell, his heart thudding slowly in his chest, his tongue dry as sand.

"You know I'm right. You know we're condemning other people to die, doing this. *Allowing* it to happen."

Chris turned, teeth bared, speaking low. "What the fuck you want me to do, Sarge? I was face to face with that little boy. You're right. But the captain's right too. And if anyone spits out that 'greater good' bullshit or any collateral damage bullshit I swear to God—" He clamped his jaws shut, shook his head, and looked away again, breathing hard.

He expected a reprimand for going after the sergeant like that, but Drake only gave him a grim nod. "Now you're talking like a soldier. But this ain't shiny fairytale land. You can't have it both ways. You can't say I'm right, and the captain's right. You can't straddle. You're a knight, and you take a stand."

"Yeah. When you need a knight, I'm a knight, when you need a soldier, I'm a soldier, right?" Dammit, why wouldn't the guy just go, just get out of his face for a minute? And why wasn't the captain back yet?

Drake stared at him, his face angry, then his mouth quirked upward. "Like Buddha said, 'Life's a bitch, don't ask why.'"

Chris smirked back, mostly just to get the sergeant to leave him alone, go away so he could get this mission done, and please God, the kid home safe. Easy to hate Drake, but he wouldn't fall into that trap either. It was also easy to sell out other people's lives in service to something abstract. People did it all the time. But he'd looked Michael straight in the eyes, had promised to get him back to his mom. Take a stand? Yeah, he'd take a stand on the side of saving the kid. If he had the blood of fifty future people on his hands because of this, he'd just have to deal with it when the time came. There were no high, abstract ethics in the goddamn trenches. You saved the people near you. That was all you could be expected to do. And he was going to save this kid.

Captain Garcia walked back inside. He gave Chris and Sergeant Drake a very long look.

Drake said, "Stay frosty, Hill," and moved back to his position on the other side of the room, with a nod to the captain. Captain Garcia didn't nod back.

Ten long minutes later, the ghouls started down the stairs.

CHAPTER TWENTY
Two A.M.

He recognized the first ghoul that crept down the stairs. It was the female ghoul who'd peeked at him around the door frame and sang the one verse over and over again. She walked hunched over, one hand on the banister and the other raised as if warding them off.

"Steady, people," Captain Garcia said over the radio. Their weapons were up, cocked and ready to rock, but no one aimed directly at her.

The ghoul paused, then scampered down the rest of the stairs and stood in the brilliant glare from the flood lights, licking at her wounded lips with a pink tongue mottled with black.

More ghouls came down. Male and female, fat and thin, most of them half-naked, and what little clothing they wore was a crazy mismatch of styles. One of them hopped the railing and landed on the floorboards in a crouch. It scratched at the wood with the claws on both its pointer fingers and blinked around at them. Ropes of saliva dripped from its flayed jaws.

Quiet blanketed the room. The air felt muggy and oppressive. Chris flexed his hands and tried to keep from fidgeting, tried to keep his heart from pounding away like a frenetic bass drummer.

Where was Michael?

The stairs groaned as the broodsire descended. At first all he could see were its thick legs. Most of the long black talon on each foot thrust out over the edge of the steps. More of the broodsire came into view as it moved down the staircase. Its spoiled-cream skin appeared wet and almost gelatinous in the light from the flood lamps.

Michael was clamped in the broodsire's arms, a little rabbit in the claws of a grizzly bear. The broodsire's gaze roamed around the room, inhuman and hostile. More ghouls trailed behind it, now maybe eleven, twelve or so in view. The broodsire stepped onto the first floor with a thud. Chris felt the tremor through the floorboards. Something began a rapid, high-pitched beep.

"Perimeter alarms!" Sergeant Drake yelled. "*Ambush!*"

Chris had only started to glance in his direction when the bright flare of muzzle flash spat from the sergeant's assault rifle and the deafening crack of shots ripped through the air.

Oh shit oh shit—

A flabby male ghoul near the stair risers jerked and collapsed with a hole in its forehead. A bullet clipped the broodsire as it turned toward them, holding the boy out as a shield.

"Cease fire!" the captain screamed. "Cease fire! *Hold your fire!*"

But Roth and Tyson had already opened up and several ghouls dropped. The broodsire launched itself up the stairs. One of its heavy feet crashed through the wooden step. It stumbled and almost fell on top of the boy, but caught itself on its elbow at the last instant. An explosion of plaster dust burst an inch away from its head. Drake still fired at it, despite the captain's continual yells to "fucking cease fire!"

Bullets tore into the banister and drywall, hitting close to Michael. The goddamn monster was using the kid as a shield. The broodsire bled in several places from multiple hits, and bellowed in rage and pain, so loud it shook the house. It wrenched its foot from the hole in the stair and launched itself back toward the second floor as rounds continued to strike all around it.

Chris swung his weapon toward Sergeant Drake. His finger tightened on the trigger. He should've known. Should've *known* Drake would try some stupid shit like this, after his last minute spiel. Chris hadn't believed anyone could be so cold as to put a child in harm's way, throwing the boy on the altar as a sacrifice.

And he'd been wrong.

He had two pounds of pressure on the trigger, aiming at Drake's face, every sound too loud, too distorted, but everything happening so damn fast. Two pounds of pressure and squeezing tighter, when Captain Garcia threw himself at the sergeant and slammed him into the wall. Chris checked his fire at the last instant.

An accidental shot from the sergeant's M4 buried itself in the floorboards not three feet away. Captain Garcia pinned Drake against the wall with a forearm across his throat, still screaming into the radio for everyone to hold their fire.

The broodsire barreled up the stairs, clutching the crying, terrified boy, and vanished. Seeing Michael so close, then losing him again, shanked into Chris's heart, pierced his lungs so he could hardly suck in a sip of air.

Most of the ghouls fled up the stairs after their broodsire. But one of them leaped at Tashelle. She drew her falcata and hacked away a chunk of its skull and brain with one vicious slice of the blade. Other ghouls screeched as they fled. It sounded like a zoo full of shrieking animals on the second floor. More gunfire roared, insanely loud inside the house. The Thorn knights outside called frantically over the radio, demanding their status.

Tyson and Roth were the last to stop shooting. Six ghoul bodies sprawled on the floorboards. The air reeked of burned powder and blood. The outraged screeching upstairs cut off all at once. The house was very quiet in the aftermath of the shooting and screaming, but the air seemed to ring, to vibrate with its echo.

Chris sagged against the wall. He'd never fired a shot. Almost, though. Almost shot Sergeant Drake in the head, but the captain got to him first. Jesus. God, what had he been thinking?

He leaned there, feeling dizzy, the edges of his vision graying. He was listening for a scream or a cry from Michael and dreading every passing silent second. Waiting for something that would tell him they were killing the boy as revenge for breaking the truce. Everyone else seemed to be listening for the same thing. No one moved. Everyone stared at the bullet-riddled staircase.

No sound. Nothing.

Captain Garcia grabbed Drake by his armor, spun and threw him. The sergeant hit the floor hard and slid toward the door, losing his rifle. Captain Garcia stared at him with his fists clenched. Sergeant Drake stared back. Neither of them moved.

"Specter Actual this is Specter Three, rifle two," Peralta's frantic voice came over the radio. "What's your status, over?"

Chris thought the captain would say something, call the sergeant out for disobeying orders, promise retribution, demote him. Something. But Captain Garcia only stared at Drake as his hands slowly clenched and unclenched.

"Specter Actual this is Specter Three. Do you need back up? Please advise, over."

Captain Garcia finally spoke. "This is Specter Actual. Hold your position. Out."

Chris stepped forward. The air felt too thick to breathe. This tension of waiting for some sound from above was sawing into his skin, coring him out. "Captain. I'll go up. Try and see if the kid's okay—"

"They'll tear Hill apart, Captain," Sergeant Drake said. "He goes up alone, he dies. There's only one option now. We have to see this through."

"Shut up." The captain took a step toward Drake,

but stopped. He turned and looked at Chris with hollow eyes. "Go."

He hurried to the stairs. He had to step over two of the fallen ghouls and left a boot print in a spray of blood and brain matter. This time he brought all his weapons, though he let the MP7 dangle on its sling and kept his sword in the sheath on his back. He raised his hands to show they were empty. On the landing, a ghoul shadow flitted in and out of sight along the wall.

Tyson crouched nearby, covering the staircase with his rifle. "Be careful."

Chris didn't look at him, didn't take his eyes off the shifting shadows up there as he set his foot on the first stair. "What time is it?"

Tyson glanced at his watch. "Two sixteen."

"Shit." Two a.m. Of course. He took a steadying breath and started up the stairs. He opened his mouth to say something to the broodsire as he climbed, but he had no idea how to make this right.

He carefully jumped over the step the broodsire's foot had smashed through. The trouble light had been crushed like a stomped soda can. Whispers hissed back and forth on the landing and second floor rooms. Somewhere, he heard the faint sound of Michael sobbing. His stomach did a slow clench at the sound. But at least the boy was still alive. There was that.

He glanced down the stairs again and saw the other Thorn knights standing there, watching him. He turned his back on them.

"Hey!" He called out, and his voice echoed back to him. "I'm coming up. No weapons in my hands."

Furtive whispers echoed off the walls, the ceiling, and down the staircase, sounding heavy with hate. He pushed on, step-by-step until he stood at the top of the stairs. There were ghouls in every doorway, glaring at him, gnashing their teeth. He ignored them. No sign of the broodsire or the boy. He took a step toward the bedroom where they'd been before.

"Stop there, knight errant." The broodsire's voice boomed through the damaged door frame. Its words seethed with disdain. "Come no closer."

"Is the boy all right?"

A long silence drew out. Just as he was about to risk another step toward the bedroom, the broodsire finally answered.

"If he were dead, do you think I'd tell you, as craven, as honor-less as you be?"

What the hell could he say to that? Sorry we lit you guys up. Our mistake. Let's try take two, from the top. Yeah right. But he tried anyway. "We can still work this out. Maybe you send out the kid, we pull out, let you leave whenever—"

"No more deals. No more lies."

He stood there, racking his brain for something to say, anything to convince it to let the boy go. Part of him also listened for sounds from downstairs. Yelling, gunfire, he had no idea, but listening for some kind of confrontation between the captain and the sergeant.

"All right, all right." He took a deep breath. "Let me switch out with the kid. You can have me as a hostage instead."

"So heroic, maggot bag. So *valiant* an attempt to redeem the stained honor of the knighthood. And yet your attempt has failed."

"There's a helluva lot more meat on my bones than some kid. You can have more fun with me. Just let the boy go downstairs."

There was another long pause. Chris took a step toward the door, now halfway there across the landing. He could feel the dread clinching tight to his body, squeezing him.

A ghoul watched him through the crack in the bathroom door where the hinges met the frame. It pushed its fingers through the gap and scraped its claws on the wood, scoring it. He tried to ignore it, waiting for an answer.

"No," the broodsire finally said.

He iced up inside, but tried to keep his voice

calm, bordering on dismissive. He didn't want the broodsire to catch on to how badly he wanted Michael away from it. "Think about it harder. Like I said, I got more meat on my bones and more blood on my hands."

"I don't care about blood on your filthy hands."

"Yeah? You got a tiny peanut brain in that misshapen skull pan of yours? Whose blood could I be talking about? I fucking iced a dozen of your freaky progeny already. They all die the same. Little screechy puppets with their strings cut—"

A roar as loud as a jet engine split the air. He grabbed at his submachine gun as a massive off-white wall of flesh barreled through the doorway like an oncoming train. The broodsire charged straight at him, teeth bared, amber eyes blazing. He had time to feel new fear spike through his veins but not enough time to scream.

The broodsire smashed into him. He twisted away, trying to bring his weapon muzzle to bear on it. Its jaws snapped closed just inches from his neck, those see-through white eyelids flipping shut over eyes full of insane rage, its nostrils flattening and sealing against the blood it wanted to spill. Pain exploded in his shoulder, where he'd been half turned toward the doorway. The world wheeled and spun. His guts felt like they'd hit his abdominal wall so hard they'd burst free like streamers from a party favor.

He flew back through the open air above the stairs. The broodsire's reeking carrion breath washed over him, and he felt the incredible heat burning off its clammy skin. He flailed for his MP7 again. He'd lost hold of it somehow as he fell backward through the air. His hand hesitated between grabbing for his knife and his pistol.

Shouting. Yelling from below him. Someone started shooting. He had time to think how badly he'd gambled and lost, time enough to taste the bitterness of having failed Michael. Then he hit the bottom of the stairs and the world went black.

CHAPTER TWENTY-ONE

Danger Close

For a time there were only random flashes of images. Bursts of sound. A roaring like a freight train rushing past, and an atonal *clink, clink, clink*, like metal raindrops hitting concrete. Brass shell casings. Falling like water.

More darkness, and then came a bright flare of sunlight, and he stared up at a high column of floodlights, a strange metal alien tower against the bright blue, cloudless sky. His mind reeled, trying to piece this image of pristine sky with the other place of darkness and pounding gunfire and pain, but he couldn't.

He could smell wet grass. He looked down and found himself center field, staring past the second baseman, past the pitcher on the mound, toward home plate. Just a bunch of kids playing baseball, and he was young like them. The pitcher threw and the batter swung and the bat cracked. He followed the ball up into the air with his gaze, back-peddling as fast as he could, but he lost it in the sun, and the glare was so bright it washed out the world…

…and he was back, breathing in gasps, flat on his ass, and staring up at the stairs that climbed into shadow. Burning hot shell casings were falling on him, on his face and neck, searing his skin. Someone stood over him, firing up into the darkness, painting the walls with muzzle flare. Yells, screams, gunfire. He could hear them all but they were distant, as if coming from miles away. His view jerked and shifted as someone grabbed his harness and dragged him away across the floor. He tried to turn over and only shifted enough to have his view filled with black boots. The pain exploded and he lost everything to the darkness again.

Sand dunes. Grass in shades of light green and yellow. Wind swirled sand off the tops of the dunes with a steady hiss. The sky was cloudy. Layers of fast-moving clouds stretched above him. The water was steel gray, forbidding, an ocean that promised to suck the breath right out of him with its cold. Small waves curled, charged up the beach and withdrew, leaving the sand covered in foam, bubbles popping and vanishing.

Allison crouched at the edge of where the waves

reached. She stared down at the wet sand. He stood behind her, a ways off on the dunes, watching her. Allison, a girl he'd loved for awhile, years ago, long before he'd sworn his oaths. He remembered this day. He remembered drinking beer at the beach on a day without sun, remembered how the wind off the water was cold enough that Allison had to wear his jacket over her one-piece swimsuit, so he missed the view of her curves. Her long brown hair hung down over her face, but she glanced back at him, holding up a small seashell and smiling, her eyes bright. He noticed her lips and remembered how much he'd loved kissing them, and the feel of them on his skin...

"I thought you wanted vengeance," a man said from beside him, voice as cold as the wind. Chris turned to see the man from the grocery store, the gray-eyed, hard-faced man who'd held the milk. Maddox. The Thorn lord who'd knighted him. No milk in his hands this time. He only stared out at the water. An entire ocean the color of his eyes.

Chris looked back to the drifts of blowing sand without replying. Maddox wasn't part of this scene. He shouldn't be here, staining this memory, one of the last he had of the beach before everything had changed forever.

Allison started playing some game with the surf

rolling in. She charged forward as the waves withdrew, retreated back up the beach when they came crashing in again, not paying attention to either of them over here on the dunes.

"That young man I met sure as hell wanted some payback," Maddox said. "You remember that?"

"I just wanted to be a knight."

"Do you even know what that means?"

Things started to streak and blur. A curtain of darkness slammed down again, and the beach dream-memory-hallucination vanished. He opened his eyes. The world shook as his helmet bumped along the floorboards. He was still on the ground. Someone he couldn't see still dragged him along, pulling him through the living room toward the front door.

What he could see was chaotic. The flood lamps had been knocked over and threw crazy shadows everywhere. Tashelle backed up as she pushed shells into her shotgun's magazine. A ghoul's body flopped around against the far wall without much of a head left. He saw Chen near the hallway, standing near the mattress and couch barricade, and that surprised him because Chen was supposed to be outside, guarding Richards and his dog. But here he was firing his 9-mil, his face sickly pale, and fresh blood on his bandages.

The mattress shifted. Something started to push

past the couch, worming its way through the barricade and shoving the mattress aside. Chen was looking in the wrong direction. Chris tried to call out to him, but his voice came out as a hoarse, rattling whisper and he wasn't even sure what he tried to yell. He was still being dragged, but he struggled to lift himself toward Chen. He tried to point, even though his shoulder felt as if he'd been walloped with a splitting maul.

Chen never heard him, never saw the threat until the ghoul wriggled between the mattress and the door frame and leaped on him. It dragged him down and ripped at his throat with its hands. Chen screamed and shot it pointblank. The ghoul jerked as the 9mm rounds tore into its chest, but it still yanked away Chen's throat guard with no care for the silver or the holy symbols on the armor. It darted its head forward and sank its teeth into his throat.

Chris fumbled for his Beretta in its holster, still trying to yell, still trying to point with his other hand. Another ghoul climbed over the mattress that still partially blocked the entrance. It was laughing.

Jessica ran past him like a heavily armored juggernaut. She thrust her lance toward the ghoul on top of Chen and depressed the triggers. A huge coughing roar shattered the air. Most of the ghoul's upper body disintegrated into pink and gray mist. The wall erupted with hundreds of pellet holes that blasted away chunks of drywall and wood. The concussion back-blast hit Chris like a punch, knocking the breath out of him. White-gray smoke billowed everywhere.

The lower-half remains of the ghoul flopped to the side. The blast and pellets had also shredded the laughing ghoul and most of the remaining barricade. The laughter had stopped.

More ripping gunfire. Adrenaline-charged voices yelling over the radio, punctuated with chaotic battle sounds. And upstairs, something massive and inhuman screaming and raging, smashing walls and destroying things.

Michael…oh, God.

Time focused down, became strange and slow and disconnected while his thoughts seemed to burn with the intensity of an incendiary grenade. His mind flashed on the memory of Michael as he crouched in the corner of the junk-filled room. He'd had so much fear in his eyes, but his face had changed when he'd looked at Chris because of that new hope…the vow made to him by a knight who killed monsters.

The kid had to be all right. Had to be. He wasn't sure if he could live with himself if he'd caused the boy's death. What would he say to the mother? What could he say to anyone after something like that? The fact that, before this mission, before tonight, he might've shaken his head and said something stupid and flippant like "shit happens," and how it was a goddamn shame but they were here for the greater good, etc, etc, amen—now that fact was a shiv to his guts. Truth was, you didn't ever get out from under that kind of thing.

Never ever.

He grayed out again, but didn't completely lose consciousness this time. He still heard the roar and crack of the gunfire and the melee, the *hiss* and *thunk* of a sword shearing into flesh, and repeated yells of "Specter Two fall back!" Heard the rapid radio chatter as the captain struggled to establish another perimeter around the house. Heard someone swearing in a low, savage and unrelenting stream. But these seemed disconnected and unreal. He gradually became aware he wasn't being dragged anymore. The night air felt warm, almost humid. The pain in his shoulder and neck grew in intensity, throbbing, while his head still pounded away and he felt sick to his stomach.

He opened his eyes on the night sky. The moonlight was pale white and brilliant, but the moon was moving toward the horizon and the shadows steadily deepened their hold. He groaned and turned on his side and vomited on the dead grass, then rolled away from the stink. He gasped when the pain flared to new heights.

Then something attacked his face with a tongue and some powerful dog breath. He groaned again and managed to push his dog away enough to suck in a breath of night air that stank of gunpowder and blood.

His dog whined at him. He relented and petted her, though his head was still filled with cobwebs and bright stabbing pains. "Hey there, pretty girl. Give you a scare, did I? Sorry 'bout that. One word of warning, though. If you eat my vomit, I'm disowning you."

She looked at him. If he had to testify, he would've sworn she looked affronted.

"Don't look at me like that. I'm only establishing boundaries."

"You're talking to your dog as if she understands you again," Tashelle said from nearby. Turning his head hurt, made him dizzy and sick to his stomach, but he spotted her crouched by the van's bumper with her shotgun in her arms. She glanced at him and frowned. "How you doing?"

"Puking."

"Yeah. Noticed that. And thanks for scaring me to death, you jerk." She turned back to watching the house with the intensity of a predator haunting a watering hole.

Roth's voice crackled over the radio, making Chris start and the unexpected burst of sound. "Specter Two in position. No contact with tangos. No visible movement in the house, over."

"Roger that," came back Captain Garcia's voice. So the captain had survived at least.

Chris slowly levered himself into a sitting position, groaning at the sharp pinch of pain in his side and at his pounding head. He'd somehow lost his MP7, despite the fact he'd had it on a goddamn sling. He unsnapped his thigh holster and pulled the Beretta 9mm and chambered a round. He frowned at the pistol. It seemed so damn small. Almost a joke.

"Is Michael okay?" he asked.

"We haven't seen the kid since things went to hell. But I think he's still in there alive. He's still leverage."

"What happened?"

"They tried to break out, but we contained them. Barely."

"Back to square one." It hurt to talk. Hurt more to admit that.

"Yeah."

"What happened?"

Tashelle double-checked her radio to make sure it was off. "You went upstairs like an idiot. I thought the captain was fit to shoot Drake in the head, for what he'd done. I don't know what the hell would've happened. Something bad anyway. Then we heard the monster go all ragey and the shit hits the fan and here comes Hill, bouncing down the damn stairs like a rubber ball." She glanced at him again. The moonlight frosted half her dark skin in silvered light, and her helmet straps dangled down by the curve of her neck. "You break anything?"

"Don't think so," he said. "I'm pretty much invincible even though I'm still really good-looking. Some say it's a curse." He tried stretching, intending to work out the pain in his back, shoulder, and neck. It didn't help; in fact, it hurt like a bitch. He wished he had something for the damn pounding headache. Maybe a magical beer-pissing unicorn too, while he was busy wishing.

"You need to take it easy, man. Second time tonight I thought you were dead."

"Yeah, I'll keep it in mind." He pulled the dog closer to him as he stared at the house. Run down carcass of a building, seeming to slump across the dead lawn, wrapping itself around its porch as if jealously guarding a secret from view. "So the ghouls came after us…"

"Big time. Bounding down the stairs, sneaking

up from the basement, through the kitchen, creeping out of the hall. We lost Chen."

He said nothing. The memory of seeing Chen die was very close. Too close to deal with, and nothing he could do about it now anyway. That was two. Two buddies gone and nothing to show for it.

Tashelle went on. "We had to pull back. They retook the first floor. Captain didn't want to push again until we knew if the kid was still okay."

"Sarge still alive?"

She snorted, sliding her hand along the barrel of the Benelli. "Things are bad."

"What do you mean?" But he knew already. Something to do with Sergeant Drake.

"I mean I didn't sign on to fight against other people. Monsters, yeah. Give me a good vampire and I'll riddle that thing with silver, watch 'em smoke. But other people? Damn. I wanted that, I'd have gone regular army, you know? I'd have kept myself ignorant of all this shit."

"Yeah." He waited for her to give more detail, but she didn't. She didn't look at him either, as if she wanted to drop the whole subject. So he asked, "Where's the captain now?"

She jerked her chin. "Back of the house, last time I saw him. You shouldn't be moving around though."

"What am I, a pussy? I'm not even bleeding."

"What are you? You're a damn fool, that's what." She shook her head. "Be careful. For once, all right?"

He kept his face as grim as he could make it. "You know what kind of boxers I'm wearing?"

"What…?"

"Superman. That's right. Man of Steel."

"Yeah, you were Superman bouncing down the damn stairs."

He started to laugh, but the flare of pain in his head and his right side made him wince and grit his teeth. And just like that he didn't feel like laughing anymore. God, he was pathetic. Never mind that it hurt. It felt wrong to make jokes with Chen and Weeger dead and the kid still in danger. He wished he'd kept his mouth shut instead of trying to say something to bleed off the pressure.

He looked at his dog. "You coming with me, or you gonna sit this one out?"

She cocked her head, panting and wagging her curled tail. He took that as a yes.

It felt as if it took him twenty minutes to get his feet under him again. He left Tashelle, and moved crouched-over along the side of the van with his dog following at his side. His aching head thudded along with the beat of his heart. The first couple of steps were hard. His knees almost gave out, nearly sending him face-first into the grass. He put a hand on the van to steady himself and waited until the lightheaded sensation went away.

When he finally reached the van's passenger door he found it locked up tight. He debated knocking but was pretty sure Richards would get bent about any interruption. Still, Chris needed to pick up a better primary weapon than his 9mm and sword. Maybe a grenade launcher and a chainsaw for starters.

The radio had been silent since Roth's status call. He had to check in with the captain, let him know he was back in the game and find out the current orders. Also, he needed to learn exactly what Tashelle had been talking about when she'd said things were real bad. Things had been real bad before the damn monster had tried to bite his face off.

He keyed his radio. "Specter Actual, this is Hill reporting in, over."

"Roger that, Hill. Sit tight your location. I'm incoming to you, out."

He waited, staring at the house, hating it. The plywood hanging over the bay window resembled a bandage pasted over a wound. The first floor windows were all blind except the one where Chen had peeled off the tinfoil. The windows above the porch roof were gaping, methodic stab wounds filled with darkness. The heavy black power cord leading from the generator lay in a tangle near the porch steps, its end severed. He glanced at his watch, discovered the face had been smashed. Shit.

Captain Garcia eased around the side of the house, moving in a combat crouch, keeping his assault rifle trained on the windows and doorway. Jessica followed behind him, covering his six. Chris raised his hand when they cleared the porch. The captain started toward the van, but Pin moved off to take up a defensive position near Bowen.

Lines of strain etched the captain's face, and dark circles curved under his eyes. "Good to see you on your feet. I was worried. How bad?"

He debated playing it off, but the captain's expression told him he wanted a no bullshit answer.

"My head feels like somebody dropped a grenade in my skull." True, enough, but he didn't mention the constant taste of blood in his mouth. He also didn't mention the ringing in his ears, or how he'd puked his guts up. Kept quiet about the sharp pinch in his right side where he might've cracked a rib. He tried not to stare at the house where it seemed to brood in the center of the swath of dead grass like a wounded lion. But he failed that too.

"We'll get you checked out when we get back. Right now, if you can pull a trigger, I need you on the line."

"Got it, Captain." He'd do his best. For the captain. For the boy. "Any word on Michael?"

Captain Garcia frowned and looked away. "Unknown."

"We can't leave him in there if—"

The captain leaned in close and spoke in a harsh whisper. "Don't you think I know that, Hill? Don't you think I'm very well *aware* of that? We've lost two people in that fucking rat's nest so far, and sunrise is two hours off. We're running out of time."

"Sorry, Captain."

Garcia shook his head, a curt back-and-forth motion, but he stared at the house's front door and said nothing. A black strip of darkness seeped along the door's edge where it wouldn't close. Anything could be watching them.

"What now, sir?" he said. "We got reinforcements on the way?"

"No." His scowl deepened. "We've been given a termination hour. This operation ends at first dawn. Reinforcements won't get here in time."

"So what's that mean for us?"

"Means we get another watcher, and after that

we're on our own. Command just gave standing orders to destroy all hostiles before the deadline, regardless of the status of hostages."

"That's—"

"That's standard protocol for situations like this. You know it." The captain slung his rifle and leaned against the van's hood. He looked about as bad as Chris felt.

Michael didn't have much time left, if he was even still alive after that fucked up disaster that had just gone down. If they were going to risk another assault, they'd have to wait until the watcher arrived so she could infiltrate and check his status. Anything else was too dangerous for the boy. He glanced at his watch before he remembered it was busted. Now if only the damn watcher would hurry the hell up and get here.

"I heard what you said up there," Captain Garcia said. "To the broodsire."

Chris shook his head. He'd said a lot of things, including the taunt that had set the damn monster off and left him a mass of bruises and, judging from the pain, sporting a cracked rib to go with his concussion.

"You offered to switch places with the boy," the captain continued. "I knew I was right about you."

Chris looked away and said nothing. His offer had come to nothing, so it shouldn't even count.

"I'm done after this," Garcia said, and that made Chris look at him again. The captain snorted, his smile cynical. "Sergeant Drake's filing a complaint with Command."

"He fucking deep-sixed that hand-off, Captain. There was no fucking ambush."

"We could say that in front of the highranks, before all lords and ladies, but there's no way to prove it. I was pounding thin ice with a sledgehammer anyway, making that agreement. The sergeant had more than enough ammo against me even before things went tits up."

"He was planning something," Chris said in a low voice. "I saw him talking with his people before I went up. The crew that was with him from before—"

"Hill, it doesn't fucking *matter*. You understand? All that matters is getting Michael back safe to his mom. I thought you were with me on that."

"I am, Captain. One hundred percent. But nothing's over—"

"The highranks will strip my command. And they're right to do it. I lost two knights so far this operation. Two. Drake's gonna make the case that we lost people because I hesitated, too worried about the boy's safety to maintain operational integrity. And it's true." He wiped a hand across his face, scrubbing at his chin. "It's true."

"They'll understand we were trying to get him out in one piece—"

"Nah, Hill. Just shut up about it. You don't know anything." He met Chris's eyes and gave him a different smile—this one almost warm. "You know why I took you under my wing this mission? Let you see things? Because you're an optimist. Like I used to be—hell, still am most of the time if I can swing it. Drake's right though. You understand? Putting the kid's safety above ours has endangered our primary objective, which isn't to save the boy, no matter what I might want. According to protocol, our primary objective was always to kill the broodsire and all the ghouls before they hurt anyone else. The greater good. Bigger picture. I get stuck on the smaller stuff, because the small picture's only a child. And no one else is there to save him. No angels. No superheroes. Just the monsters and us kicking the shit out of each other in the darkness while the world grinds on about its fucking business."

"That's bullshit, Captain," he said. "We're knights. If we ain't gonna care about people like Michael, who the hell will?"

The captain closed his eyes, leaned his head back. "You say the things I want to hear. Shows I have a keen judge of character."

"I tried to stay neutral, sir, because the sergeant, what he's saying, sometimes makes sense. But this is a kid. And I can't swallow that, can't stay on the fence. A knight doesn't stay neutral here. I made my choice and I'll live with it. Same as you."

"Yeah. Yeah, you're right. So you know what? This watcher shows up, we find out Michael's status and position, and I think it's time to be more aggressive. One last assault, for all the goddamn potato chips this time around. Me, you, Jessica, Tashelle. The only ones left I can count on."

"Jessica's not part of our old crew."

"She's good people. Heart's in the right place."

Well, it was the captain's call. With Weeger and Chen KIA, the number of Thorn Knights in the unit who'd served under Garcia was now very low. "What if Michael's already dead?"

The captain stared at the upper windows. "Then we kill them all. Burn the house to the ground. Mourn later."

CHAPTER TWENTY-TWO

Bleed Time

A man could be haunted, not by ghosts but by questions. They were always worse.

Sergeant Drake had deep-sixed the handoff, but Chris couldn't wrap his mind around why he'd done it. For a shot at the broodsire? The sergeant had been up front about what he believed...but he'd had orders, and Drake had seemed a hardass when it came to orders. And what was going on inside that house now? Nothing. And that bothered him more than he could say, fed his fear to near-panic levels. Michael should be free, on his way home to his mom, but he wasn't. Because of Drake. Chris remembered staring down his gun sights at the sergeant, his finger on the trigger and tightening. Would he have shot Drake, back there when all hell was free and gone, everything chaos, when the sergeant had been shooting at the broodsire, and Michael had been in the line of fire? Could he have shot another knight?

Too many questions and not enough distraction to drive them from his brain.

The only thing keeping him from losing his shit right now was his dog. She sat quietly at his side, a comforting presence he found himself increasingly grateful for, especially as his battered body started to blare the pain-alarm with an idiot's focus and dedication. His dog seemed to know at a glance every ache he shrugged off and all the turmoil in his mind. He tried to think up a good name for her. Nothing would come to him.

The watcher hadn't astral jumped here yet. Specter team needed her to recon the house if they had any hope of getting Michael out in one piece. That meant more waiting, even as time bled away.

He'd taken up a support position on the dead front lawn, near one of the Chevy Suburbans, where he could cover the front of the house. A big truck rumbled by on one of the main streets. He glanced its way, looking the city lights, unable to shake his unease. Soon the horizon would grow brighter over eastern Providence. The city would stagger awake. Commuters. Businesses. A steady stream of planes in and out of T.F. Green instead of only the occasional one. Same old everyday shit, with no care that some kid was facing life or death in a room full of junk in a house full of monsters.

He turned his focus back to the house and spotted Jessica Deering double-timing it across the yard. He covered her movement until she reached the protection of the van. She crouched down, put the safety shield on her lance, and carefully set it aside. Then she yanked off her heavy-duty helmet. Her dark hair was sweaty and matted to her head.

She began peeling off top sections of her armor, working through what seemed like a million and a half buckles and clasps. She finished pushing off the top half of her armored suit but still stayed in the bottom half. Plates and sections of armor hung down around her like the peel of a banana. Underneath she wore a lancer's tight black body suit of Kevlar with a built-in layer of anti-compression gel. She grabbed a water bottle from the haphazard pile near the van's rear fender, twisted off the cap, leaned back and started chugging water. He admired her, watching her throat work as she swallowed, her eyes closed, head tilted back, lost in the simplest act of slaking thirst.

She finished drinking and dumped the rest of the water over her head. That made him smile.

Carefully, he checked around. Captain Garcia

was talking with Bowen. The rest of the Thorn knights that he could see all maintained defensive positions. Sergeant Drake was around the back with the rest of Specter Two. The house was still and silent. Nothing moved. The moon gone, the darkness deeper. A car drove by on the street with a vague, shadowed shape hunched behind the wheel. The car continued on, never slowing, the driver having no reason to glance at the rundown house. Richards's wards made the world appear in its normal state of disinterested disrepair, and why would anyone question that? When Chris was a kid, he'd believed magic would make things wonderful instead of simply reflecting back the decay. Not the first time he'd been wrong.

He slowly stood and managed not to groan as he tried to work out the stiffness. His dog trotted around him in a circle, waiting for him to hurry the hell up.

"Take pity on the walking wounded," he said to her. She only wagged her tail and circled him again as if showing off.

The first step was the worst. It brought all the pain to the forefront and pinned it under a microscope for his brain to study. His head ached something fierce; his cheek and jaw throbbed where he'd been hit by the stupid fuse on the flashbang. His left shoulder was all fucked up, and moving his arm was agony. His back felt like a mass of bruises, not surprising after he'd bounced down the stairs like a superball, adding cracked or bruised ribs to the end tally. Every time he moved, some other part of him protested with an explosion of hurt.

After they got the kid home safe, he was gonna find a Jacuzzi and live in it for a month straight.

He holstered his pistol and headed for Jessica, trying not to limp or stagger. His dog friend paced alongside him as if this were a weekend stroll in the park. He circled as far from the front of the house as possible, approaching the edge of the wards. The hair on his arms lifted when he neared all the directed power maintaining the illusions. His dog whined and scooted away from the invisible barriers.

"It's all right, girl," he soothed, keeping his eyes on Jessica.

Jessica glanced at him as he reached her. He thought he spotted a flash of annoyance, betrayed by the tightening of her mouth and eyes, but it was there and gone again quickly enough that he felt safe pretending he'd never noticed.

He crouched next to her, gritting his teeth at the multiple explosions of pain that set off all over his body. His dog laid her muzzle on his thigh, looking up at him with sympathetic eyes even as she marked his fatigues with dog slobber.

Chris checked his mike, making sure it was off, and kept his voice low as he spoke to Jessica. "You ran with Drake. What's he like?"

"Why are you asking me?"

"I've seen you watching the captain's back." He shrugged. "So maybe you aren't in one camp or the other. And you seem like you'd give a straight answer."

"I don't know you."

"Yeah. So maybe we can be straight with each other. We got nothing to prove. No lies to tell."

"That means I don't trust you, Hill."

"I don't care." He said it with more savagery than he intended, but it got her to look him in the eye at least. "This isn't about me. It's about Michael."

Some of the wary defensiveness left her face. She didn't answer, didn't nod, but he took her silence as consent to pursue the subject.

"I want to know if the sergeant is a guy you can talk to," he said. "Yeah, he's a hard ass. Yeah, he's balls-to-the-wall, full-out, hardcore, whatever. But if I go and see him, will he listen to me?"

"What do you need to talk to him for?"

"He's gonna hang the captain out to dry on this. Blame him for Weeger and Chen."

She stared at him. "What do you think?"

"You ever answer a question? I know what I think. I'm hoping you say different."

She fiddled with the front edge of her bomb suit but seemed unaware of what her hands were doing. He did his best to fight back his impatience.

"I can't tell you want you want to hear," she said. "Sergeant Drake...I don't know."

"What?"

"He doesn't get close to you. But he feels responsible for you. Understand?"

"No."

"It's like you're his kid or something. But he doesn't want to get too close, in case of stuff like...Weeger and Chen. It's why he went along with the captain until knights started dying. Then..."

"Then he sabotaged the handover so the fucking ghouls wouldn't get away."

"He values us more than the civilians. He doesn't say it, but..." She shook her head.

"That's a kid in there, in danger."

"Everybody's got a different take on what it means to be a knight."

"Bullshit. The codes are clear as day in my mind."

She shrugged and looked back at the house. He could sense that she didn't want to talk about it anymore, and that made him angry.

"So you think he should destroy the captain just 'cause we lost some people? I saw Weeger die. He made a goddamn mistake. This business, you make a mistake and you end up dead and your name on the lists. The captain's a good man."

"The captain cares too much," she said, very quietly.

"Yeah? And when did caring too much become a fucking crime?"

"Listen to you. You don't hear anything I say. *Drake* thinks it's a crime when it costs us people. You wanted to know if you could talk to him, convince him to lay off. I told you the truth, but it's truth you don't want to hear, so you're going to ignore me."

"You're right. I don't want to hear that truth. And you know what? I'm going to try anyway."

She didn't say anything. He could tell from her face she thought his chances were less than zero. He didn't care. If he didn't try, it'd be like stabbing the captain in the back.

"You know what?" he continued, still all revved. "When this shit's over, when we got the kid home to his mom and the captain's clear and things are peachy, I'm gonna take you out for a beer or something. Just to gloat about how I was right and you were wrong."

"I don't owe you anything, Hill," she snarled. "And I don't wanna hear it."

"Fine. I won't say a word. You'll just know. You'll sit there with the beer I bought you, knowing."

She gaped at him. "I don't even like beer."

"How about coffee?"

"No."

"No beer, no coffee. You're crazy."

She gave him a little half smile and started to pull on all her armor again. Yeah. Definitely crazy.

Sergeant Drake was in the backyard, so he stood, called his dog, and started to walk toward the east side of the house. Jessica hadn't been any help, and he wasn't even sure why he'd approached her. Had he really believed she'd share some touching story about how the sergeant was a real sentimental guy underneath two metric tons of steel plating and reinforced concrete and everything would work out okay? What the hell was wrong with his head lately?

There were no touching stories. All the same, he meant to talk with Drake before the watcher arrived and they made a last play in this game. Time was running out.

"Hey, Hill," Jessica called before he'd walked more than a few feet. He glanced back, waiting.

"I like bagels." She said it fiercely, as though he'd

pissed her off somehow. She put on her helmet, slapped the visor down, grabbed her lance and moved off.

He grinned...but the grin didn't last.

CHAPTER TWENTY-THREE

If Blues Were a Bullet

To get to the backyard where Sergeant Drake was, Chris had to skirt the side of the house and sneak along the nine-foot gap between the clapboard siding and a rusting chain link fence. Skeletal rose bushes clawed up from the ground, their leaves black, their thorns gray. The ground was dirt and patches of desert-dry grass, studded with chunks of lava rock. He paused before running the gauntlet, not wanting to get grabbed by any creepy hiding inside the house or shot by his own guys.

He spotted Tyson crouched among the tall weeds in the corner of the backyard, covering the back porch and the east side of the house. He took a deep breath and keyed his mike. "Specter Two, this is Hill. On my way to your position, over."

Captain Garcia turned and looked at him. Chris

felt his armpits grow damp, sweat beading on his forehead and under his helmet, as he waited for the captain to order him off, maybe reprimand him for acting on his own initiative. Luckily, he didn't have an assigned AOR. He'd been too banged up in the last go round with the broodsire and the ghouls. All the same, this was a deal more unexplained initiative than a knight of his rank could usually get away with. But the captain only watched and said nothing.

Sergeant Drake's rough voice came back over the radio. "Roger that. Tyson will cover. Keep sharp, over." The right words, every one of them, but Chris couldn't tell from his voice what Drake thought about him paying a visit.

He pulled his Beretta from the holster on his thigh again, pushed the safety off, and looked at the house. It made him think of something—an image that came spinning out of absolute left field. The Wicker Man. The huge wooden human statue where people were supposedly trapped inside and burned alive. He'd watched some weird '70s movie about it once. He stared at the house as it squatted over the dead lawn, hunched between the borders of the overgrown lot and the chain link with half its eyes blinded and every other window empty. Waiting to burn. Huddled with its decaying porches held close against itself like wounded arms and waiting to burn.

"What do you say, girl?" he asked his dog. "Is this crazy or is this stupid crazy?"

She chuffed and pressed herself against his lower leg, leaning her weight on him as if for comfort.

"Yeah, exactly. So let's get this over with. Stay close."

He started along the side of the house. The dog kept pace. He felt watched and didn't like it. Tyson watched him from the backyard and he felt eyes on his back—the rest of the team in the front watching him go. Maybe something watching him from the windows.

He approached the bay window. Glass shards and splinters were scattered on the ground beneath the busted-out frame. He raised his pistol and moved in a careful Weaver stance as far from the plywood-covered window as possible, keeping the front pistol sight on the wood. His dog started to growl low in her throat. The hairs on the back of his neck stood up.

Carefully, he edged past the bay window, now approaching another small window covered over in tinfoil. He continued to face the side of the house as he moved so he could cover as much of it as possible.

Wood creaked behind him, followed by a tiny, stealthy scrape.

He swung the pistol back to the bay window. His

breath hissed in. His teeth bared in a silent snarl. His finger tightened on the trigger and his heart punched a rapid alarm. The growl from his dog deepened. Her attention was locked on the bay window.

The narrow gap between the battered window frame and the plywood pushed open a little wider, making an expanding slit of darkness. Wood groaned on metal. The crack opened an inch, maybe a little more. He aimed at it, but couldn't see into the blackness beyond. His night vision device was broken and his flashlight still mounted to the rail of his lost MP7. All the same, he knew something watched him back. He could feel it like the gooseflesh rippling up and down his arms.

A liquid whisper seeped out of the crack. "Je-*sus* loves the little chil-*dren*. All the children in the *world*."

"I got movement," he said into his mike with a calmness he didn't feel. "Hostile at the bay window."

The whisper continued, loud enough to be heard over his dog's low growling. "Je-sus loves the little..." A pause, and then a bone-weary sigh. "All the children in the win-*dow*."

Out of the corner of his eye, Chris saw Karen approach in a combat crouch with her shotgun aimed at the bay window. He could hear another dog barking, far in the distance. Nearer, across the back alley maybe, glass bottles rattled together, playing a clinking chord before falling silent again.

He took a step backward, giving himself more distance from the window in case the ghoul shoved through it and charged. Distance was good. Distance was his friend.

The plywood creaked again, pushed another inch wider. The darkness only widened its grin, revealing nothing from inside the house.

"Don't you want to be pretty?" the sing-song voice asked.

He didn't answer. His gun was steady. The gun sight didn't even waver. He was stone cold—but that verse kept echoing in his head and he wanted to shoot something for putting it there.

"Come closer," the voice cajoled. "Please. Bring your poochie-pooch."

"Fuck you," Chris said. "Stick your head out and show me how pretty you are."

Captain Garcia said over the radio. "Don't talk to them, Hill."

The plywood fell closed so fast it bounced against the frame. No more dark crack. No more voice. He hurried the rest of the way to the backyard, not quite running but definitely hauling some ass. He thought he heard something laugh inside the house.

Sergeant Drake stood near the backyard gate, watching him come, no expression on his face. "I hope this is worth risking your ass, Hill."

"Yeah, Sergeant. It is."

Drake scanned the windows above the back porch roof. He held his M4 carbine loosely in his hands. His night vision goggles were up on his helmet, aimed toward the sky. "You ever get the feeling somebody's watching you?"

Chris stared at him, not quite sure if the sergeant was joking.

Drake saw his look and gave him a slow grin. "Just bustin' your balls, Hill. So why you back here with the knights fallen from grace? Running secret messages for the captain?"

"I wanted to talk. Offline."

Drake's grin widened, but his gaze was sharp and wary. "You showed a lot of initiative back there, but I didn't think you were gonna make it when I saw your ass rolling down the stairs. You got brass balls almost as big as mine, kid."

Chris shook his head. He hadn't come to hear that kind of shit. "I wanted to ask—" He stopped. Now that he was here, facing Drake, all the words seemed to slam together in a car wreck of loud, disjointed thoughts.

"Captain send you back to beg me not to report all this to Command, that it?"

"I came on my own."

"Still showing that initiative. Maybe he was right to take you under his little wing. Maybe you got the spark." Drake glanced him over and then returned his stare to the upper floors of the house. "Maybe not."

"The boy... Michael—"

Drake pointed at the Beretta in Chris's hand. "Nine millimeter blues."

"What the hell's that?"

"A guy stuck with a handgun at a sniper battle has a righteous case of the nine millimeter blues. That's what we have. Trying to maintain the Silence. Intentionally handicapping ourselves. Putting our asses in danger, not just to save people, but to keep them ignorant of the real threats out there. And it's bullshit. Always was. Always will be."

"That doesn't matter now," Chris said.

"The fuck it doesn't. You got it, too, right now, but you're too starry-eyed, white-knighting, running around with your dick up to know it. Trying to win a long-range war with the wrong fucking weapon. Stupid. Hopeless. Like your arguments here."

"The captain's a good man. He's trying to get that boy back."

"And I don't seem to care what happens to the kid, that it? You're wrong about me. I want the kid safe. But you know what? We're here to contain suffering, not to stop it."

"Bullshit. We can stop it. Right here, for one little boy. That's enough for me."

Drake shook his head in disgust. "See? That's where you're wrong. You can't stop suffering. Nothing stops it. Look around. We stop any suffering here tonight? Someone's got to go tell Weeger's wife and kid he's dead. Chen's got a mother. Same old song and dance. You, you're practically suicidal out there, trying to do the right thing. You got someone who cares about you?"

Chris looked at him. Didn't answer.

"Point is," the sergeant continued as if Chris had replied, "the captain was gonna trade that boy's life for the broodsire's freedom. Letting it escape, letting it inflict its obscene fucking degradations on people all over again. Don't give me bullshit about how they'd leave and go back to eating corpses. Bull-fucking-shit. Fucking naïve. They're gonna go to ground somewhere else, and it'll be tough as shit tracking them down again. They'll kill other innocent people, take more little kids, before we finally fucking put an end to it. You think those ghouls in there *wanted* to become that way?

Fuck you, Hill. The suffering, it just spreads."

Chris leaned toward him. "I don't care about any of that. It's just words and bullshit. Because there's a kid in there who needs me. And we need more men like the captain who see people as more than...just weights on some kind of cosmic suffering scale."

"We ain't meat for the grinder, like your heroic captain seems to think. You don't easily replace a knight in this world."

"You fucking deep-sixed the handoff." Chris's free hand clenched. "You put a little boy in danger. Just like that monster."

The sergeant showed some teeth as a sneer twisted his lips. "Yeah? You know that for a fact? What? You didn't hear our little motion sensor alarms go off right as the broodsire came down the stairs? You know what that meant? You were in the basement, so you sure as shit should know. The fucking ghouls were crawling down the walls again, sneaking in, flanking us while all our focus was on the boy. What part of *ambush* you not get?"

Now that Drake mentioned it, he did remember something beeping an instant before everything had gone to shit and the sergeant had opened fire. But damn it, even if the ghouls had been pulling some bullshit, that didn't justify any full-on rock and roll response with a kid in the line of fire.

Chris forced himself to take a deep breath. "All I'm saying is, I think the captain's doing the right thing, and it's wrong to destroy a guy like him. The world needs more like him. So I'm asking you to think about it. That's all."

"He'll get his chance to defend himself, don't worry," Sergeant Drake said. "To the highranks, and to Weeger and Chen's people."

There was nothing more to say. He'd risked his ass coming over here, for what? A pipe dream. Had he really believed he could change the sergeant's mind? Him and the captain were on opposite ends of the stadium, everybody believing they were doing the right thing.

Chris called his dog to his side. She licked at his hand and nudged her head against him until he petted her. He started toward the west side of the house next to the chain link fence that held off the overgrown lot next door and she followed. It'd be stupid to risk moving past the bay window again.

"Remember what I said," Sergeant Drake called after him as he walked away.

He didn't reply. He wasn't likely to forget.

CHAPTER TWENTY-FOUR

Watcher

It seemed as if all eyes were on him and his dog as they shag-assed back to the front yard. The scrutiny scraped his last nerve raw. Nothing like failure for a good kick in the balls, knock the fire right out of him.

He spotted Garcia, but the captain only turned away without a word. He'd probably guessed what Chris had gone to talk to the sergeant about—shit, it had been obvious enough, and the captain was far from stupid. But hell, Chris had expected Drake to agree to at least let things sit, not drag everyone through the mud and the shit with the mission still hot. Turned out he'd been naïve. As usual, one play behind in the game. Things always seemed to break that way for him.

He finally made it to one of the SUVs and broke out a bottle of water from inside.

"Thirsty, girl?" he murmured. He poured the

water into an unused tactical helmet and set it down for her to drink.

She lapped away eagerly. He took another bottle for himself, turning his back on the house and drinking deep. Yet, he could feel the damn house looming there behind him. Just another crack house rotting away, hiding corruption in its guts. Made him wonder what other things old houses had seen, what shadows they kept secret. He glanced out past the wards, at the houses pressing right up against the street. Made him wonder what went on behind the blinds all over, hidden on every street.

Stupid thoughts, fueled by exhaustion and pain. He needed to focus. Block out the pain, fight off the stiffness relentlessly clamping down on his body. The sun would be up in less than two hours. The illusion from the wards would be nearly impossible to maintain by one mage in the daylight, with more people around, cars in the street, and the city waking up. Richards had to be exhausted anyway. He'd been holding the wards in place all night. Shaping energy had a price.

In fact, they were all exhausted. He could see it in the way everybody held themselves: shoulders sagging, gun barrels not quite as steady, movements short and jerky. Chris felt so deep down weary that the thought of a bed with clean sheets pulled at him from the center, the way dreams of playing baseball for a living had pulled him when he'd been a kid. Hell, even his dog kept yawning.

A spark flared in mid-air in the center of the yard. It split into a line, racing in opposite directions, and then flared into one of the strange two-dimensional doorways the watchers used.

"About damn time," he whispered. His dog glanced up at him, her tail wagging.

The door warped and shivered as the watcher's female form pushed through it, wrapping the light around her limbs as the details of her body slowly filled in. A different watcher this time, younger, very thin, but wearing the same Psi-suit.

The watcher scanned around the yard, saw Captain Garcia, and streaked right for him. The relief on the captain's face when he spotted her made him look a different man. He spoke with the watcher, but Chris wasn't close enough to hear what was said, either aloud or across her telepathic feed. Part of him wanted to be in on the conversation. He'd grown used to being a central spoke on the wheel. Yeah, he was still just a grunt, but the captain had pulled him into the middle of this. Now it was a letdown to remain in position and wait to be told, like everyone else.

Captain Garcia said something to her and

pointed to the house. The watcher nodded and blurred toward the front door, leaving a trail of streaked afterimages. Her image sliced into the porch floor, cutting her off at the knees, and then she ghosted through the front wall.

For him, waiting was always the worst when he knew the waiting was almost over. It over-torqued the bolts, stripping the hell of them, making the last few infinitely long moments of delay almost unbearable. Think wind-up before a pitch at the end of a game, runs needed, men on base, last inning. Or staring at the lights at a drag race, afraid to blink, watching for green.

The watcher streaked out of the house wall, straight toward Captain Garcia, moving so fast her form smeared behind her like watercolors running down a canvas. She stopped in front of the captain and leaned toward him, speaking quickly, her face urgent. Chris crouched next to his dog as he watched, his free hand on her back and the other holding his pistol, as his stomach sank. Didn't look good, whatever it was.

The captain glanced his way and motioned him over. He caught looks from Jessica and Tashelle as he hurried toward the van. He ran with his dog by his side, ignoring all his aches and pains, to where the captain waited with the watcher. Even though he'd just been bitching about not knowing, now that the captain wanted him, he felt uneasiness gnawing away his cool. He hoped the captain didn't want him to talk to the goddamn broodsire again. That hand had been played out. If he saw the monster again there'd be no words, nothing but guns and teeth.

Captain Garcia nodded to him as he closed in. "Hill, this is Perry. She's got a fix on the boy. He's still alive."

"Thank God. Where's he at?"

Watcher Perry stared at him with eyes that glowed with their own muted light. Her mind-voice echoed in his head. *"Near the broodsire, in the north-facing bedroom with the damaged doorway. No ghouls in the room."*

"That's where he was before. He hurt?"

"Bruised and battered. There's no life threatening wound that I could see." She wrapped her arms around herself and her image suddenly flickered and blurred before snapping back into focus. *"He's terrified though. That…thing. That thing was licking him. On the face. Like a dog."*

"Christ," he whispered, hating the gut-punched feeling that smashed into his stomach. Captain Garcia looked at him. Chris met his stare. They understood each other without saying a word.

Watcher Perry glanced back and forth between them. *"Where do you need me now, Captain?"*

"How many ghouls are left? Last watcher didn't get an accurate count."

She turned back to the house, scowling. "*Six. I counted six. I checked the attic and the crawlspaces and those fake walls. Basement, too. There's lots of bodies. But I only saw six still...functional. And they're not afraid.*"

"Doesn't matter," Chris said. "A bullet doesn't care if you're afraid." But the watcher only looked his way and said nothing.

Captain Garcia tapped his fingers on his rifle's stock as he stared at the second story windows. "Where are the ghouls?"

"*All six were downstairs, near both entrances.*"

"They think we're gonna push again," Chris said. "Through ground floor. Like last time."

The captain nodded slowly. "All right. Perry, I need you back inside. Anything changes with the broodsire or the boy, you let me know right away." He ejected the SIG 553's magazine and checked the rounds remaining, then slapped it back home.

Watcher Perry raced back toward the house. As she moved she shot off the ground, rushing toward the second story like a plane breaking free of the runway. She pierced through the second story wall and disappeared. He stared at the spot she'd vanished. A trick like that would make things a helluva lot less painful the next time somebody threw him down the stairs.

Captain Garcia headed to the back of the van and Chris and his dog followed. He unlocked the double doors and swung them wide. Inside, Richards sat in a lotus position within the casting circle. His face sagged with exhaustion, dark bruises pooled under his eyes, and a sheen of sweat spread all across his pale skin. The crackling white flames around the edge of the circle flickered and shimmered, but burned lower than Chris ever remembered seeing before. Their light was muted and uncertain.

The captain eyed the mage, frowning. "How you holding up?"

"It's all peaches and cream, Captain," Richards answered, but his smile was sickly.

"You look like roadkill," Chris told him.

"Thanks, Hill. You look like an asshole, but you don't hear me mentioning it in public, do you?"

The captain held up a hand for quiet. "How much longer can you keep the wards up?"

"I can go to dawn, easy. Maintaining wards is nothing."

Richards had to be lying through his teeth, but neither of them called him on it. He looked as if he'd start sweating blood any minute. Maintaining wards might be nothing, like he'd claimed, but he'd been doing it for hours and hours with no break. Chris might not know much about the fox mike spell-slinging end of things, but he did know mages could die from mindlock, where their brains imploded or something from pushing their will on the energies they summoned.

"Carry on, then," Captain Garcia finally said. He shut the doors again. They shared another look, grim as before, and then he keyed his radio. "Specter One this is Specter Actual, form up on me, over."

"Specter Actual, this is Specter Two," came Sergeant Drake's voice over the headsets. "Please advise. What's your status, over?"

"Hold your position, Specter Two."

"Say again, Specter Actual, over."

"Specter Two, *hold…your…position.*"

A long pause. "Copy that, Specter Actual. Out."

Shit. It would be only Specter One this time then. No Sergeant Drake. No second team. Jessica and Tashelle hurried toward the van from their picket positions. Just the four of them on this, the battered remains of Specter One. He hoped it would be enough, but swallowed his doubts. Instead he kept quiet and turned to face the house, feeling hollow, his heart drumming echoes inside his chest.

"You name that dog yet?" the captain asked, surprising him.

"No, sir."

"It's not good for a dog to have no name."

Jessica and Tashelle reached them. Jessica stood with her lance horizontal across her shoulders, staring at the captain with her game face on. Tashelle kept glancing at the second story of the house. Her helmet sat slightly crooked on her head, giving her an off balanced look.

"Double check your radios," Captain Garcia said. "Make sure they're off." When that was done, he turned to Jessica. "I need you to get the Halligan bar, flashbangs, ladder, and the brake-n-rake out of the trucks."

"We're going in, Captain?" Tashelle asked.

"We're gonna get that boy out safe. And here's how we do it."

CHAPTER TWENTY-FIVE
Assault

"'Once more unto the breach,'" Tashelle whispered to him as they huddled in the deeper shadows near the front porch. She grinned at him over her shoulder, but there was no humor in the flash of teeth.

"Let the good times roll," he whispered back, but his heart wasn't in it either. He remembered Drake's words about pistols and rifles and the world and the Thorn. Guy was an asshole. No doubt about it.

They were arranged in a line behind Captain Garcia along the front side of the house. The captain had point. He carried the Halligan breaching tool on his back instead of his sword. Tashelle was next on shotgun. Chris behind her, carrying an unwieldy extendable aluminum ladder with his pistol holstered and sword slung. Jessica brought up the rear. She squatted near the corner edge of the porch with two long poles, one balanced on each shoulder. One was her explosive-tipped lance, the other the brake-n-rake tool, a long shaft, hooked and with a serrated edge designed for busting out windows and clearing the glass from the frame.

The dog crouched beside Chris, her ears lowered, her tail down. They'd considered locking her inside one of the SUVs, but it had been the captain's call. He'd stared at her for a long moment and then said she was part of the team. If she wanted to come along, maybe that was a sign she should.

Tyson spotted them from his corner position in the backyard, but his facemask was up and Chris could only see his eyes, watching them over the top of the Steyr-AUG's scope. No sound came from inside the house. He could hear the breeze trickling through the leaves of bushes and scrub brush in the lot next door, but he couldn't feel it. He was hot, exhausted, and he hurt…but he was going to see this done.

Captain Garcia signaled and started forward, keeping tight to the side of the house, and they followed close behind, silent as ghosts. Even the dog was quiet.

If someone had told Chris a half hour ago he'd

feel another adrenaline flood tonight, Chris would've laughed in disbelief. He'd mainlined adrenaline all night. His body had to be drained. It damn well *felt* empty, victim of the kind of weariness that coiled in the marrow. And yet, from somewhere, the old flesh machine managed to squeeze out some more and pump it into his veins. His heart sped up, his breath came faster, the ladder seemed to have very little weight, while sights and sounds and smells intensified, hitting him with almost painful clarity.

They swung wide around the plywood bay window, covering it as they passed, but the boards didn't move and there was no sound from inside.

They reached the back porch. Captain Garcia took a defensive position covering the rear door. Chris swung around Tashelle and set the ladder against the slanted porch roof that ran beneath the second story windows at the back of the house.

The captain slung his rifle and started to climb. Chris pulled his 9-mil and joined Tashelle in covering him.

Sergeant Drake watched them, his expression unreadable. Chris had been afraid he'd do something to sabotage this final rescue attempt, but Drake maintained radio silence and didn't leave his position.

The captain cleared the ladder onto the porch

roof and pressed himself against the side of the house, out of Chris's line of sight. Chris holstered his pistol and climbed, careful to be as quiet as he could, trying not scrape the tread of his boots on the ridged aluminum steps or rattle the ladder. He swung out onto the gritty shingles of the porch roof, looked over the ledge at Tashelle and Jessica and gave them the OK sign.

Tashelle nodded. She and Jessica moved to their position. The dog hesitated, glancing between them as if unsure, until Tashelle made "come here" motions and the dog trotted over to her.

Their role was simple. Jessica would smash out the second floor window on the landing with the brake-n-rake and toss in a flashbang while Tashelle covered her and the dog watched them both. Captain Garcia had rescinded his orders and cleared the use of flashbangs— which said all that was needed about how desperate things were.

The sky in the east grew steadily lighter, from a deep purple, almost black, to a hazy dark blue. Chris unsnapped his thigh holster and drew his Beretta again. It felt like a toy when he imagined using it on something as nasty as the broodsire. The porch shingles crackled as his boots scraped the grit, though he tried to move as quietly as possible.

He took position behind the captain, who crouched near a window. He pressed his back against the house and nodded his readiness. Command's orders to burn the house and purge the broodsire regardless of Michael's safety haunted him. It shadow-slipped behind every motion, every breath, jacking up the pressure. He'd seen the same knowledge in the captain's eyes, stark as a bleeding wound.

There were four windows on the north side of the house's second story, each of them above the porch roof. The last two opened into the bedroom with Michael and the broodsire. Captain Garcia pulled a small dental mirror from his harness, moving slowly but surely, and tilted it around the window frame. Chris crouched beside him, pistol in both hands, not aware he was holding his breath until he had to force himself to suck in air.

The captain drew back the tiny mirror. He signaled for Chris to follow and pointed to the second to last window. The windowsills were low enough that they'd have to belly crawl across the porch roof to move unseen.

Captain Garcia edged forward. His boots crackled and crunched on the shingles, seeming so loud that Chris wondered how anyone inside could fail to hear them moving around out here, closed windows or not.

The captain crawled past the first two windows. Chris followed, pressing low, feeling the grit biting into his skin, trying to keep himself steady. His body let him know how much it resented moving after all the abuse it had taken tonight. He ignored the pain, shoved it in a box, and kicked it to the curb.

They reached the second-to-last window. The captain set his rifle across his lap as he leaned against the clapboard. Again he pulled the dental mirror out and moved it to the edge of the window frame with smooth but painfully slow motion. He turned the mirror this way and that as he scanned inside. Then he put away the mirror and turned to Chris. He pointed two fingers at his eyes and gave the hand signal for one hostile and one hostage. He pointed to the Halligan bar on his back.

Chris carefully unstrapped the heavy tool and handed it to the captain. The tool had a heavy steel forked end and an adze and pick on the other. This one had a serrated edge just below the pick for clearing glass from the frame. Captain Garcia settled the bar in his hands and shifted, readying himself to swing.

It stayed eerily quiet. The night seemed very still, everything compressed into this one place and nothing else mattered, as if there were no city around them and no world beyond.

Captain Garcia half stood in a ready-crouch, Halligan bar in one hand, his rifle held by the stock in the other. He gave Chris the three-nod go signal. Chris reached up, heart slamming away, teeth clamped together so hard his jaw ached, and keyed his radio three times—*click, click, click.* The execute signal.

Then he waited for the explosion.

He couldn't see Jessica from this position. She was around the east side of the house. He only heard the sharp crash as she broke the window second-story window.

One, two, three, he counted. *Four, five, six*—and the flashbang went off with a huge crashing blast. The window nearest their ladder shattered, spitting glass out onto the shingles.

Captain Garcia immediately swung the Halligan bar and smashed the window next to him. Chris flinched at the shattering crash, even though he'd expected it. The captain slid the serrated edge along the frame to clear the glass shards still jutting from the wood like jagged shark teeth. Pieces of glass chimed and tinkled as they fell to the floor. He jumped through the broken window and vanished into the room.

Chris moved forward and knelt. He peered inside the dark room along his pistol sights, watching

Captain Garcia's back as he ran toward the corner.

A deep, massive shadow shifted near the broken doorway. The broodsire. It had been peering into the landing, where they'd set off the flashbang. Now it wheeled around to face them. Its amber eyes flashed with surprise and venomous hate. Its glistening, translucent skin pulsed with veins, so pale it seemed to glow in the darkness.

The captain dropped his rifle, letting it dangle on the sling. He grabbed Michael in his arms. He spun back to the window with the boy clutched to his chest. He was less than five feet away and moving fast, back toward Chris and the open window.

The broodsire loosed a bellowing roar as loud as the flashbang. It lurched forward, charging out of the gloom. Michael was crying, screaming. Chris barely heard him over the harsh rasp of his own breath.

No chance for a clear shot. Captain Garcia was too close, moving too fast. Chris couldn't risk hitting the kid.

The walls shook as the broodsire pounded toward them, roaring. A picture of red roses fell off the wall and broke. Deeper in the house, the ghouls began to keen and wail.

The captain gripped the boy in both arms, tight against his body, shielding him as he ran. He made it to the window and shoved the boy at Chris. The broodsire loomed over the captain. It grabbed for him. Its hideous face leered with mad rage. It seemed all teeth and eyes.

No choice. No time. Chris dropped the pistol and caught the boy. He needed both hands and didn't have time to shove the gun back in the holster.

He pulled Michael through the window, careful as he could be while moving fast not to cut him on any of the shards still in the frame. He yanked the boy clear and stepped backward. His rear boot slammed down on the slanted roof, treads grating as his heel slid for a couple inches before stopping.

The broodsire seized Captain Garcia in both hands and jerked him back to its chest, crushing him in a bear hug from behind as it shrieked and roared like a train. Then it reared its head back and clamped its huge jaws down on his neck.

Chris staggered, clutching the boy to him as tightly as he dared. Then he spun and ran for the ladder at the edge of the roof. *For the boy.* The wild thought careened around in his mind. He left the captain for the boy.

He sucked in a big lungful of air and screamed into his mike, "Hostage clear! Engage! *Engage!*"

The Thorn knights charged. Chris reached the edge of the porch roof. Michael clutched him, his little fingers digging into Chris's skin and muscle, but the boy seemed to weigh nothing at all. Chris's heart thundered away. His mouth tasted like he'd licked the inside of an exhaust pipe. Michael shook in his arms like a running engine. Heat poured off him in waves.

Chris glanced over his shoulder. His pistol lay on the shingles near the window and the discarded Halligan bar. A heavily muscled, inhuman arm shoved through the broken window. It waved around, snatching at the air as if trying to grab him, but he was far out of reach.

Tashelle stood below him near the bottom of the ladder with both her hands lifted. His dog paced back and forth, staring up at him and making those mournful *barooo* sounds. He knelt and handed Michael down to her, dangling the boy by his arms. She grabbed him around his legs and stepped backward to keep her balance as she took his full weight. Jessica stood guard behind her with her lance in both hands.

Gunfire erupted—a rapid chatter and crack. Ghouls were screeching and wailing. It sounded like a Hell and South Los Angeles apocalyptic remix.

A grinding, wrenching crunch sounded right behind him. He flinched and risked a look over his shoulder again.

The huge broodsire was shoving itself through

the too-small window frame by sheer force. The wood buckled and broke. The broodsire clawed at the shingles, trying to get enough grip to pull itself out. Shards of glass lodged in its slimy, gleaming skin. It stared at him with insane fury burning in its amber eyes, panting and snorting, red foam speckling its bloody gray lips.

He turned and jumped off the ledge. Behind him, the broodsire shrieked and raged and ripped at the house frame. Chris landed in the dead grass to the right of Tashelle and Michael. The jolt of impact made him grunt. His roll was a pathetic thing, more of a flopping fall because of the explosion of pain in his shoulder, head, and ribs. His dog danced around his head, licking at his face. Wearily, he scrambled back to his feet, ignoring the agony.

Tashelle cradled Michael to her chest. Her shotgun lay on the ground near her boots.

"I'll carry him," Chris said, taking Michael back from her. He didn't have a gun and he could move faster while carrying the boy. "Cover us."

"Where's the captain?" she yelled.

"Fighting it off!" He wouldn't allow himself to think about the last time he'd seen Garcia, with the monster biting into him. "Now let's get out here!"

As he spoke, another wrenching crunch of

breaking wood nearly drowned out his words. The broodsire roared again.

He had to get Michael to safety. He ran along the side of the house toward the front yard. Tashelle and his dog ran alongside him, while Jessica lingered behind, covering their retreat. Running with Michael started to hurt after only a couple steps. Jumping off the porch hadn't been his most brilliant idea. He felt slower with every step, each footfall a jarring hit. He was panting, slowing, almost staggering, as if his adrenal glands had finally been squeezed dry.

He gritted his teeth and tightened down. He could hurt later. There was no time for that shit now.

The plywood covering the broken bay window swung outward. A ghoul leaped out of the darkness. Its eyes gleamed, its jaws snapped, and the pattern of scars on its chest resembled stylized waves. It raised its scar-striped arms as if to grab Michael. His dog leaped on the ghoul, sinking her teeth into its forearm and dragging them both down before the ghoul could touch them.

Chris cursed and dodged away. His dog snarled, her teeth ripping into the ghoul's flesh. The ghoul hissed and cursed. Tashelle skidded to a stop and raised her shotgun.

Chris whistled sharply and yelled at the dog,

"Get over here, fur-face! Now!"

She immediately released the ghoul and ran to him. The ghoul bounded back to its feet, unfazed by its shredded arm. Its hungry, maddened stare locked on Michael again. Drool poured through its flayed lips as it clicked its teeth.

But the instant the dog was clear of the line of fire, Tashelle blew off half the ghoul's head with her shotgun. The ghoul flopped back against the clapboard where its brains and blood had painted an abstract blotch in gore before it slumped down to the grass.

He kept running and didn't slow. He heard Tashelle start running after him again but didn't look back. His dog sped past, running out ahead of them as if taking point.

The closest SUV was parked near the edge of the wards, a few feet short of the sidewalk and asphalt. When he cleared the side of the house and first spotted it, the SUV seemed a football field's length away. A bleak thought hissed through his mind like an arrow: He'd never make this last stretch because that goddamn monster would throw itself out the window and run him down. He didn't even have a gun anymore and he'd have to fight it with his sword—

—and then he reached the SUV's driver-side door. Michael still clutched him so tightly it was hard to breathe. His ribs groaned in protest. He reached out, grabbed the door handle, and wrenched it open. Tashelle ran up beside him and stopped, swinging her shotgun back on the house.

"Get in the seat, Michael." He tried to pry the boy loose, but Michael only held him tighter. "It's okay now. Tashelle's gonna take you somewhere safe. C'mon."

But Michael wouldn't let go.

Chris patted the seat and whistled. His dog, God love her, jumped up into the SUV and ran back and forth on the seat.

"Get inside with my doggie, Michael," Chris urged. "She needs some attention. See if you can think up a name for her."

"We don't have a lot of time here, Hill," Tashelle said out of the side of her mouth.

"C'mon, Michael. My dog's really nice. You'll like her."

The boy finally released his hold. Chris set him on the driver's seat and pointed to the passenger seat. Michael clambered over to it as the dog tried to lick his face, her tail whipping back and forth.

More gunfire cracked nearby—Bowen opening up with his M21 rifle. A ghoul dragged itself toward them along the front porch and down the steps, but

Bowen shot it in the forehead.

"Get Michael clear," he said to Tashelle. "Get him to the safe house."

Tashelle nodded and scrambled into the driver's seat. The keys were in the ignition, a grim standard procedure—never knew when someone would get blown to bits or dragged away with the car keys in their pocket, stranding everyone. She handed him her shotgun. "You got six shells left. Make 'em count."

He nodded. "Hurry. Get him out of here."

He couldn't shake the oppressive feeling of the broodsire bearing down on them like a tank at the last minute, now that they were so damn close to getting the boy away safe. He slammed the door and backed away, his guts roiling with dread.

She started the SUV, glanced at the house again, threw it into reverse. The tires spit dirt as she backed up. She swung out into the street and the ward image shimmered and rippled as the SUV broke the barrier. He watched her go, his heart thundering away, his breath rasping in and out, his body a roadmap of aches. Michael stared toward him through the passenger window, but he knew the boy could no longer see him from outside the wards. All he'd see was the dark house, lifeless, decaying, empty of people, and empty of monsters. The boy's small face appeared so pale, so haggard, that it hurt Chris in ways his physical injuries never could.

Tashelle slammed the SUV into drive and screamed away down the street. He couldn't help but watch until she was out of sight. Then he turned back to the house with Tashelle's semi-auto shotgun in his hands.

"Specter Two look sharp!" Sergeant Drake ordered over the radio. "Clear those corners! Clear those goddamn corners!" His words were followed by the crack of gunfire, heard over the radio and echoing from the house, a disconcerting stereo effect.

Chris hurried toward the side of the house where he could see Jessica slowly retreating from the back porch, staring up at the second story with her lance ready. He felt tired—weary to every nerve—and strangely lonely without his dog at his side, even though he'd only had her around for a short while. They were strange, out-of-place feelings for the middle of a firefight, as if he no longer held a stake in what happened. He'd been so focused on rescuing Michael for so long, now that the boy was safely away, he felt curiously empty, almost disconnected, as if the rest of this were the ending to some movie he'd only half cared about. But then he remembered Captain Garcia and it all came crashing back into razor-shard intensity.

"Get to the captain!" Chris yelled as he ran toward Jessica. Part of him was certain it was already too late, but he'd be damned if he'd give up until he knew for sure. "He needs support!"

More gunfire. "Fire in the hole!" someone—he thought it was Roth—yelled over the radio. A few seconds later an explosion ripped through the air. The concussion wave made his ears pop.

"Got one! Secure those stairs!"

"Drop that fucker! Nine o'clock! Nine o'clock!"

A fusillade of gunshots rang out. Then silence, broken by a resounding boom from upstairs that rattled all the windows.

Chris finally reached Jessica at the side of the house. She'd halted her retreat and stood fast, digging her heels in and holding her lance at the ready. When he stopped beside her, she pointed to the porch roof, her face grim and her skin pale through her armor's blast visor.

Another deep boom was chased by the crack and crunch of breaking wood. The broodsire roared again— a deafening blast of sound. Its footfalls thundered on the porch roof, pounding toward them like an artillery barrage.

"Primary target out of the house, in the open!" Chris yelled into the mike. He raised the shotgun, standing clear of Jessica. "Need backup, east side!"

The broodsire's huge grayish-white mass appeared at the edge of the porch. The support posts groaned and cracked under its weight. Peralta shot it with his sniper rifle. It jerked as the round ripped through its sleek flesh. But Peralta had missed its head, and it flung itself off the porch roof. It landed close, with a thud Chris felt through his boot heels, up into his shinbones.

The broodsire crouched, nearly filling the narrow path from clapboard to fence, and its strange amber eyes locked on him. Its jaws gaped open. It lifted its arm and from its hand, the pale tentacles with the blade tips of bone pushed out toward him. Neurotoxin dripped from the ends. It rasped its tongue across the bleeding wound in its torso like a cat licking fur. Then it sucked its tongue back in and gave him a frighteningly vicious smile.

"Time to suffer," it rumbled, eyes widening, nostrils flaring. "Time to—"

Jessica charged and shoved the lance into its chest with a running lunge. Chris clearly saw her fingers tighten on the lance's dual triggers an instant before the world shattered into a coughing explosion as all the charges went off pointblank.

The broodsire disappeared from the chest up,

parts of its odd skull driven into the clapboard like white shrapnel as its black blood sprayed everywhere. The concussion wave slammed into Chris, hammering him to his knees. Smoke and dust billowed all around them. The air filled with a nauseating reek: gore, burned explosives, and chemical stink all intermixed.

The end of Jessica's lance smoked. She'd been driven to one knee, despite her armor and blast shields. She was leaning back into the butt of the lance to keep herself upright, her left arm dangling at her side. The remains of the broodsire's body fell into the side of the house, scraping along the clapboard. The exposed jagged bone made a fingernail-chalkboard screech he knew he'd hear again in his dreams.

"Specter One! What's your status, over?"

Sergeant Drake. Over the radio. Chris could barely hear because his ears were ringing again. He'd probably come out of this FUBAR mission deaf as well as beat-to-shit. Incredibly, he coughed out laughter. Jessica flashed him a look as if he were completely mad.

"Specter One, how do you copy, over?"

"Jessica fragged the broodsire." Chris's voice shook, but he didn't care. He managed to haul himself to his feet. "Painted the fucking house with it."

"Use proper voice procedure, Hill."

Chris laughed again, over the radio just so the

sergeant could hear him. Fuck voice procedure. They'd saved the kid. Killed the monster. Drake was lucky Chris didn't break out singing "The Star Spangled Banner" over every available frequency.

"Pin, can you confirm?" Sergeant Drake radioed. "Is primary destroyed, over?"

Jessica dropped the spent lance. It hit the ground with a thud and lay there smoking. She flipped up her suit's visor with her right hand. The motion made her suck in breath and clutch her left shoulder.

"Confirmed, Specter Two," she said through gritted teeth. "I say again, primary target destroyed, over."

"Where's the captain?" Chris broke in, his elation vanishing as fast as it had spiked. A sick dread replaced it and had him cold all the way through. "What's his status?"

"Captain Garcia is KIA," Drake replied. "What's the status on the hostage, over?"

KIA. Killed in action. Chris couldn't speak. It was as though the breath had been sucked right out of him. He could only stand there, his ears ringing, his body hurting in half a hundred places, and stare at the blasted remains of the monster and hate the fucking thing. His mind filled with the memory of the captain running toward him with the boy in his arms, the broodsire right behind him.

The news didn't surprise him. He'd known all along hadn't he? And still...those flat, precise words over the radio confirming the captain was dead rocked him like a slap with their cold finality.

The sergeant's voice broke through Chris's stunned thoughts. "Repeat, what's the status of the hostage, over?"

"The hostage is safe and secured," Jessica finally answered when it was clear Chris wouldn't.

"Roger that," Sergeant Drake said. "Gather the corpses in a central location in the house. Roth, Tyson, Bowen, help them drag the broodsire inside. Get our honored dead back in the van, we don't leave anyone behind. We got fifteen minutes and then we set off incendiaries. Out."

Chris and Jessica stood there staring at each other. Her armor was covered with a dusting of fine gray ash. There were dark circles under her eyes. Her face was very pale and covered with sweat.

He glanced at her left arm hanging limp at her side. "You're hurt."

"Back-blast broke my arm. Maybe dislocated my shoulder too. Second time this year."

"I ever tell you you're crazy?"

She frowned and dismissed his words with one

sharp shake of her head. "If you get to Tashelle, you can take the boy home before anyone else is in contact with him. If he stays at the safe house…" She looked away.

He'd been thinking the same thing. He didn't want the boy debriefed, or worse, taken away as a ward of the Thorn because of the things he'd seen. He was ninety percent sure even Sergeant Drake wouldn't be that much of a prick with a little kid, but… No, he wouldn't take any chances. Too much had happened for him to risk it. He had to get Michael back to his mother. The captain had promised her.

Chris nodded and limped past Jessica, headed toward the front yard and the second SUV. Every step sent lightning bolts of agony zigzagging up his spine. His nerve-endings still relentlessly informed him his body was rather banged up and would like to stop all the moving around, please and thank you very much — as if he didn't realize that already.

He ignored the pain. Sometimes you had to ride a machine hard.

"Hey, Hill," Sergeant Drake called from the front porch as Chris rounded the side of the house. "Hold up."

Shit. He stopped and stared at the sergeant.

Drake walked down the porch stairs holding Chris's MP7 by the sling in one hand and his Beretta in the other. Chris waited, watching, too exhausted to guess what would happen next.

He held the weapons out to Chris. "You're the sloppiest fucking soldier ever, tossing your gear everywhere."

Chris didn't reply. Drake had one of those unreadable expressions on his face, closed up and guarded, so he tried to keep his own face the same level of neutral. He took back his pistol first, checked it and put it back in the holster, then took the MP7, checked the safety and the magazine and slung it again.

The sergeant's expression hardened. He pointed to the horizon where the sky grew steadily lighter. "What the fuck you doing out here, Hill? We got body disposal and it's almost sun up."

"I'm taking the SUV and bringing the kid home."

"That right?"

"That's right."

They stared at each other.

"What makes you think you got clearance for something like that?"

"The captain was right." He lifted his hand and pointed at Drake. "He was *right*."

"I won't speak ill of a fallen knight."

"I almost want to make you talk to the kid. To Michael. You can look him in the eyes, understand who you would've written off."

The sergeant's jaw muscles clenched for a moment. "You think it'd make a difference?"

"It'd better make a difference," Chris said. "You want to call yourself a knight, it'd *better* make a fucking difference."

"You don't know jack shit. You want to be the hero who brings the kid back to his mother, go right ahead. Get in that truck and get the fuck out of here. But send Tashelle back with the other SUV. We need the room to haul back the bodies of Weeger, Chen, and Captain Garcia while you prance around in your shining armor, doing what's *right*."

"This ain't over. Command's gonna hear about you deep-sixing the hand-off, putting a kid in danger. I'll see you busted down to squire for that."

"Go right ahead and squeal," Drake said. "Everything I've done has been righteous, and the highranks will see it the same. You got a hard-on for me, that's fine too. But I suggest you mind me when I say get the fuck outta here before I lose my patience."

Sergeant Drake turned away and walked up the porch steps. He started calling orders over the radio, but Chris turned off his radio and pulled off his helmet so he didn't have to hear anymore. The slight morning breeze on his face and sweat-soaked hair felt wonderfully cool.

He walked to the SUV, paused, and glanced at the house one last time—the ugly, flaking paint, the curling shingles, and the windows like bullet wounds. He could close his eyes and remember every detail burned into his memory, all the things that had happened. The dreams would be bad. That was simply how things went down.

The sun was nearly up, the world gray and dim, the color of concrete and mop water. He opened the door, took off his harness, tossed his sword and MP7 in the back, and climbed inside. For a moment he sat there with his hands on the wheel, shaking. He couldn't get his hands to stop shaking. His breath came in jagged gasps. He held on until the shakes passed. He glanced at the house again, but nothing watched him and the place was silent. Dead.

He drove away.

CHAPTER TWENTY-SIX

Return

Tashelle and his dog both met him at the door to the safe house.

His dog greeted him with exuberant face licking when he crouched to pet her. She almost knocked him on his ass. Her tail was wagging so hard it seemed to shake her whole hindquarters. It was hard not to smile when something loved you that much.

Tashelle greeted him with a semi-auto pistol in her hand, still dressed in all her combat gear. She didn't smile, but he could read the relief in her face. She stepped back to let him inside the small foyer with the hideous yellow and brown linoleum and the carpet mat with a green cartoon frog.

"Where's he at?" Chris asked, keeping his voice low.

"In the living room watching cartoons. On his

third bowl of cereal."

Now they grinned at each other, a hundred unspoken things passing between them in an instant. But the moment didn't last because of what he had to say next. "The captain's dead. He died getting the boy to me."

Tashelle closed her eyes. She held herself very still, as if any movement, the slightest tremble, would shake her apart.

"I'm taking Michael home." He jerked a thumb toward the driveway where the two SUVs sat parked. "Drake needs you to head back with the other SUV. They're gonna burn the place and bug out, but they need more wheels."

She nodded and moved past him. She paused before she went out the door. "Captain Garcia didn't have anybody. No one who wasn't a knight, anyway. But who's gonna tell Weeger and Chen's people, now that the captain's gone?"

He read what she meant between the lines. She didn't want Sergeant Drake doing it. Weeger and Chen had served alongside Chris and Tashelle in the captain's unit. They'd been buddies, seen fire and boredom and all the shit that went with being a soldier, and all the hidden glory that went with being a knight.

"I'll take care of it," he said.

She nodded again and hurried to the SUV, concealing the handgun from view behind her back, though she still looked like nothing if not a soldier.

He watched her back out and speed down the street in the early morning gray. He turned and walked down the entrance hall, past the kitchen, to the living room with his dog following.

Michael sat on the couch. A huge box of cereal had tipped over on the glazed driftwood coffee table, spilling tiny pieces in a yellow flood. Next to it sat an empty bowl and spoon in the middle of a puddle of milk. The TV screen threw flickering light across the walls, painting Michael's face in flashes of blues and whites.

His dog ran into the room and jumped on the couch. She curled up next to Michael and put her muzzle on his thigh. The boy began to pet her without glancing away from the television.

Chris hesitated in the doorway. "Hey, Michael."

The boy didn't turn from the animated action on the screen. The sound was turned low, almost inaudible. Or was that only hearing damage from all the recent explosions going off right next to his head all night? Whatever. Didn't matter now.

He walked to the couch and sat next to Michael and the dog, trying to be mindful of his shoulder and ribs and failing miserably. At least he didn't groan, though the couch springs creaked and the smell of mildew wafted up from the cushion.

He set a hand on the boy's shoulder. God, the kid was so small. His hand seemed to envelope half his back. "Mike, I'm gonna take you home to your Mom."

Michael whipped his head around and stared up at him. "Now?"

"Yeah. Now."

"I asked, but that other lady said I had to wait."

"She didn't know where you lived," Chris said. "I do."

The boy stood up, walked to the TV with solemn steps and turned it off. Then he turned back to watch as Chris hauled his sorry carcass back off the couch.

"Sorry the cereal somehow spilled," Michael said, staring at the mess and frowning. "And some milk too."

He smiled. "Don't worry about it. We'll leave it for my sergeant to clean up." He glanced at his dog. "You coming too, girl?"

She barked out a *barooo*, and Michael laughed.

"She sounds weird."

"Yeah, she does, but I like her."

"What's her name?"

"Doesn't have one yet. I just got her. Say, can you

think of a good name for her?"

Michael stared at the dog, his face scrunched up in concentration. "I think...Pepper."

Chris grinned. "Pepper?" He eyed the dog critically. "She doesn't look very peppery, though."

"Pepper's good on eggs," Michael informed him, as if that settled the debate. And maybe it did.

"Pepper it is, then." He scratched her behind the ears. "You like that, pretty girl? You like the name Pepper?"

She turned in a circle, wagging her tail and trying to lick him. Looked like a yes.

Together the three of them walked through the house and out the door. He didn't know how much time he had before the rest of the team returned, but he guessed not much. He opened the passenger door. Pepper clambered in immediately, but the boy just stared at the seat.

"That's not my seat," he said. "I'm not supposed to ride in the front. And there's no car seat."

"I don't have a car seat, big guy." He frowned, remembering something about kids and air bags in the front seat. "Guess we'll have to risk the middle row." He gently grabbed Michael under the arms and lifted him inside. "Sometimes you gotta make do."

He couldn't get over how small the boy seemed.

He already felt uneasy about hauling him around without a car seat. How did parents constantly deal with stuff like this? A thousand little worries. He'd be a nervous wreck until he finally returned the boy home safe.

Finally, he climbed in and started the SUV. He was about to shift into reverse when he spotted a rising plume of smoke off to the east. He stared at the black smoke for a moment, the engine patiently rumbling as it idled. Then he backed into the street and put thoughts of the smoke out of his mind. He glanced in the rearview mirror at Michael. "You want some music?"

Michael shrugged. He stared out the window and yawned.

The memory of Captain Garcia running toward the window with the boy in his arms flashed back into his mind again. He turned on the radio, hoping for distraction. The chorus on Dobie Gray's "Drift Away" came over the speakers. Not usually his style, but he liked the song because it made him think of his mom. She used to always have one of those mellow rock stations going in the background when he was a kid, a steady stream of stuff by America and Jimmy Buffet and whatever. He turned it up as he drove, singing along on the chorus, the only part he knew.

Mike watched him from the rear seats. When the

song was over, he said, "Can we change the music?"

Chris laughed—the first time in what felt like forever. "Don't like that, huh? All right, I'll scan the stations. Tell me when you hear something you like."

And Michael smiled. Not much. Just a little curve of the lips. But enough.

CHAPTER TWENTY-SEVEN

Home

The walkway to the front door of the boy's house seemed at least a mile and a half long. Michael led the way. Chris limped alongside him, and Pepper was busy running here and there, smelling the grass and the bushes. The distant column of smoke had drifted high in the air and started smearing off to the south making a black smudge stain in the sky. Fire engine sirens wailed in the distance.

No cop was parked out in front of the house this time. Michael didn't run to the door, as Chris had expected. He walked calmly, as if in line at school, climbed the steps, and rang the doorbell. Pepper hurried over to join them as they waited. They waited for so long that Michael pushed the doorbell again, twice this time.

The front door opened, then the screen door. Ms.

Cantwell stared at Michael, unblinking, her face and body absolutely still, as if she feared her slightest movement, slightest breath, might make her son disappear again.

Michael jumped up the last stair and threw himself at his mother. When he moved, it broke her paralysis and she grabbed him up in her arms and clutched him to her. She was shaking and tears streamed down her cheeks. She began crying so hard it wrenched through her body, but without a sound. She pressed her face against Michael's, covering him with kisses, quick fierce kisses all over his face and hair. He wrapped himself around her, his legs around her waist, and his head on her shoulder. He closed his eyes.

Chris was grinning so hard his mouth hurt and his jaw ached. He watched them and couldn't help but stare. He didn't want to miss a second of the boy back with his mother. It was a scene he hadn't dared imagine when he'd been in the guts of the house with gunfire echoing off the walls and the ghouls screaming.

But another part of him felt like a voyeur, peering in at something he wasn't meant to be a part of. Michael's mother was crying into his hair now, one hand clasped there as she rocked him back and forth, her silence finally broken. "Oh my God, Michael," she said, over and over again.

He stepped off the bottom stair and tried to sear that image into his memory, to burn it there over all the other dark, horrible things scratched into his brain. This was the image to keep forever.

He finally turned to go. Best to leave them without interrupting their joy. Life already excelled at diminishing moments like this, shoving in with its petty details, dragging something that shined bright as chrome in sunlight down into the browns and grays of the mundane.

"Wait," Ms. Cantwell said.

He glanced back to see her staring at him, her eyes red from crying. She still clutched Michael to her, still rocked him back and forth. Michael's eyes were closed, and Chris thought he might be asleep.

"Thank you." There was so much emotion packed into the words that her voice cracked and broke. She sobbed out a laugh and swiped at her cheeks with one hand, before dropping it back down to keep holding Michael. "Thank you. I can't even say…"

He smiled. "You don't have to say."

"The other man. The one who was here before…?" She looked at the SUV as if expecting to see Captain Garcia inside.

He felt the smile fade from his face. He drew in breath, but paused before replying. It hurt to think, and he was damn tired. Just...tired. Still, he had to make a choice. He could lie. Tell her the captain was just fine, back at headquarters booking the bad guys, yadda yadda, and had sent Chris to bring the boy home. Spare her any guilt. Diminish none of the joy on her face. He could do that.

Or he could tell her the truth. After a moment, he knew which to choose. A sacrifice had to be honored. She needed to know the reason he wasn't standing here beside him, bringing the boy home as he'd promised.

"He was killed in action. We got Michael away safe because of him."

"Oh my God." She closed her eyes, rocked her boy. New tears ran down her cheeks. "I'm so sorry. So, so very sorry."

He watched her with her son, feeling a red-hot wire gouging into his neck, between his windpipe and the muscles, because he was fighting so hard to keep his emotions in and his face professional. She cried, yes. The news had rocked her, he could see that. But...all the same, he also could tell it didn't hit her the same way it hit him. And he couldn't blame her. She had the most important thing in her world back in her arms, safe, whole, after she'd faced the possibility that her boy might never be with her again. If he'd stood in her shoes, he'd have felt exactly the same: sorry a man had lost his life, but his mind and soul soaring at having someone he loved returned safe and sound. The sorrow and the happiness were all tangled and intertwined to the point where he couldn't touch one without touching the other. Maybe that'd be his job, his duty, a cross to bear, feeling both of those emotions. Maybe for a long time.

He looked at the boy again and the pain in his throat intensified, eclipsing all the other bruises and aches throbbing throughout his body. He couldn't look for long. He had to drop his eyes.

"He'll need help." Chris gestured at Michael, a helpless, almost ineffectual motion. "Counseling. The things he's seen. Nightmares."

She kissed her son's head again and leaned her forehead against his. She still trembled, her muscles shaking beneath her skin. "My baby. My little baby. I'm sorry. I'm sorry."

"It's not your fault."

The wrong thing to say, maybe, but he remembered her the first time he'd seen her. The empty stare. The self-blame. More than anything he wanted to heal these wounds, both hers and the boy's. But maybe words could never do so. Not his words anyway.

She looked at him, and her eyes were fierce. "It's always a mother's duty," was all she said.

"He's a good kid. Brave. Be proud of him." He nodded to her and turned away. He started back toward the SUV with Pepper. His eyes hurt. His throat felt as if he'd swallowed a white-hot fishhook.

"You're not FBI," she called after him.

He paused again, glanced back and met her gaze. "No."

She nodded very slowly. Rocking her boy, her cheek on his forehead, holding him so tightly it was as though she wanted to pull him back into her. Keep him safe forever. Michael was indeed asleep, his face smooth and unworried. Peaceful.

Chris walked to the SUV, held the door for Pepper, and then hauled himself in. Not an easy task. His body had started to stiffen up something wicked. He could see the distant smoke through the windshield. The black cloud had diminished—fire crews battling back the flames, no doubt. There'd be little left of the house after all those incendiaries.

It took three tries to get the key into the ignition. The damn key was shaking. Pepper watched him, her doggie expression serious.

"You ready?" he asked.

She cocked her head and her ears twitched. He took that as a yes.

He started the engine. Ms. Cantwell watched him

go. It made him feel a little better, that she cared enough to see him off. Right now he wanted nothing more than to head back to the safe house and collapse in bed for the next sixteen hours. Then, if he could move and wasn't confined for medical attention, he'd bring a bagel to a certain broken-armed crazy woman.

Just a thought. Just an interesting possibility.

He shifted into drive, but kept his foot on the brake. He was greedy. He stole a last look, desperate to burn the image of Michael and his mother together again into his permanent memory: the boy sleeping in her arms while she cried with joy so powerful it seemed closer to pain. He had to take these moments and save them for as long as he could, because the world might not understand, and even if it did, it would always forget.

Some things were worth every sacrifice.

He turned up the radio and drove away.

END

AUTHOR'S NOTE

I started writing *9mm Blues* in October 2010 and finished in December of the same year. Since finishing, the book has seen a seemingly never-ending series of setbacks and delays, to the point where I feared it would never be published. So I'm very pleased to be able to finally offer it to the world, even if it is five years late.

I like Chris and his dog. If readers like him too, we'll be seeing more of them both.

—Keith Melton

ACKNOWLEDGEMENTS

A special thank you to Robin and Jared, my beta readers extraordinaire, and to Sara.

ABOUT THE AUTHOR

Keith Melton is a fantasy author. His first book was *Blood Vice*, a vampire/crime novel and part of the Nightfall Syndicate series. *Ghost Soldiers*, the second book in the series, was published in 2011. His fantasy comedy series, The Zero Dog Missions, has a completely different flavor. *The Zero Dog War* and *Dark Ride Dogs* are books one and two in that series. He is currently working on his novel *Spanner Jack* and considering a sequel to *9mm Blues*.

Discover more about Keith Melton here

Website: http://keithmelton.wordpress.com/

Twitter: http://twitter.com/KeithMelton99

Facebook: http://www.facebook.com/pages/Keith-Melton/199082863480486

www.ingramcontent.com/pod-product-compliance
Lightning Source LLC
Chambersburg PA
CBHW021445240626
47153CB00001B/305